TRAWLER TRASH

C.P. JAMES

BY C.P. JAMES

The Reassembly Series

Rocket Repo

Trawler Trash

Ship Show

Xeno Xoo

Fleet Feat

Dark Dodgers

The Cytocorp Saga

Dome Six

Into the Burn

Out of the Seam

For everyone who's ever shown up for me.

Vinci Books

vinci-books.com

Published by Vinci Books Ltd in 2025

1

A CIP catalogue record for this book is available from the British Library.
Paperback ISBN: 9781036701314

CHAPTER 1
ALONE TOGETHER

I f the crew of *For Sale Make Offer* was smart, they'd have jumped away by now. Circling back for him, a black bubble in the eternal ocean of stars over Kigantu, was suicide. Geddy Starheart just used his ship as a missile and turned his former boss' spectacularly expensive cruiser into space dust. One way or another, that would have repercussions. Reinforcements were already scrambling to return the favor to the *Fizmo*, and without shields, their only option was burn ass out of there and hide.

He'd just have to trust that that's what happened. It would comfort him in his final moments. Was it selfish of him to want this ending? To actually be the captain who sacrificed himself and his most prized possession to enable his crew's escape? Of course not. That was the kind of story told around campfires in hushed, reverent tones. *Have I ever told you boys about the bravest, most selfless captain to ever sail the infinite sea? His name was Geddy Starheart, and you'd do well to know it.*

Still, the moment felt bittersweet, tainted as it was by the fact that the *Penetrator*, the one-of-a-kind vessel he and Eli built together, was a direct casualty of his actions. He knew she was a tough ship, but it ripped the *Auctionaut* in half and kept going. Such a delicious moment for it to come through unscathed, only then for it to be swallowed by Beebit Tompanov in the *Red Raven*. Anything would've been better. Exploding with the *Auctionaut*. Tumbling into Kigantu's atmosphere and burning up. Not becoming someone's *salvage*.

But man, if there was ever a time to let go of shit you couldn't control, it was right fucking now.

It briefly occurred to Geddy that he should pull up his pants, but celestial beings had little need for such things. Now that the *Fizmo* had escaped Tretiak's ship, and the *Penetrator* was swallowed up by the rival trawler *Red Raven*, there was nothing left to do but enjoy the uncluttered view of Kigantu and its nearest moon, Balox.

Exposing himself to such stark beauty just felt right, like he was saying, *This is me. This is my body. Human. Fragile. Balls half frozen.*

It was much warmer now inside the Morpho-bubble, though that was a low bar. Somewhere in the vicinity of minus twenty, he guessed. Whatever process his biosynthetic savior used to convert electromagnetic radiation to convective heat had reached equilibrium with the punishing cold of space.

Crystals of frozen urine surrounded him like a cluster of sparkly yellow stars. Somehow, peeing out into the vacuum was among the least interesting things he'd done that day.

For a guy who wanted nothing more than to be forgotten, this should've been the perfect exit. But all he could think about was Eli, his longtime companion, and Morpho, the Zelnad booger that had saved his life several times over. A very weird little family of three, alone together at the end.

— Will I freeze first or run out of oxygen?

Normally, he'd talk out loud to Eli if they were alone, but his tongue had swelled to where he had to breathe through his nose. They'd chat in their quiet way. The only way for Eli.

— *Don't trouble yourself with such thoughts.*

— Not like I can save them for later.

— *This moment is about acceptance, Geddy.*

— I reject that theory.

— *Want a story?*

During those first several weeks after Eli revealed himself as a literal voice in his head, Geddy fought it. He had more than enough internal conversations, thank you very much. But as he came to see that Eli meant him no harm and that his plight to return to Sagacea was now Geddy's as well, they reached a sort of truce.

Eli enjoyed providing color commentary on Geddy's sad little life on Earth 2, but building the *Penetrator* together focused their interactions on the task.

He knew the broad strokes of Eli's home world, but precious few details. It was at the center of the universe, which could only be a metaphor, and his race had existed since the Big Bang. Its mission was to disperse the seeds of intelligence far and wide, giving any number of species the insight and inspiration to evolve into civilizations.

It now appeared that the Zelnads, the shadowy cult that spread faster than Vyephian blue fever, were little more than disgruntled Sagaceans that decided to go way, way off-book.

Eli could, and did, talk for hours about Sagacea and all the questions he thought about while floating through space for seventeen million years, but to that point, he'd never heard Eli tell a single story.

— I'm kinda busy dying, but sure. Let's hear it.

— *Once upon a time, an immortal being named Neil Armstrong found himself alone. The only one of his kind.*

— Wait. As in *the* Neil Armstrong?

— *The being's name is irrelevant. I thought it would make it easier to conceive if I used that of your favorite historical figure.*

— Neil Armstrong it is. Apologies in advance if I die before you get to the end.

— *Neil became so lonely that he forced his soul to split in two, like a cell, so he would have a friend.*

— Can we call that one Armstrong?

— *Of course. This other half of him — Armstrong — was an exact copy. For a time, Neil and Armstrong were very happy. But as the years rolled on, Armstrong turned bitter and resentful, opposing Neil at every turn and belittling him. What began as simple disagreements degraded into spite, and finally to cruelty. And so it went for all eternity.*

— Great story. Ending needs work.

— *Don't you see? Rather than accept his circumstances, he split in two. As a result, he was forever at war with himself.*

Geddy paused to consider the story's meaning. There were worse things to occupy your mind at the end. But it was asking too much of his oxygen-starved brain. He kept losing the threads. Oblivion beckoned. Kigantu and Balox were little more than blurry shapes now, frozen in the ether like ghosts.

His eyes were useless, so he closed them. It melted the crystals forming on his eyeballs and helped focus his thoughts just enough to understand why Eli shared this particular parable at this particular time. The other half of Geddy Starheart was little Eddie Kepler.

That doe-eyed kid who loved spaceships and Old Earth stories was still in there somewhere, but Geddy felt no more connected to that boy than a bird to its eggshell. Nothing about his ridiculously easy, absurdly happy life before his parents died struck a chord.

His long and distinguished career as a henchman wasn't a path. It was a retreat. But he didn't leave it behind because he *wanted* to. He left because he *needed* to. Somehow, that kid from Earth 2 reached clean through time and shook Geddy awake. *Come back,* he said. *You're better than this. Let me help.*

And so that's what he did.

What the boy with the pilot dad and docent mom wanted more than anything was a best friend. Someone worthy of trust and fully in sync with him. There were kids at the Planetary Defense Force base, of course, and he made a lot of friends, but never like he imagined a best friend being.

Eli became that friend. After all this time, the kid finally got what he wanted. Geddy Starheart would still be fighting the voice in his head, but Eddie Kepler? Eddie was just grateful for someone to talk to.

— I'm not at war anymore.

— *Nice feeling, isn't it?*

That was Eli's point all along. Of all people, Geddy Muthafuckin' Starheart was going to rest in peace after all. Who'd have guessed?

His right cheek pressed against the Morpho-balloon. The warmth felt luscious. A tingling, electric sensation pulsed through it, and again, Morpho joined the party in his head.

— You're too late, Morph. I don't have any energy for you.

— **I have all I require.**

— Then why are you here?

— **To get your attention.**

— Sorry, but it's important I let go. That's how my journey ends. Thanks for everything.

— **Open your damn eyes!**

The same electric tingle in his cheek surged through him with increased power, a jolt of adrenaline that made him gasp as his eyes popped open. At first, all he could see was the dim outline of Kigantu and a nearby chunk of Tretiak's ship, but a tiny puff of air from Morpho pivoted the balloon around. Morpho released him, and the flow of energy stopped.

Lights, not stars, in a symmetrical pattern.

— *Geddy? What is th–*

From the center came a supernova, a brilliant and blinding

explosion of light that burned a hole through his foggy eyes. Either he'd just witnessed the death of a star or this was the light, as in *the light*. The closer it drew to him, the more he wanted to be in it. He was ready.

— This is the end, pal. It's finally here.

— *I'm not so sure.*

Quite suddenly, the light disappeared. Something was blocking it. But what? Had it judged him unworthy, or was it just another piece of debris from the *Auctionaut*?

A moment later, the shape obscured all lights in the pattern, allowing it to reflect the bright glow of the moon. It was a chunky, artificial object that moved, one claw closing around the Morpho-balloon. And atop its strange form was a shiny bubble with a face inside that, at least to Geddy's addled brain, bore a striking resemblance to Oz.

CHAPTER 2

GEDDY UP

Everything hurt. His throat burned. His eyes were raisins. And his dick? He couldn't bring himself to look.

If they'd jumped away after plucking him out of space, he hadn't felt it. Not that he would, considering his condition. Either it was the darkest place he'd ever been, or he was blind. He swore his eyes were open, but got nothing. Nothing! Living totally ruined his honorable and legendary death, and what kind of life would he live now? Begging for credits on Caloth? Drawing disability on Earth 3?

— I shouldn't be alive. This is bogus.

— *But that means we both are.*

Fair point. Maybe he just needed to feel a little sorry for himself.

— Are we on the *Fiz?*

— *Yes.*

— Whoa, slow down, Eli. I can only keep track of so many details.

Not two seconds later, a voice, clear as a bell, met his grateful ears.

"Geddy, this is Dr. Tardigan. Are you able to move?"

With tremendous effort, he lifted his left hand and extended his middle finger. It was too perfect a setup.

Doc chuckled. "I'd call that a good sign."

Still, not a single photon had gotten in. "Am I blind?

"We won't know for sure until the bandages come off, but I don't think so." Geddy felt a warm hand slide under his shoulder, lifting him up slightly. "Here. Drink some water."

A plastic straw passed between his lips, and he took a grateful pull. He launched into a coughing fit as soon as the liquid hit his throat.

"Whoopsy. Let's sit you up."

From behind the small of his back came the whine of a motor, and the bed pivoted under him.

"All right, this should be better." The straw brushed his lips before sliding between them.

This time, he took a tentative pull from the bottle, making sure he could swallow. It only partly doused the fire, but he'd take it.

"You have some frostbite, including the inside of your nose and throat. And your tongue is still swollen, so it may be difficult or impossible to speak. But I'd like you to try."

Geddy tried to talk, but his vocal cords were too thick to vibrate. A whisper was all he could manage. "Does this count?" It sounded like *buh biph comp?*

"No, but at least I can hear you. How are you feeling?"

"Like Silver Surfer just shot my curl."

"I don't know what that means," said Tardigan.

"Forget it. How long have I been here?"

"Two days. It was touch and go for a while."

He'd been unconscious plenty of times, but only ever for a few minutes. It would make one helluva story someday.

"How'd you find me?" he rasped.

"Denk circled back after the explosion to search the debris

field. At some point he detected Morpho's heat signature. Another minute or two and–"

"Tretiak ..."

"Sent out a search party, yes. We hid on the dark side of Kigantu's largest moon, Balox, where we remain."

"Must be a good hiding spot."

"A patrol has passed over the area several times. They know we're here somewhere."

A shiver ran through his body, and it wasn't just some mild shock. It was cold enough that his unsteady breath escaped in clouds. "Did I get frostbite from space or this damn ship?"

"We're running on life support to avoid detection. The heating system uses too much juice, so we're cycling it."

Geddy wasn't one to hide and wait, but sometimes, playing dead was how you stayed alive.

— *The key, Geddy. Ask him if he found it.*

"Listen, Doc, I had this metal piece ..."

"Ah, yes," Tardigan said. "I didn't know what it was, so I've kept it in my pocket. What is it?"

He pulled out the key and Geddy and Eli breathed a sigh of relief at the same time.

"The key to my ship."

"The one the *Red Raven* took and jumped away with?"

"That's the one. Where are they others?"

"Everyone's fine, thanks to you. I must say, I have never heard of anyone bailing out of a spaceship."

"That's a new one to me, as well," Geddy said.

"Why were your pants around your ankles?"

"Because I needed the key."

"Where was it?"

Geddy flared his eyebrows.

"Ah, I see. I'm ah ... going to go wash my hands."

———

Dr. Tardigan's hands unwrapped the bandage slowly, each pass making his head feel less constricted. The *Fizmo's* pathetic medkit had plenty of gauze but little else. Eventually, only two pucks of soft material separated his eyes from the light.

"Okay," said Tardigan. "Moment of truth. Hold on to these sunglasses in case it's too bright. Let's hope it is."

He guided Geddy's hands to a pair of plastic sunglasses. Geddy fidgeted with them as Doc gently removed the pads. Even with his eyes closed, the light of the tiny infirmary assaulted his senses like needles. He slipped them on, hot tears streaming down his cheeks, and opened his eyes. Closed them. Opened them. Each time, they adjusted a bit more. Once he could handle the brightness, he kept going until he could make out shapes.

"Well?"

"Getting better." His voice was rough, but stronger than it had been.

"You're lucky your eyeballs didn't burst," Tardigan said.

"I've seen 'em get big in cartoons. They never burst."

A rap came at the door. "Aww, you took off the bandages already?" asked Oz, leaning in for a closer look. She recoiled. "Gross! Put 'em back on!"

"What's the good of being half blind if I can still see Oz?" Geddy croaked.

She plunked down on the edge of the bed next to him, laughing and jostling his tender limbs. "Nice shades. I'm betting Denk won those at Underground Daze on Durandia."

"Oh god, what are they?"

"They have, like, a beach scene on the lenses. They're ridiculous." She sniggered and shook her head.

That was already enough humiliation for one day. Back to business. "I don't imagine you saw where the *Raven* went."

"It jumped in the direction of the Triad, but that's all we know. Sorry."

Great. Now he only had to search half the galaxy for it. The rusty machinery of his brain sputtered briefly to life. Where might an opportunistic salvage ship take it besides the Double A on Kigantu? Dozens of possibilities came to mind. Virtually every developed planet had a market for such rarities.

— *Could Tompanov have known you took it from Tretiak?*

— It's not crazy talk.

"Who does your old pal Beebit sell to?" Geddy asked.

"Hard to say. Next to Caloth, Aku's got the biggest black market."

Aku. Home to the Screvari, a fearsome race friendly to the Zelnads. The Ring War cost them dearly. Three generations of Screvari had grown up wanting revenge. Were they doing more than just supplying them with tukrium?

"Then that's where we need to go," said Geddy matter-of-factly.

Oz's eyes drifted down to the bed. "Um, about that …"

"I'll give you two a minute." Tardigan disappeared through the door.

A sinking feeling gripped his stomach. "What's wrong?"

"While we were picking you up, six fighters took off from Aquebba. That interceptor you blew up took out our rear shield. One more direct hit and we're toast. But life support's running low, and those fighters aren't giving up. They know we're here and that we can't outrun them."

Had they not come for him when they did, Balox would've been the last thing he ever saw. Now they were trapped there, pinned down by determined patrols from Tretiak's private army.

"This is about me, not the *Fiz*. I'll surrender."

"Like hell you will. But without repairs, novaspheres, and supplies, we're stuck here."

As usual, the *Fizmo* had no prospects and no money other

than what they'd saved from their winnings on Caloth and Kriggy's meager advance.

"What's our food situation?" he asked.

She blew air out the sides of her mouth. "Not great. When it was just three of us, we could make it a couple months, easy. But with six, we're looking at less than a month."

He wasn't all that good at math, but if the crew doubled, wouldn't food be cut in half? Also, weren't there five of them? Oz, Denk, Morpho, Doc, himself, and …

Oh, *hell* no.

"Tell me you didn't take in an eight-foot-tall lizard who talks like Tarzan."

She threw up her arms. "We barely made it back to the ship after you punched out of Tretiak's compound. What were we supposed to do? Leave him to the Saraks?"

Part of him wanted to scream yes, that is what they should've done. But they had bigger problems now. Their scanners would only pick up those fighters if they were on the same side of the moon, so if they weren't on the scopes, it might give them a window to make a run for it and burn away before the patrol knew they were gone.

— *What are you thinking?*

— It's a risk, but we sure as hell can't stay here.

He shook his head as though to clear it. "What's our weapons situation?"

"Same as before. One working disruptor bank on the starboard side. No torpedoes, no mines, no nothing. Our assets are Nutrimush and recycled pee."

"We could always shoot Voprot at them. What about the *Dom*?"

"Disruptors and an antimatter cannon. Oh, and a couple of plasma missiles. Why?"

Geddy flared his eyebrows. "Because we've gotta get out of here and I've been spoiling for a proper fight."

CHAPTER 3

THE DAPPER GENTLEMAN

Recovering from a half-naked spacewalk took more out of Geddy than he expected. The blotches of frostbite healed quickly enough, and the ache in his joints eased a bit more each day, but the fatigue drove him into the ground. Because he spent most days in bed, his input-starved brain would take him on random journeys into the past, punctuated by fitful bouts of half sleep. It gave him lots of time to think.

Anyone could think, but to do it properly took discipline. Being stuck on The Deuce all those years taught him that. Rumination was the ultimate enemy. Revisiting his many, many mistakes only gave them the power they needed to become regrets, and regrets drove people mad.

Not every experience working for Tretiak was bad. True, he'd made a lot more enemies than friends, but he only appreciated his friends all the more. One such friend, and an unlikely one at that, was Zirhof of Zorr.

Zirhof was a cordial and instantly likable businessman who had frequent dealings with the Double A. Geddy rarely dealt with buyers, instead either taking possession of items from sellers or, in some cases, stealing them when they weren't for sale. But Zirhof didn't fit the typical mold. Most people in the Double A's broader network were brokers or small-time dealers who occasionally wound up with something exceedingly valuable but dangerous like weapons or ships. But a few times a year, he got to deal with collectors like Zirhof.

If the galaxy had a historian, it would be him, and if it had a museum, it would be his palatial home above Nova Auris, Zorr's legendary capital. He collected artifacts from myriad worlds and dedicated himself to learning their history. The rarer the better, it seemed. Visiting him was a welcome respite from the backstabbing, violent, and criminal world of the Double A.

To Zirhof, Old Earth arcana were the ultimate scores. Very few material items of historical significance were important enough to make the journey from Old Earth. Considering the eye-watering cost of bringing anyone or anything to another galaxy, it's a wonder any of it was saved.

For that reason, practically everything on display at the Museum of Space Exploration where his mother worked was a replica. She'd always maintained that Neil Armstrong's suit was the real deal, and may have been told as much herself, but even that turned out to be fake. Originals were kept in a climate-controlled vault at the back that she let him see only once, on his tenth birthday. Most of it was either small, like a collection of crew patches from the Apollo missions or quantum cubes containing hundreds of years' worth of scientific research and data collected from the space programs.

A handful of these authentic items had gone missing over the years, including the patches and at least one of the quantum cubes. If there were backups, his mother never said.

The last time he saw Zirhof had nothing to do with the Double A. He'd reached out to Geddy to see if he was interested in doing a job for him. The money was good, and he had no obligations, so he agreed.

Zirhof welcomed Geddy to his villa and led him to the enormous room where his many, many pieces were on display. He went to the safe in his office, unlocked it, and handed Geddy a small, latched metal case.

"Open it."

Ordinarily, he never questioned the provenance of any item. It was rude or even dangerous to inquire, and usually better to not know. But this wasn't a typical job.

Geddy hesitated. Was he being for real, or was this a test? Zirhof nodded encouragingly, so he undid the latch. Inside the foam-lined case was a quantum cube. He had a pretty good idea where it came from, and it must have registered on his face.

"You know what this is?"

"A quantum cube. A mass storage device."

Zirhof seemed genuinely impressed. "Very good. You must be steeped in Old Earth. The planet, I mean, not the whisky."

"You might say I'm steeped in both," Geddy replied.

"I was unable to break the encryption. Given your … unique connections, I thought you might be able to help."

Geddy's ears twitched. Surely Zirhof knew people who could open a quantum cube like a book.

"What's supposed to be on it?"

"Research. I'd hoped it could solve a mystery."

"Oh?"

Zirhof paused a moment before replying. "Some students of Old Earth history doubt the account of how humans came to our galaxy."

"Oh?"

Growing up, that was unchallenged gospel. A fleet of transports left Old Earth in 2129 carrying a hundred thousand humans ostensibly chosen by lottery. They drifted through space for 82 years before discovering an anomaly in spacetime and sent a probe through. The data it sent back suggested many habitable worlds, so the whole fleet went through and found themselves in a whole new galaxy, eventually settling — and that certainly was the word — on Earth 2.

"The chances of running into a stable natural wormhole are incalculably small," Zirhof explained. "Let alone one that led to multiple star systems capable of sustaining life. As far as stories go, it's a fairytale."

"Okay, so what do you think really happened?"

The old man's eyes glinted with excitement. Boy, did he love a good mystery. "Some believe the technology to create artificial wormholes originated on Old Earth."

Geddy stared at him for a moment, blinking. "You mean blue b– er, novaspheres were created on Earth?"

He dismissed the thought with a wave of his hand. "Nova-spheres create jumpgates through brute force. I'm talking about something far more elegant."

His mind raced to decipher Zirhof's meaning. "Like what?"

"Even now, we don't know the way to Old Earth. Hell, we wouldn't even know where the Milky Way was if humans hadn't shown up. But they couldn't have known the way to ours either. The only logical explanation is that they learned how to manipulate spacetime at a level we have yet to achieve."

Geddy stopped in front of a painting that depicted an early Sumbakh, a famous Zorran holiday. Villagers in loincloths pointed at the sky with their mouths open, freaking out at the perfect alignment of the three suns.

"How is that possible?"

"I don't know, but the idea that they simply stumbled upon a wormhole that dumped them out here doesn't hold up to a moment's scrutiny."

Geddy blinked, incredulous. "Humans couldn't have

figured that out. We only got rid of pennies because a committee decided they were too heavy. Even then, the vote was 52-48."

He shrugged as though acknowledging the idea was fundamentally silly — the fanciful indulgence of an old collector. "Like I said, it's just a theory. But you must admit, it's a tantalizing one."

"I'll see what I can do," Geddy said, patting the case in his hand.

"I know you will," Zirhof said, gesturing toward the door.

Behind him, Nova Auris' endless crescent of slim white buildings curled around the purple-tinged ocean like a beckoning finger. Except for Sumbakh, its three suns formed a triangle of orange, red, and blue. He nodded and headed out to his ship.

An old friend from Stemir was able to decrypt portions of the data on the cube. While it contained references to NASA research on Einstein-Rosen bridges, a.k.a. wormholes, there was nothing to indicate that such technology was ever developed. Even so, he occasionally indulged a little fantasy that someday, after he brought Eli to his ancestral home, Geddy might one day pay a visit to his.

CHAPTER 4

I'M THE CAPTAIN NOW

The morning after Geddy's little trip down memory lane with Zirhof, Dr. Tardigan cleared him to move about the ship. Everyone made time to stop in and keep him company, which he appreciated, but no one deserved his gratitude more than Morpho, who was inexplicably dedicated to keeping him alive.

But that was only part of the story now. Morpho had plugged himself into Geddy, ostensibly to borrow a bit of energy, and in the process discovered Eli. In the heat of the moment, there was no time to explain, though he seemed to understand.

All of which led back to whether the crew needed or deserved to know about Eli. If they did, would they even believe him? And what if they knew about the link between Eli and the Zelnads?

Right now, they had bigger fish to fry.

Between the three crew members and the very capable Dr. Tardigan, they had the foundation of a proper working ship. If only the ship worked.

Having only seen the inside of the infirmary for the past

several days, it struck him how unfamiliar everything looked at first. If anything, it was dingier than he remembered. He kept his steps small, almost at a shuffle, with Doc right beside him in case he lost his balance.

"Heyyyy." Denk spun around in his pilot chair as Geddy entered the bridge. "It lives!"

"I see no one bothered to clean," he said as his eyes roamed over the grimy walls.

Oz rose from her chair to give him a hug. Whether she'd just cleaned up or emanated some natural Temerurian musk, he couldn't have said. Either way, it imbued him with fresh energy.

"Glad you're upright. Feeling better?"

"Mostly just sore. My eyes are a lot better, though."

A thin, slurpy sound came from overhead as Morpho swung into view. He landed on Geddy's shoulder with a wet plop.

"Hey, funky gunky." Seeing him stirred surprisingly strong emotions, chief among them gratitude. "Last time I saw you, you were stretched pretty thin."

Geddy laughed at his own joke, but his reverie was interrupted by a sound from behind him. The door to the hold had slid open, and a sinking feeling sprouted deep in his stomach as he slowly turned around.

Their giant Kigantean friend was hunkered in the doorway looking for all the world like a T-rex with scoliosis.

"Hi Geddy!" He awkwardly extended his arms as he lurched forward.

Oz took a couple steps back, leaving room for Geddy to be wrapped up in his scaly meathooks. He smelled as lizards generally did, which was to say vaguely rotten. Yes, he'd proven himself a powerful ally against the Sarak goons back in Aquebba, but he was supposed to get on another ship. *Any* other ship.

"Hey, big guy," Geddy muttered. "I can't breathe."

Voprot released him and pulled back, his eyes glassy. "Sorry. Voprot excited. Forget immense strength."

Geddy pleadingly searched his friends' eyes for some indication that Voprot's presence was only temporary, and that dropping him off was the next priority, but none came.

He heaved a sigh. "Look, none of you would be in this situation if it weren't for me, and I'm sorry about that. But we can't hide out here forever. Looks like we've only got about three weeks of food and water, probably less. Denk, what systems are within that range?"

"Only one with the supplies we need," Denk replied. "Thegus."

Thegus was the most remote planet of the former Alliance and closest to the center of the galaxy. It was originally established as a jumping-off point for exploration of the core systems, but in the wake of the Alliance's collapse, the spaceport was sold off to private investors who wanted to make it a tourist destination. They'd likely have everything the *Fiz* needed, but it wouldn't come cheap.

He hadn't been there in thirteen years. For all he knew, it could be Zelnad Central by now. But what choice did they have?

"What's the plan?" asked Oz.

"Plan? This is just a discussion."

She gave him an *Oh, please* look. "That's not how a ship works and you know it. The captain leads, the crew follows."

"But I'm not the ..."

The look in their eyes said Geddy didn't have to finish that sentence. For good or ill, they looked up to him now. Charm and charisma were such burdens sometimes.

"You are," Oz assured him with a smile. "You're just the last to know."

— *Told you.*

"What say you, Voprot?" asked Denk.

"Voprot??" Geddy asked. "What does he have to do with anything? No offense."

"Voprot understand," he muttered.

Geddy looked at him askance. "Can we, like, drop you off somewhere? Maybe Thegus?"

Oz cleared her throat. "Look, Ged, between us getting away and you being out, there were some conversations ..."

— Oh, god, don't tell me. Please d–

"We invited Voprot to join our crew," she finished. "We figured it wouldn't hurt to have some muscle."

— *I happen to agree.*

— Nobody asked you.

"What about the *Penetrator*?" inquired Oz.

After their earlier conversation, Geddy gave that a good, long think. The *Red Raven* was in the wind and so was his ship, at least for now. The same patience that got him through seven years on The Deuce with only Eli as company would have to serve him once again.

He forced a pained smile. "Looks like she'll have to wait."

"Your orders, Captain?" Denk asked hopefully.

Geddy approached the front display, which provided the only light in the bridge besides the emergency lights along the floor. The scans appeared to be empty, but that meant nothing. Tretiak's patrol could show up at any second, and even if they timed their escape perfectly, they likely couldn't outrun them in the *Fiz*.

"Well, we're almost out of food and power, we can't stay, and we can't run. Luckily, humans have a time-tested method of dealing with these situations."

"What's that?"

"We shoot our way out."

CHAPTER 5

THE DOG IN DOGFIGHT

Most dropships were the starship equivalent of a family sedan, designed for atmospheric entry and with minimal defenses. Some freighters had room for a light, one-man fighter in lieu of escape pods, but the *Fiz* wasn't half the size of your average freighter. It had been heavily modified to accommodate the *Dominic*, in which the late Captain Bykite's had deserted the Kailorian army.

That made it old, but old wasn't necessarily bad when it came to starships. In the Alliance days, certain weapons were banned by treaty, so newer ships weren't as well-armed as they used to be. The *Dom* had dual recoilless KSA Quasitaser disruptors on its stubby wings and a Brightbreaker antimatter cannon in the nose. Two banks of guided plasma missiles were mounted on top.

Though he'd piloted the *Dom* through the difficult approach to Earth 3, he hadn't examined it that closely. Several blaster marks were still visible on the outside. A few rivets were missing, and the left rear engine's finish was a different color. Even so, he could tell it was innovative in its day. Now it was just ... cool.

"They don't make 'em like this anymore, Denk." He ran his fingers along the top of one disruptor barrel. "She was made for an honest fight."

"Ol' Cap took pretty good care of her. You're sure you don't want a crash course on the weapon controls? They're not exactly intuitive."

Geddy couldn't help but smirk. Fighters were fighters. The kid just wanted to be helpful. "How's about we go over the plan one more time instead?"

"As soon as we dust off, I'll do a full burn toward Thegus while you guard our tail. If they come after us, we'll pivot and hit 'em with the starboard disruptors."

He gave Denk a reassuring pat on the shoulder. "See? Easy-peasy."

"Yeah, but I really think you should–"

"Relax, kid," Geddy interrupted. "You'll do great. Now let's get the fuck out of here."

He ducked under the wing and moved around to the rear of the craft, only to realize he didn't know how to open the door. Confusion must have registered on his face, because Denk hurried over to tap an unseen button that lowered the steps.

— *Well, this doesn't bode well.*

— Jeez, you, too? How am I supposed to captain if nobody trusts me?

———

Kailoria's reputation for elegant design was on full display in the *Dominic*. The fit and finish were gorgeous, from the combination of materials to the ergonomic controls. Though everything was designed to fit taller, thinner Kailorian bodies and hands, Geddy still felt it could've been custom made for him.

For Denk's sake, he'd downplayed the risks of this plan.

Tretiak was out for blood. If the squadron searching for them were Screvari-made like most merc ships were, then he would have his hands full.

He settled into the pilot's chair, powered her up and surveyed the control bank. All he'd really used to fly her into Earth 3 was the stick, the throttle, and the button that lowered the skids, which he'd guessed correctly. The smooth buttons and front display were all marked with Kailorian symbols he didn't recognize.

"You ready to roll, chief?" asked Denk through the comm. "Still no sign of the squadron."

"Good. Let's fly the unfriendly skies," he affirmed, fastening his restraints.

— I don't suppose you know any Kailorian.

— *Seriously?*

— Forget it. I'll figure it out.

A low whine came from overhead as Denk restored power to the *Fiz*. A second later, the engines shuddered as it lifted off, sending up billowing clouds of moon dust as it pivoted toward Thegus. He already had an idea how to dig them out of the financial hole they were in, but the first order of business was making it out alive.

The rumble of a full burn pressed at his back as the *Fiz* accelerated. A typical fighter's scanners could only reach maybe half a parsec into space, so he figured they had about twenty minutes to get clear, maybe less if they could put one of Kigantu's moons between them and the patrol.

His eyes fixed on the front display, a translucent blue sphere indicating the outer limit of the *Dom's* scan range. Five minutes passed without incident, but then the sphere flipped to red. Bright, diamond-shaped contacts appeared in the lower left corner and were closing fast. The system automatically zoomed in and revealed the merc squadron. Six Screvari Broadswords flying in a tight V.

"We've got company!" Denk said.

"I see them. Lemme show you how it's done." Underfoot, motors engaged and retracted the doors. "Remember, keep the pedal to the metal. I've got your back."

"Give 'em hell, chief. Releasing dropouts in one … two …"

From overhead came a sharp *clank*, and the *Dom* dropped free of the *Fiz*. Geddy tapped the stick to spin her around the other way and hit the thrusters.

— *I really hope you know what you're doing.*

— Watch and learn, my friend. Watch and learn.

Comms were open, but the merc squadron didn't bother to hail him. They knew what this was.

— All right. Let's see what these buttons do.

He pulled the trigger on the stick. As expected, bright green bolts fired from the wings in the general direction of the approaching fighters.

— Disruptors, okay …

A button next to the stick looked like an upside-down U that flared out with a circle on top. It looked vaguely like the cannon, so he pressed it. Immediately, a blast shield slammed down over the front display and the interior lights turned red.

— Definitely not the cannon.

He pressed it again, expecting it to toggle back, but it didn't work. He scanned the controls looking for another similar symbol, perhaps flipped the other way, but no such luck. The button right next to that one resembled a letter K but with two lower slants and a curly top.

He pressed it, and the whole ship powered down.

— Umm …

— *I knew this would happen!*

"Denk, do you copy?"

But Denk couldn't hear him because the ship's comms were powered down, too. Why was the off switch so far from the on switch? Maybe Kailorian design wasn't all it was cracked up to be. At least he knew where the on switch was. Of course, he couldn't discern it from the others in the darkness.

— I don't know which one to hit.

— *Then hit them all!*

He opened his hand and started just mashing buttons with his palm like an idiot. At once, the ship powered up, the blast shield retracted, and one of the missiles launched from underneath. Geddy looked up in time to see it streak toward the rapidly approaching ships. They scattered, and it missed, sailing off into the void because it didn't lock.

"Geddy, do you copy??" Denk asked frantically.

"Loud and clear, kid. Just, um, working through a slight malfunction."

"What kind of shot was that? You just wasted a missile!"

"It's, umm … an advanced tactic."

— *Leave it to you to shoot prematurely.*

The advancing squadron returned to their formation and launched their own missiles all at once.

"All right," he muttered. "Let's see what this puppy can do."

He lined up with them and punched it. Alarms blared, the display flashed a recommended evasion maneuver, but he wasn't about to do that. He put the *Dom* into a wobbly roll and squeezed the trigger, spraying a cone of blaster bolts in front of him that took out all but one of the missiles. At the last second, he dove right under it.

As expected, it did a hard U-turn and followed him.

"Denk, countermeasures?"

"Are you serious?" whined Denk. "You said–"

"No time to argue."

"It kinda looks like a stick man taking a dump."

His eyes raced over the buttons until he saw a zigzag shape with a dark triangle under the bend.

"Wow, it really does," he said, and pressed it.

Pop pop pop. A staccato knock sounded from behind and he banked hard up and left to see what happened. A ring of soft-ball-sized spheres had deployed from the rear, activating lasers that spun at high speed. The laser wall turned the last missile to space dust.

— *Very nice!*

Half the squadron stayed on the *Fiz* but the others broke off to attack him.

"Denk, sorry to bother you again, but which one's the cannon?"

"Oh god, they're coming straight for us!"

"The cannon, Denk."

"Two snails playing catch with a stick."

Geddy spied a button with two spiral shapes and a short horizontal line between. "Wow, you are weirdly good at this. But how in hell could that possibly mean ..."

"Just get these guys off me!" he pleaded.

"Right. Be there in a jiff."

He angled toward the three fighters and pressed the button. A haunting sound like the gathering of a storm came from directly above as the enemy unleashed a barrage of disruptor bolts at him. A pulse of yellow light bright as the sun fired from the cannon, boring a hole through the red streaks and slamming into the lead ship. It exploded with such force that it sent the other two spinning sideways into space.

"Ha! Now that is some old-school shit right there. Woo, boy, it's like riding a bicycle!"

He punched it and got one of the disabled fighters in his sights just as it righted itself. The hapless pilot looked up just as Geddy squeezed the trigger again, the bright yellow flash lighting up his terrified face like a firework right before it exploded. Geddy giggled to himself.

— I haven't seen that look in ages. Takes me back.

— Of all the heads in all the worlds in all the galaxy, I had wind up in yours.

Geddy accelerated again and swung wide to take out the other disabled fighter, flying straight through the debris as he raced to catch up to the *Fizmo*.

"Hey, Denk? Quick question about that missile I fired earlier. Can it still acquire?"

"As long as it has enough fuel."

"I don't suppose you–"

"A bird beak flying into the sun!"

He found a hook shape inside a circle and pressed it. The nearest ship to him flashed red, and the missile he'd fired earlier came back onscreen.

Again, he gunned the engine and rocketed off toward the *Fiz*, which was taking heavy fire from the merc ship. When the reticle at the center of the screen settled on the rearmost ship, a spiked ring spun around it. A moment later, the stray missile zipped by overhead, slamming into the back of the fighter and turning it into a fireball instantly swallowed by the vacuum.

Another alarm blared and two more ships entered the sphere from behind him. Apparently the two knocked off course by the first blast weren't out of commission. They reformed and made straight for the *Fiz*.

He spoke into the comm. "Denk, I need you to shoot Voprot out of the cargo hold. With any luck, these guys take the bait."

"What?! I'm not doing that!"

— He's been nothing but nice to you.

— Worth a try.

"Are your weapons hot?" Geddy asked.

"Aye, Cap," Denk replied.

He glanced up at the display long enough to see the fighters bearing down on them and preparing to unleash on him.

"When I give the word, hit the brakes and square up to them. We'll both fire at the same time."

"Roger that."

Denk had the *Fiz* wide open but Geddy barely felt like he was moving. The remaining fighters were much faster and would be in firing range in a few seconds.

"Okay, buddy, let's see what that hunk o' junk's packing. Three ... two ... one ... now!"

Denk pivoted the *Fiz* ninety degrees right at the same time Geddy looped around and leveled out. As soon as they were in position, Geddy pulled the trigger that launched the last missile. The *Fiz's* disruptors sent a bright orange volley into space.

The enemy ships fired at the exact same time, uncorking a red torrent of laser bolts. But the *Fiz* was too fragile to take the hits. Geddy darted in front of the ship and sped toward the hail of fire, unleashing the antimatter cannon. It swallowed the bolts while their barrage connected with the enemy targets, turning them into fireballs that flashed once, then went black.

"Yeah!" shouted Denk. Geddy could hear the others cheering in the background. "That's the last of 'em!"

He had to smile. "Good. Now let me back in so we can get the hell out of here."

He maneuvered the *Dom* under the trawler and waited for the dropouts to open, an ear-to-ear grin plastered across his face. It had been a long time since he got in a fight with anything but his fists or a blaster. That only came with practice, but this ... he'd always been good at this. Like his old man.

— Dude, you don't know how good that felt.

— *I don't think I want to know. So, what happens now?*

— I think it's high time we changed our fortunes.

CHAPTER 6

CLOSED FOR INVENTORY

What would it take to go after the *Penetrator* and, after he and Eli were gone, to set up the crew for the next several years? That was the question.

To answer it, Geddy took a slow walk through the whole ship with Denk taking notes. All the autopilot had to do was keep them on a straight line for Thegus, but even that was nerve-wracking. New nav equipment went on the list.

He'd already ordered Voprot to pull every last piece of dusty old scrap from the shelves and arrange it on the floor of the hold while Dr. Tardigan took careful inventory. Oz was below decks helping Morpho with the shield repairs.

The bridge resembled a frat house on Sunday morning. The late Captain Bykite's chair was closer to a throne and raised unnaturally high, especially considering his height. It might've given a Ghruk captain an ego boost, but Geddy didn't care for it at all. At the same time, it was weird to not sit in the captain's chair, not to mention mildly disappointing.

"Let's get rid of that stupid platform," Geddy directed. "New upholstery, too, while we're at it. Synthetic, of course." He ran his fingers along the greasy, worn arm of the captain's chair and wrinkled his nose. "This looks like it came off a hobo's corpse."

"Hobo corpse ..." Denk said, scribbling furiously in his notepad. "Got it."

"Don't write that down."

"No ... hobo ... corpse ..."

"All these buttons and gauges need a good cleaning. Get in there with a toothpick if you have to. I like my buttons clean as a Stemiran girl's areolas. How many don't light up anymore?"

Denk's eyes got big. "Their boobs? Boy, I couldn't tell ya."

Geddy gave a close-mouthed smile over his gritted teeth. "The buttons, Denk. How many buttons don't light up anymore? A starship with buttons that don't glow isn't a starship."

Denk's face fell. "Around half. At least, of the ones I use."

Geddy cocked an eyebrow. "How many don't you use?"

"Most, I'd say."

"How come?"

— *How did this kid become a pilot?*

— I was thinking the same thing.

"I don't know what they do. Cap'n Bykite never showed me." Once again, he was reminded of what a shitshow the *Fiz* really was. All he'd done was get ejected into space with a bunch of trash, and now he was somehow in charge. How did that happen? "'Course, I'm not sure he knew."

"Before we get to Thegus, you're gonna learn what they all do."

"How?"

"The fun way, obviously. Just give yourself plenty of space."

He chuckled at his own joke and approached the weapons locker at the back of the bridge. When he opened the creaky door, a musty metal smell hit his nostrils. The antique Exeter

D6 blaster he'd taken with him on Kigantu still hung on its hook, but otherwise it was bare.

"We need blasters. Rifles, pistols, grenades, the whole shebang. A working ship has to be ready for pirates."

Denk wrote it down. "Weapons. Love it."

"To the galley."

They proceeded out of the bridge and took a left down the short hallway that led to the galley and the tiny infirmary. A hexagonal metal table with built-in seats sat in the middle with a bank of aluminum cabinets along the wall, only a few of which still slid open. The nutrimush dispenser sat at the end, essentially a spigot that disappeared into the wall. The storage tank was under the floor. Voprot could only fit inside the galley if he crouched at the table and let his tail extend into the hallway. Since he couldn't get to the dispenser without knocking everything over, Denk had to fill a bowl for him as though he was a pet.

The nutrimush tank could hold six months' worth, but Voprot would change that equation. Geddy could barely stomach no more of the stuff. It was originally made for people coming out of a long hypersleep in the pre-novasphere days because it was nutritious — hence the name — and easy to digest. Not the first thing you wanted to taste on a hypersleep hangover. But that was a bygone era. Now, you could jump anywhere in the galaxy.

A good food recombinator vaulted to the top of the list. Otherwise, the galley was adequate.

Dr. Tardigan said their medical supplies and equipment were lacking, so those went on the list, too. But nothing else in the infirmary desperately needed replacing, so they moved across the way to the crew quarters and the bathroom.

"Think we need uniforms?" asked Denk.

"Screw uniforms. What we need are real clothes and softer beds."

He dutifully wrote them down. "Where's Voprot gonna sleep?"

— Is outside the ship an option?

— *Be nice.*

"I'll figure something out. Come on, let's deal with the latrine."

Denk was the only one who could stand fully upright in the weird Ghruk shower, so that, too, went on the list. Ditto for the water recycler, which left their water looking and smelling so much like piss that no one could say for sure it still worked.

"New shower, new recycler. Got it."

"All right," Geddy said, excited at the prospect of replacing all this stuff and turning the *Fizmo* into a proper starship. "Now to the hold."

Empty, the hold resembled the basketball court at a rural elementary school. It was twenty-five meters wide, forty deep, and ten high, with stacks of shipping crates on the starboard side and tall shelves on the port side, essentially making it a flying warehouse. Correction — an empty flying warehouse.

Apparently, Voprot and Tardigan had made quick work of things because the shelves were bare and everything was neatly arranged on the floor. Denk's private stash still appeared to be behind the ratty old blanket on the bottom shelf.

He narrowed his eyes at Voprot. "You better not have touched my stuff."

"Voprot respect boundaries," said the Kigantean.

"Captain, there's something you should see," said Tardigan.

He led them over to a corner of the shelving just below a vent. Even empty, it was hard to see all the way under. When he crouched beside Doc, he discovered a desiccated skeleton slumped against the wall still wearing a ratty set of gray clothes.

Denk joined them and his eyes widened. "Yikes. So *that's* where that smell was coming from." He shook his head and chuckled at the memory. "And here we thought he hopped off on Doxx-Mora. Wait 'til Oz sees."

"You know this guy??" Geddy asked.

"Some hitcher. I don't remember his name. It was years ago now."

When Geddy came on board, they were giving a lift to three rough characters who would've been put to work if there was any. One got sucked out through a cantaloupe-sized hole and the other two took off running the instant they reached Caloth. Considering how many nooks and crannies were on the shelves, it wasn't hard to imagine some poor bastard getting stuck. Kind of a bad look, though.

"Deal with him." Geddy rose to his feet and stretched.

"We could use him for target practice," offered Denk.

"Good idea." He sauntered between the metal pieces with his hands in his pockets, frowning. "Is it just me, or did most of this crap come from the same ship?"

"I had the exact same thought, Captain," said Doc, arms akimbo.

"Can you tell what kind of ship?"

"Kailorian. Roughly the same vintage as the *Dominic*, if I'm not mistaken."

Geddy and Denk exchanged a long look just as Oz came strolling in with Morpho on her shoulder.

"What's up?" she asked.

"All this is from the same Kailorian ship," said Geddy, nodding at the assorted pieces of fuselage and bent control panels.

She paused briefly. "You don't think Captain Bykite ..."

The ship's late captain was a world-class weenie who had no business running a trawler, but he may have been trying to find parts from some old ship. Was it his or someone else's?

"He hung on to this stuff for a reason," said Geddy.

Maybe he and Bykite weren't so different after all. He took it as a sign that this was the right ship and the right crew to help retrieve the *Penetrator*.

"Whatever it meant to him, it isn't worth jack to us," Oz noted. "How's the list coming?"

"Long and growing," said Geddy, holding her gaze. Oz smirked at the double entendre, which was entirely accidental. "The shields?"

"Gone-zo."

Denk went line by line through the list of stuff they needed, batting estimates back and forth with Oz until they settled on a figure. Conservatively, they were looking at eight hundred thousand credits, and that was at a place like Caloth. Thegus would have half of what they needed and cost half again as much. At least a million.

A heavy silence descended over them. That was a boatload of money. Double-A sized money. Even with a run of good luck, it would take years to fix everything. No wonder she was practically held together with twine.

— *What are we going to do? If we wait too long, we'll never find out where our ship is.*

— I dunno, pal. It's a pickle.

— *What's a pickle?*

— Something you rip off a sandwich and throw in the trash.

— *What's it have to do with–*

— Never mind.

"Aw, man," lamented Denk. "We'll never get that kind of money! Especially not way out here."

"Not out here," Geddy said. "But Thegus may offer us a unique opportunity."

Thegus' lone claim to fame was a legendary race that he'd always dreamt of running. It felt like kismet.

"There's good salvage on Thegus?" Denk asked, clueless.

Oz, however, knew exactly what he meant. "Oh, *hell* no."

"What?" Denk asked eagerly. "What's on Thegus?"

A sly smile crept across Geddy's face and he flared his eyebrows. "Ponley Point."

"A race where rich assholes go to die," Oz said gravely. "Winner takes all."

"There are frequent accidents, yeah, but the pot's usually a million credits or more," Geddy explained. "I think the *Dom* could hold her own."

He'd never seen Oz's lilywhite face redden until now. "A word, Captain?"

"Excuse us a moment." He backed up as she approached, her arms folded tightly. Once they were out of earshot, he said, "I suppose you're gonna tell me this is a dumb idea."

"It absolutely is."

"But ..."

"But I don't have a better one."

"So what's the problem?"

"Who's gonna fly it?" she asked.

"Me, obviously. I know the course and I'm the best."

She rolled her eyes so hard he could almost hear it. "You're our captain, Ged. It pains me to say it, but you're no longer expendable."

His eyes narrowed. "You want me to teach Voprot how to fly?"

She huffed and looked away, exasperated. He glanced past her at Denk and his chest tightened. The kid was far too nice for Ponley Point, but they could work on that. And he needed the confidence boost. The question was, could he live with himself if things went sideways?

He heaved a sigh. "Think we can teach him how to race between now and then?"

She cracked her knuckles and shrugged. "What the hell else are we gonna do for the next three weeks?"

CHAPTER 7

DENK THE DARING

Ponley Point. Last stop on the midlife crisis express for desperate, lonely has-beens with a fat wallet, a fast ship, and an itch to stare death in the face.

Winner-take-all didn't mean everyone else died. Some races never recorded a single casualty. But those were bad for business. Ponley was all about the carnage. People still talked about the forty-two ship pileup at the bottom of the Plunge, and that was sixty-odd years ago.

Geddy had never actually raced there himself, but he'd grown up playing the video games and always went to the race when he had business on Thegus. He knew every turn, every gate like the back of his hand. He used to know all the racers, but not anymore.

Even if you could run it alone, the course was fiendishly difficult. Throw a few dozen racers in the mix, and it turned into a meat grinder. Big, circular gates registered your ship as it passed through, but they were only wide enough for one ship. If you weren't among the leaders after the first three gates, you'd be playing catch-up for the last three and had to get in line for the gate.

The *Fiz* didn't exactly have a library of games, so they improvised a course in the hold built roughly to scale. Using Bykite's ship parts, Geddy lovingly laid it out from memory and walked Denk through it over and over until he knew it cold.

When the time came, he plopped Denk down on a chair beside the breakdown bench wearing a blindfold, a wrench in one hand and an electric screwdriver in the other. He looked for all the world like a raccoon, but the course had many blind spots even if you weren't eating someone's dust.

Denk assured him he'd do well because games were big on Durandia, like Where Does This Tunnel Go? and Who Chewed the Root?

— *He's gonna die.*

— Maybe. Let's see how he does with a little pressure.

Oz and Tardigan were racked out, leaving just Voprot and Morpho to watch this little scene. Voprot had no earthly idea what they were doing.

"Okay," Geddy set his hands on his knees as he crouched beside his young protégé. "You're crowded behind the starting line. Every ship looks faster than yours, every pilot looks better. Where's your head?"

"On top of my neck."

"What are you thinking about?"

"Oh! I'm thinking about the first corner, the Razor."

"What about it?"

"I need to set up high and left."

Geddy smacked his forehead. "High and right. It's a left turn."

"High and right was what I meant. Sorry, I'm nervous."

"Forget it. Talk to me about the curve."

"It looks like a right turn until you're almost on top of it. You're jockeying for position," said Denk, his rodent-like face puckered with determination.

"That's right. But what happens if you set up *too* high?"

"You hit the wall."

"Good. Then what?" asked Geddy.

"Set up low through the Crotch Gate where the canyon pinches off, then start climbing for the Moonshot."

"And what's most important in this section?"

"Steady acceleration." Denk pushed the faux thruster forward and pulled back on the stick. "Don't get too anxious. Start looking for the gate once you hit the ionosphere."

"Exactly. You can't use scopes, so rely on your eyes. It's hard to see. What's after Moonshot gate?"

"The Suicide Plunge," he said reverently.

"A ten thousand-meter, asshole-puckering dive straight into the mouth of a dormant volcano. Like thrusting a dagger into the black, oily heart of hell."

He flashed back to that most treacherous part of the game where he'd crashed so many times. You eased through the Moonshot ring so slowly, you almost came to a stop. But then you nosed her straight down and punched it like you intended to die.

"Ooh, I like that!" said Denk.

"No, you don't!" Geddy barked, his adrenaline building. "You'll be pulling so many G's you'll think it's an H. Your eyeballs suck into the back of your skull and there's nothing to do but scream. But you can't because your tongue's stuffed down your throat and it feels like Voprot's sitting on your chest. Meanwhile, you've got to nail the volcano dead-center."

"I thought you only played the video g—"

"Focus, Denk!"

"Okay, sorry," he muttered.

"You're flying blind through the dark at 4,000 kph. Your lights won't pick anything up until it's too late, so you count. A one, and a two, on that exact cadence until you hit six. Then what?"

" ... I flip upright and hit the brakes. Then I choose my line through the ship-pile, pull up, and punch it straight through the DTC."

The Devil's Transcending Colon. How many ships had bottomed out where Suicide ended and it began, exploding in flames? He'd died there a thousand times. But if you made the transition from vertical to horizontal, the DTC was your best chance to make up time. The old lava tube was big and smooth, with few obstacles save for the giant stalagmites. The ceiling was largely clear. If you were good at flying upside down, you could pass a dozen competitors before you came out the other side into the most famous stretch of all.

"You've passed a few ships in the DTC and you're feeling good about yourself. It's a barrel and you're a bullet. What's the next thing you hit?"

"Shoelace Canyon." Denk's voice went low and hushed, as though speaking a forbidden curse.

The DTC shat you out into a deep canyon thousands of meters above a winding river. Over eons, it carved sheer walls in the rock that took a circuitous and treacherous path back to the home stretch, each corner sharper than the last. To slalom through it was exhilarating, but slow compared to the second, more tantalizing option, whence came the canyon's name.

Holes like shoelaces were bored through each fold in the canyon, creating an alternate and nearly straight route that could shorten the distance considerably. But the holes were tight, even for ships smaller than the *Dom*. And there was no room for error because the two routes crossed five times. The penultimate gate was perched atop the canyon rim.

"You're third coming into Shoelace," Geddy continued. "Do you try to outmaneuver them in the curves or take the straight route?"

Almost no one ever took it, but those who did became legends. If you had the skill, it was a heroic way to pull ahead before the final wide-open stretch to Ponley Point, a former military outpost whose entire economy was now built around this race. The winner got eighty percent of the purse, a big celebration, a commemorative mug, and free entry to the Ponley Point Heritage Museum.

"I'll follow my gut," Denk growled.

"Either way requires perfect execution just to survive, let alone triumph. But if you pull it off, they'll sing songs about you."

Denk took off his blindfold, and wiped the sweat beaded on his small nose away, before looking hopefully up at Geddy as though awaiting praise. But champions didn't need praise. They needed to hate losing more than they hated themselves, and he doubted Denk could ever get there.

"Again!"

———

After a few more trips around the track, Geddy sent Denk to rest. Morpho went off to clean the CO_2 scrubbers and Voprot had found a spot in the shelves, lying on his back and looking for all the world like he might be dead.

The two chairs next to the breakdown bench were bolted to the floor but rotated freely. Knowing he couldn't possibly sleep, he leaned back and placed his feet against the bench, then spun himself around, reversing direction each time and thinking how this whole predicament was his fault.

— *I rarely find you lost in thought.*

— Haven't heard from you in a while.

— *I was observing Denk's training.*

— I'm guessing you don't approve.

— *You must know he can't do this.*

"Captain Starheart!" Oz's voice echoed through the large open space.

He spun himself toward the bridge door and found her standing in the threshold, arms akimbo.

"Why are you yelling at me?"

"You were in some kind of daze. I was practically screaming your name."

— *Oh, god. Don't make a joke about her screaming your name. Resist the urge, just this once.*

— Relax, pal, I'm practically a feminist icon.

"Sorry, I was thinking about the race. Denk says we're two days out from Thegus."

"I want real food and a real drink." She closed her big, beautiful eyes and imagined it. "And a hot shower with clean water."

"I want that for you, too. The shower, I mean." He sniffed loudly in her direction, then grinned as she rolled her eyes. "What's up?"

She plopped down on the other chair and started spinning herself around in the opposite direction. Their feet occasionally bumped when they passed, but she didn't seem to mind.

"It's about Denk."

"What about him?" Geddy asked.

"He's a kid."

"Twenty-six in Durandian years," he reminded her.

She barked a laugh. "You believed that line? He's been saying that since I met him."

"Then how old is he?"

"In human years? Nineteen, maybe? Like I said, a kid."

"Don't worry, he's not gonna race. Even if he wanted to."

Her eyes drifted down to the floor. "Which means you are."

Was Oz only worried about him racing because he was the captain or because she cared about him? "I promise I won't die."

She smiled warmly. "You never really intended for him to do it, did you?"

"Someday, maybe he will. But not now."

— *Good. You had me worried.*

— He's not ready. Yet.

"There you went again," Oz said as she studied his face. Somehow, she could tell when he was conversing with Eli. "You must need sleep," she patted his leg.

Eventually, he would have to come clean about Eli, but it never seemed like the right time. She'd given him an off-ramp from this conversation and he'd be a fool not to take it. After Thegus, he'd tell her everything.

"Y'know, I am kind of tired," he said, rising from the chair. "Guess I'll see you in the morning?" She nodded. "Thanks for the spin."

He hurried away, berating himself for being so careless when talking to Eli.

"I'm gonna figure you out, Starheart. One of these days, I'm gonna crack you wide open."

"Can't wait!" he called over his shoulder.

CHAPTER 8

ZERETH-TINN

Denk's voice came over the speaker to announce they'd reached Thegus' outer marker just as the last of the nutrimush spattered out of the clear tube into Geddy's bowl, ruining the perfect little coil he'd formed. He forced it down in three huge spoonfuls and hurried to the bridge.

The control tower at Thegus station cleared the *Fiz* for landing on platform 6B. There was a brief debate about whether she could handle the entry, but it was nowhere near as rough as Caloth or Earth 3. Denk and Morpho expressed confidence she wouldn't break in half, which would have to be good enough.

Off in the distance, just a tiny speck from where they were, was the glowing ring of the Moonshot Gate.

With their approach vector loaded in, they began their descent through the atmosphere. There was no way to buckle Voprot in, so he simply got into a low crouch at the back of the bridge and braced himself between the walls, remaining surprisingly steady while the ship shuddered and creaked.

The same couldn't be said for Oz, whose tightly pinched

face formed a sweaty sheen as Thegus opened up through the clouds. Geddy sat in the jump seat beside her, just as worried about the *Fiz* breaking up but better at hiding it. Instead, he focused on the pleasures of terra firma. They'd left Kigantu almost a month ago, and that wasn't exactly rejuvenating.

Thegus was a small, arid, rocky planet with a slowly dying sun that bathed the mountains and plateaus in a blood-orange hue. He'd always felt very much at ease there. He hadn't racked up any debts or pissed off anyone as far as he knew, so maybe he could relax and get a good night's sleep before tomorrow's race.

— *Would the* Penetrator *do well here?*

— I hardly got to fly her, but I'd like to think so.

"You excited for the race, Mr. Junt?"

He adopted a look of phony bravado. "You bet, Cap! Can't wait to mix it up with those ... dozens of giant racing ships."

Geddy glanced over his shoulder at Oz, who had loosened her restraints. She gave him one of those, *really?* looks, but he wanted to jerk Denk's chain a little. The kid needed to lighten up.

"I wonder if they'll run it forwards or backwards today," he mused.

"Uhh, what?" Denk asked nervously.

"Well, sometimes they start at Shoelace and work their way back. It's not a big deal, you just have to think in reverse."

Watching Denk squirm shouldn't have delighted him as much as it did.

"You never said anything about that!"

"Geez, I'm sorry, it never occurred to me. Did we talk about beneficiaries?"

His eyes widened. "What do you mean?"

"Who gets all your stuff if you die? Better give some thought to that because they'll ask you at check-in. I've got dibs on that old spacesuit."

Denk lowered the gear and pivoted the ship to line up with platform 6B, his hands shaking on the controls. He looked like he might hyperventilate. Oz gave him a final cautioning look over the tops of her eyes.

A bit more clumsy than usual, Denk set the *Fiz* down and killed the engines, his eyes fixed straight ahead, his face pale. Geddy rose from his chair, stretched, and patted him on the shoulder.

"Relax, Denk, I'm just messing with you."

"What do you mean?" he asked hopefully. "Which part?"

"I got us in this mess, I'll get us out of it," Geddy said, smiling. "I'll run the race."

All the air escaped from Denk as he relaxed, folding over and burying his face in his hands. "Oh, thank god!"

———

After pooling their remaining cash from the fight on Caloth, they had ninety-six thousand and change left. Back in the day, the entry fee was fifty grand. Geddy had no idea what it was now, but either way, there wouldn't be much of a cushion. Plus, they still had to eat and sleep. He stuffed a handful of credit squares in his inside jacket pocket and tucked the antique blaster into its holster.

Voprot, Morpho, and Denk were going to see about parts and prices while Geddy, Oz, and Doc went to secure a spot in tomorrow's race. The plan was to reconvene at the spaceport around noon and go from there.

It was perched atop a mountain, much closer to the city than most. A long, wide set of steps led down to the main drag, which was distressingly uncrowded. Once, you'd be shoulder to shoulder with huge crowds but still spot the racers just by the hungry, slightly unhinged look in their eye. Now, everyone looked like they were on their way back from yoga.

Oz took a deep breath with her eyes closed, a satisfied grin decorating her smooth face. "I never get tired of fresh air."

Tardigan inhaled deeply himself, nodding. "Truer words were never said."

"What's your longest turn off-world?" Geddy asked Oz.

"Eleven weeks and change. You?"

"Less than half that," he admitted, recalling the longish haul from Xellara back to Kigantu. That was only because Tev lost all their blue balls betting on wuk-wuk fights.

They'd delivered a huge load of rifles to a crime syndicate and spent the night celebrating. Not until they were nearing their jump vector back home did Tev remember he gambled away their shortcut. It took four-plus weeks to get to Aku and purchase more, during which they had to live on half rations.

"Where do you register for the race?" asked Tardigan.

"It always used to be at this bar called Lil' Bash's. Not sure if that's still the case, but someone there ought to know."

"Can't you just ask around?" Doc inquired.

"Yeah, but it doesn't seem like you should have to."

But by the looks of things, nobody here needed more cash. As they headed toward the entertainment district, Geddy noticed that a lot of the old shops and food stands were gone, replaced by stuffy art galleries and spice emporiums. Even the pedestrian street was nicer, dotted with nattily dressed tourists carrying bags of freshly acquired merchandise.

Had Thegus been … *gentrified?*

A few minutes later, they stood in front of where Lil' Bash's used to be. Now it was some white-tablecloth place called Nouveau Bistreau.

"Well, shit," he muttered.

"You're sure this is where it was?" Oz asked.

Of this, he was certain. Clinking glasses with strangers and watching the race projected on a giant wall was a pretty fresh memory. Panic seized him. If there was no Ponley Point race anymore, then they might be in a world of hurt.

Tardigan spotted an older couple of Orneans strolling together arm in arm. "I'll see what I can find out. Excuse me!"

Doc approached them respectfully and gave a little bow, as was customary on Ornea, while he and Oz studied a numbered map of Thegus etched into the marble plaza. There were four candle shops but nothing about a race.

The Orneans chatted amicably at first, pointing this way and that. At a certain point, though, the couple's faces pinched in disgust and they hurried away as though Tardigan was radioactive. He returned with his head lowered.

"What the hell was that about?" Geddy asked.

"A condition of my exile is that I must confess my crime to fellow Orneans," he said, referring to the so-called academic misconduct that got him booted off the planet. "They were appropriately disgusted."

"What'd they say?" Oz asked.

"That they didn't know anything about a race and that I should leave before they called the authorities."

He patted him on the back reassuringly and gestured toward Nouveau Bistreau. "Come on. Let's get you a drink."

As it had appeared from outside, Lil' Ern's was now a high-end restaurant with a big piano bar. Maybe someone would know where to send them.

Back in the day, Lil' Ern's was the only place to be. It was much too spacious to be called a dive but too small and utilitarian to be a proper sports book. Long tables that weren't at the right height for anyone were arranged in four parallel lines in the main section, useless for anything but setting your drink on. There were no stools save for the bar itself, probably so no one could use them as weapons.

The race was simulcast from a series of camera drones along the route that had wide angles on all the gates, where most of the mayhem happened. Enthusiasts would arrive the moment they opened, sometimes four or more hours before the race started, to claim their spot. By the time countdown commenced, everyone was packed in so tightly that you could've died and never hit the ground.

Now, it was just another fancy restaurant filled with fancy people. Such a shame.

It was tastefully lit and there were tables where the long bar used to be, but the bones were still there. Piano music drifted over from a platform near the new cocktail area, where a debonair older Soturian in a sport coat was playing with his eyes closed. The dining room was practically empty, but the bar was full, and a significant crowd had gathered around the piano.

They found a space at the end, and Geddy signaled the bartender, an attractive young Zorran woman who flicked coasters down in front of them like uguinok cards. Her skin was a paler orange than most and her long white hair was stacked in an elaborate conical braid. Once upon a time, he'd be putting every move he had on a girl like her. Now she looked like a kid.

"Greetings, weary travelers," she said. "What's your poison?"

"Ale," Geddy said. "Whisky back."

"Kailorian gin," said Oz. "As cold as you can get it. The good stuff."

The bartender gave a tight nod and turned to Doc. "How 'bout you, professor?"

"Just water, thank you."

The girl darted off to make their drinks. Geddy smirked. "We're gonna have to work on you."

"Alcohol dulls the mind," he said.

"That's the whole point."

He and Oz shared a laugh while the bartender returned

with their drinks. Geddy slid a hundred credits across the bar so she could see it but left his hand, motioning for her to lean in.

"For a little information, you can keep the change," he whispered.

She raised one eyebrow conspiratorially. "You think I work here because I'm plugged in?"

"You want it or not?"

"Whatcha got?" she asked.

"Ponley Point."

She chuckled to herself as she pulled his beer. "You must not have been here in a while."

"Does it still run or not?" he asked eagerly.

"Yeah, it runs, but it's this skeezy underground thing now. You've got to know the right people."

"And do you?"

"No." She nodded at the piano player. "But he does."

He turned to regard the dignified musician, still playing away in some sort of flow state. "Who's he?"

"That's Zereth-Tinn. The all-time record holder for most wins. He'll know what's up."

She looked expectantly at him. He gave the credit square a flick before her slender fingers closed around it, then she left to put some glasses in the dishwasher.

"That was money well spent," chided Oz. "You know who that guy is?"

"No, but I haven't been here in a while."

The gentleman at the piano finished his set and nodded to acknowledge the enthusiastic applause.

"Thank you so much, ladies and gentlemen," he said, his voice silky and sure. "Y'know, I've been knocking around this old town a long time, but I've never had such a generous audience. I like to think all the music that ever was is out there, just floating through the universe. All I am is a conduit … a medium, for those celestial melodies, which will return after a short break."

"Ucch," said Oz, taking a sip of her gin. "What a bunch of malarkey."

"I think it's a beautiful thought," said Tardigan with misty-eyed solemnity. "Imagine every combination of notes, just floating through space ..."

The piano man made a beeline for the bar and bellied up near them. The bartender reflexively poured him a finger of a pale green liqueur. He'd just taken possession of it when Geddy slid over to him.

"Sorry, no requests." He quartered away to make it clear he didn't want a conversation.

But this couldn't wait. If there was a race the next day, he wanted to be in it. The sooner he got the *Fiz* squared away, the sooner he could look for the *Penetrator*.

"I hear you might know something about a race."

He paused mid-sip, then swallowed and set the glass back down. "Who's asking?"

"Captain Geddy Starheart." They shook hands. "Is it true you have more wins than anyone?"

He gave the pretty bartender some stinkeye, but she just shrugged. "Ancient history. Why?"

"Do they still run it?" Geddy asked.

Zereth-Tinn studied the three of them quizzically. "The entry's a hundred grand cash now. You don't have it, you don't race."

Oz glanced nervously in his direction. They were just shy of that, but what could he say? "That's not a problem."

Zereth-Tinn tossed back the last of his drink, then paused on his way back to the stage. "Then sure, Starheart. Meet me back here after the next set and I'll take you there."

CHAPTER 9
FOUR GRAND

After Zereth-Tinn's set, he loosened his tie and led them outside. Like Sammo Yann, he was Soturian, a symmetrical branching pattern etched into his forehead that resembled scars. They all had such markings, and they were as unique as fingerprints. His hair was graying at the sides and thinning on top, suggesting he was older than Sammo, but he had the same steely blue eyes. By the way female patrons watched as he made his way to the back, it was clear he still had game.

As they followed out the door into the pedestrian mall, Oz leaned in and whispered, "We've only got ninety-six between us. Where do you plan to get the other four grand?"

He gave a passive shrug. "One of us could give GQ here a rub and tug."

"Be my guest."

"Just let me do the talking."

She rolled her eyes. "Because that always works out."

"What happened to this place?" Geddy asked him. "I remember it being more … festive."

"Oh, same thing that always happens where there's money

to be made. Investors swoop in, and suddenly everything becomes more expensive and less interesting."

"Man, that sucks. Damn vultures."

"I was among the investors."

"Love what you've done with the place, though," he hurriedly added.

— *Good save. Very smooth.*

— Shut up.

"What happened to ol' LB?"

As might be expected for a barkeep named Li'l Bash, the name was entirely ironic. He was Basoan, and his sluglike body barely fit behind the bar. It didn't matter though, because his unusually long arms reached every bottle from a stationary position, and he was incredibly fast.

"He got stuck one night after closing time and died. They had to cut him out. Just as well. It would've broken his big, greasy heart to see this place become... nice."

The ground-level shops and restaurants ended at a stairway that climbed to the second level, but they walked right past into a narrow alley. Someone had scratched PP into the old stone with a small arrow to show the way.

As though walking back into time, the fancy paint and stonework tapered off, and they spilled out into a narrower, and even busier street. Once Geddy got his bearings, he realized an entire city block was razed to form the pedestrian mall, and that the alley led to an even older part of town he didn't know existed.

At first, he was heartened. This was more like the Thegus he remembered. Street vendors handed out sticks of nonspecific meat through clouds of grill smoke. Desperate restauranteurs and shopkeepers alike goaded passerby to come inside while music wafted through open doors.

But as his eyes lingered a bit more on the façades and

patrons, he realized even this was artifice. The buildings and street *looked* old, but they really weren't.

Moreover, the people walking around were a pretty even mix of men, women, and children.

Children?

Zereth-Tinn gestured grandly, ending with air quotes. "Welcome to 'Old Thegus.'"

A narrative began to form. As so often happened, something fun and awesome had been co-opted by the rich and ruined in the process. Someone decided they should keep the "flavor" of old Thegus alive in what amounted to an amusement park. Essentially, they destroyed its old charm and tried to reproduce it at considerable expense. Where had all this money come from?

"You've gotta be kiddin' me," Geddy remarked with a scowl, his voice heavy with disappointment.

"What wrong?" asked Tardigan.

"Everything."

Zereth-Tinn gave him a knowing look. "Yeah, the race used to be the only reason to come here. Now they buy overpriced jewelry and T-shirts that say, 'I SURVIVED PONLEY POINT'."

Geddy turned haplessly to Oz. *What's the world coming to?*

"Denk's gonna want one of those," she noted.

Their guide surveyed the sad little scene and jutted his chin toward a shop called the Ponley Point Experience. A sign in the large front window read, "Race Ponley Point! Win 100,000 Credits!"

"Tourists believe the real Ponley Point hasn't been run in years. The city planners aim to keep it that way, if you get my drift."

Geddy stopped and pivoted toward him. "What do you mean, 'believe?'"

Zereth-Tinn tucked his hands in his pockets and strolled

toward the building. When they didn't follow, he looked back over his shoulder. "You said you were here to race, right?"

"Not in some lame simulation."

"Come on. There's someone I'd like you to meet."

————

They entered the Ponley Point Experience to find two long rows of fully haptic pods molded to suggest the cockpits of racing ships. About half were occupied, mostly by men and kids. One near the door tilted straight up, shook violently, then leveled out briefly before swinging straight down.

"Aaaaahhh!" screamed the young Ornean kid piloting the virtual craft, who had clearly just made the Moonshot Gate and went into the Suicide Plunge.

Geddy couldn't help but smile at the kid's enthusiasm. "Moonshot to Suicide. At least the game hasn't changed much."

"Looks like they're playing Ponley Point *Classic*," said Zereth-Tinn, indicating banks of holoscreens above the pods. "There are thirty-two, I believe, but I say the original's still the best."

"That's the one I grew up playing." He fondly recalled playing with friends for hours, learning every trick to running the course.

Zereth-Tinn made a beeline to a door at the back marked EMPLOYEES ONLY. A greasy-haired young man behind the counter leaned on his elbow, bored, barely looking up as they went through.

— *What's happening right now?*

— I'm not entirely sure.

A narrow set of stairs led into a smoky, dingy basement, the sound of a muffled conversation wafting up to their ears.

— *That bartender wasn't kidding about the underground part.*

— Or the skeezy part.

He fingered the stack of credits in his pocket, hoping whoever they were about to see would give them a break. The space was unglamorous even for a basement, with a smattering of crates and promotional banners lined up along the wall. Four men were playing uguinok — two Screvari, an Udsar, and a giant Basoan in a double-wide chair who looked eerily familiar. A pile of credit squares sat in the middle. It had to be high six figures at least.

The Basoan peered over his cards at Zereth-Tinn and gave a little nod before laying them down with a self-satisfied grin.

Uguinok. The others groaned and threw down their cards.

"How about that, Z," said the giant, blubbery Basoan, a wide grin playing across his plump, glossy lips. "You must be good luck." Oz, who was bringing up the rear, slid into his view just then and the slits of his yellow eyes traced a lazy outline around her. "Speaking of luck …"

"More like yuck," she muttered under her breath.

His spindly arms reached across the table and raked the pot toward him, bemusedly looking over Geddy and the others. "What brings you by, Z? These three wander off from the walking tour?"

"They want to race," said Zereth-Tinn.

The fat man tapped his bony fingers together thoughtfully, his eyes still locked on Oz. "I sure hope it's you."

"Yeah? Why's that?" asked Oz, wrinkling her nose.

"'Cuz you look like you're built for speed."

"And you look like you're built for sitting," she retorted.

Geddy put a cautioning hand on her shoulder. "Now, Oz, I have a feeling we might need Mr. …?"

"Pardie," he growled.

"… Mr. Party to help–" Geddy cut himself off, blinking. "Wait, your name's Party?"

"Not ParTEE," corrected Zereth-Tinn. "ParDEE. A.k.a. Big Pardie."

Suddenly, Geddy realized why he looked so familiar. Basoan skin came in such different shades and hues that he hadn't connected the dots.

"Your Li'l Bash's kid?"

— *Li'l Bash and Big Pardie? Really?*

— *Li'l Bash was a galactic treasure. I don't like this guy's chi.*

— *What's that?*

— *A life force, I suppose. It's Chinese. It's something my mom always said. 'How's your chi today?'*

— *Fascinating. And how is your chi?*

— *Better than this yutz's.*

"The only one I know about," he said with a self-amused grin. "And who might you be?"

"Name's Geddy Starheart. I'm here to race."

Li'l Bash was pretty well known in racing circles, but other than his outsized body and above-average skill behind a bar, Geddy knew nothing about the guy. At least, not enough to imply they were pals.

"I knew your old man. He was … a big presence."

Pardie's smile vanished. "He was lazy. He could've owned this town if he wanted. Too late now."

"He's gone, then?" Geddy asked, feigning sympathy for the sake of decorum.

"Thank the old gods, yes. Half my life's been cleaning up the trail of shit he left behind."

— *Geez. No love lost between those two.*

"I'm sorry. I can tell you were close."

Oz shook her head. *Why are you kissing this guy's ass?*

"Enough about that." The vertical slits of his eyes widened. "So, you want to race the famous Ponley Point."

"I take it you're the man to see."

It seemed impossible for Pardie to lean back, but somehow he did. His back pressed against the wall, spreading like a stain as a self-satisfied grin spread across his weirdly glossy lips.

"The city wanted to shut the whole thing down. Liability and what not. I convinced them not to."

"Good for you," said Geddy, unimpressed. The universe didn't want for opportunists. "I could use a little windfall myself."

Li'l Bash guffawed. "Hmuh! Heard that a thousand times, haven't we, Z?"

Geddy frowned and pivoted his head back and forth between Bash and Zereth-Tinn. "Wait — you two are partners?"

"Managing partners," clarified Zereth-Tinn. "At least for this little operation."

"You don't race anymore?"

"Oh, once in a great while. There's no real competition anymore. Guess I got tired of winning all the time."

That explained why he was so willing to escort them there. This cloak-and-dagger stuff was all part of some big act. As far as these were concerned, they were just tourists eager to drop a load of cash to compete and quite possibly die in a legendary race. It was fantasy fulfillment for anyone who had the money.

"What's the payout these days?" Geddy asked, his ire rising.

"Fifty percent," replied Zereth-Tinn.

"*Fifty percent?*" Geddy asked, incredulous. "It used to be, like, ninety! The rest went to clean up the wrecks."

"A smaller slice of a much bigger pie," Zereth-Tinn said, moving from beside them to stand next to Pardie, his arms crossed.

"How much bigger?"

Pardie tapped his thin fingers on his corpulent chin. "The winner of a typical race walks away with one to two million."

Geddy went white as a sheet. He' knew what greed did to people, but *damn*. That would set up the *Fiz* for a long time. Hell, that might buy most of a new ship. But it could only mean there were many, many more racers now.

"That's a big-ass pie."

Oz wore a shit-eating grin he mirrored, because he knew she was thinking the exact same thing: *That's what he said.*

"Pay the entry fee and you're in," said Pardie.

"How much, again?" Geddy asked, hoping the number would be lower.

"A hundred large," Pardie said.

"We have ninety-six," Geddy said. "It's all we got."

"Gosh, that's awfully close, isn't it?" Pardie exchanged a smug look with his partner and looked up at Geddy with a slippery smile.

"Please," Geddy pleaded. "We came a long way."

Pardie tapped his fingers together, clearly relishing this part of his sleazy job. "Tell you what, Starfart." He pointed back to the stairs. "The fastest way to make a few grand is right up those stairs."

"What? The video game?"

Zereth-Tinn said, "You can bet if you'd like. It's double or nothing across the board."

— *So just put down two thousand and you could win four!*

— *I may suck at math, pal, but I managed that one okay.*

If winning was all he had to do, he was a shoo-in. They might as well just give him the money now.

"And all I have to do is win at … what did you call it? Ponley Point Classic?"

"Possibly," said Pardie. "The course is random."

He'd have to see about that. In the meantime, Denk had spent hours training for a race he'd never get to run. Maybe there was a way to let him test his skill without risking death.

"We'll be back with the rest of your money." He turned on his heels and headed back toward the stairs.

CHAPTER 10

AFTER PARDIE

enk was beyond excited to race at the Point without him or anyone else dying and immediately agreed to accompany Geddy and Oz back to the Ponley Point Experience. Of course, Geddy couldn't tell the kid there would be money at stake or he'd freak out, but he didn't need to know, anyway. Tardigan stayed to go over the supply list with Voprot and work out what they could afford to buy.

When they arrived back at the Experience, Denk picked out the pod he liked best and climbed inside to await the start of the race. Other competitors had begun to trickle in, so Geddy headed over to the counter before it got too busy.

He greeted the dead-eyed kid and slid two thousand credits across the table. He regarded it like a turd. With one more finger on each hand and round pupils, he could've passed for a human. Knetosian. A long way from home, just like everyone else on this rock.

"Two grand?" he asked, wrinkling his nose.

"Is that a problem?" asked Geddy.

"Most people go bigger."

The way the kid said it made Geddy want to grab his long hair and slam his face into the counter, but maybe he had a point. Go big or go home, right? Besides, they still had to find a hotel room, and it wouldn't be cheap.

— *Don't do what I think you're going to do.*

"What's your name?" He checked behind him to make sure Oz and Denk weren't listening.

"Effer," said the kid. "Look, the race starts in five minutes, so ..."

Effer? Sometimes you went years in this galaxy and never hear the same name twice. "Effer, I don't know you, but I'll bet you like money."

He perked up but regarded him suspiciously. "Doesn't everybody?"

"You could work at any of these two-bit tourist traps, but you work here because of the juice. The action. Am I right?"

The kid paled a bit at this, and Geddy knew he had his number. Young men were easy to read. He looked down and pretended to pick something out from under one of his fingers.

"Betting's the only interesting thing in this stupid town."

He gave the counter a little slap to bring the kid's eyes back up to his. "Exactly. Problem is, this isn't *your* action. It's someone else's. What does watching somebody else's action makes you?"

"What?"

"A bystander. A nameless, faceless schmuck. Did you really come all the way from Knetos to the edge of charted space to be a wage slave?"

Effer stiffened, drawing himself taller. "No."

"Of course you didn't. Which is why ..." he slid twenty thousand across the counter and leaned in. "... I think it would be very enterprising of you to put this twenty on my boy Denk over there. Keep the two grand for yourself."

The kid glanced around and slid the money into his pocket, then wiped his sweaty brow on his sleeve. "What's the catch?"

"No catch," Geddy said, grinning. "Just make sure the next race is run on Ponley Point Classic."

— *How is that not a catch?*

— *You want to be morally superior or get back to Sagacea?*

— *I was thinking they weren't mutually exclusive.*

He shook his head. "It's random. I can't just–"

"Then un-randomize it. You can do that, right?"

He sighed, now dabbing at his cheeks as he shifted nervously back and forth. "It's just, we just ran Classic in the last race."

"I get it. There are thirty-two courses and chances of running the same race twice in a row are astronomical."

— *Technically they're one in one thousand twenty-four, which isn't–*

"But it happens sometimes, right?" Geddy asked, trying not to sound annoyed.

Effer exhaled a long breath. "Your guy's in pod six?"

"That's the one."

"Yeah, all right."

Geddy pointed a cautioning finger. "Classic. Don't let me down."

The kid nodded uncomfortably, and Geddy returned to where Oz and Denk were.

"What was that all about?" Oz asked.

"Just getting clear on the rules." He turned to Denk and rubbed his sloped shoulders. "How you feeling, Champ? You good?"

He glanced back over his shoulder, his pupils wide and haunted. "There are thirty-two courses. What if it's not the one we practiced?"

"You're a pilot," Geddy reassured him. "Go on instinct."

"Okay, racers," said Effer, adjusting a little headset. "Please enter your pods and remain still until the neural connection is established."

Denk climbed into the pod, running his trembling hands over the controls. Slinky metal tendrils with glowing blue ends extended from the headrest and settled on Denk's head, with dozens of other touch points on the rest of his body, making him squirm.

"Uh, I don't know about this ..." The snaky cables on Denk's temples lit up, making his eyes go cloudy. His jaw slackened. "... screen. Whoa, guys, this is crazy. I'm really in a ship!"

The holoscreen flicked on, mirroring what Denk saw. He was in the cockpit of some dusty, battered one-seater with playful touches like a bobblehead of a cartoon alien and family pictures taped to the edge of the steeply raked window. The other ships materialized all around him, but there was no environment yet. Just a grid.

"We see you, Pal."

"Okay," said Effer from behind the counter. "Time to select your course. Running the, um, randomizing algorithm ..."

A moment later, the grid faded out and a sweeping aerial view of Ponley Point Classic faded in — the original, rendered in loving detail. It began in the semicircular mouth of a dry canyon about twenty kilometers from town. Denk craned his neck to both sides, revealing far more ships than racers. The others must be AI-generated.

"Your randomly selected race venue is Ponley Point Classic. Watch for the flag drop and good luck."

The tourist in the next pod over grumbled, "Again with Classic? I don't think your randomizer is very random."

Denk sighed with relief. "Phew. Looks like we lucked out, Cap."

Geddy winked at Effer, who seemed to relax now that the race was underway. When he turned back, he found Oz's eyes locked on him. They narrowed as she studied his face. *What did you do now?*

"What are the chances, I wonder?" asked Oz, flattening her lips.

"One in a thousand twenty-four," he answered, evading her withering gaze. "Just focus and trust yourself. You've got this."

His ship was positioned near the front and just right of center, which was good. Setting up high for the Razor turn was easier without a big crowd in front of you at the starting line, and putting some distance between himself and the pack was crucial for everything that came next.

Denk's stubby fingers closed around the throttle, and he took a deep, cleansing breath. Up ahead, a slinky Stemirian woman in a bikini sashayed out carrying a bright red flag in her teeth and swishing her ass.

"Oh, come on ..." Oz muttered. "Why's it always some sexy babe?"

She squared up to the racers and stuck her impossibly long tongue out, wagging it lasciviously back and forth before running it over her plump lips. From the right angle, she bore a striking resemblance to Geddy's holographic girlfriend back on The Deuce.

"I think it's tastefully done," Geddy said appreciatively.

"Welcome to Ponley Point," she cooed. "Are you ready to give it your *all*?"

"Yes, Ma'am," Denk answered as though she were talking just to him. "Thanks for asking."

"Remember your training," Geddy murmured, leaning down by Denk's ear.

"I won't let ya down, Cap."

He liked that Denk called him Cap. It had a nice ring to it, and it seemed more like a nickname than a title.

"Okay, let's *do it*," teased the starter girl. "Racers ready?"

She spread her feet, raised the flag overhead, and slid her bright eyes mischievously back and forth. "Go!"

She brought it down with a sexy flourish, and hopped up and down unnecessarily, her tits practically spilling out of her bikini top. Geddy hoped it was enough to distract some of the other racers. Denk shoved the throttle forward. The ship fishtailed briefly, throwing him off, and he angled straight for the girl. Geddy assumed she would be immaterial in the game or simply fade out, but she just stood there, jumping up and down. Denk cut her off just below the waist and her face slammed into the window, her cheek sticking to the glass momentarily before she tumbled off to the side.

"Huh," remarked Geddy. "That's a surprising inclusion."

"Aw, jeez," Denk said, his voice pained. "Sorry, lady! Should I see if she's okay?"

"She's fine. Punch it!"

Denk zipped across the sea of jostling ships, trailing a pack that clearly didn't know what they were doing, because half of them misread the turn and set up left. Only a couple of other ships were positioned high and right. The others would immediately crash. Denk was in a perfect position to take an early lead.

"Get ready …" Geddy breathed as the huge turn approached. "Now!"

————

Damn, if it didn't feel good to have a little money in his pocket. Credits were all the same size, but he always thought he could tell the denominations just by feel. He picked one out that felt like a thousand and took it out just far enough to see.

Nope. Five hundred.

"Look who's back," said Big Pardie, leaning back and turning his uguinok cards face-down on the table. Again, he leered at Oz as she reached the bottom of the stairs ahead of Denk. "If you're still short, I think we could work something out."

"Not in a Zorran's age," she replied, unamused.

Geddy slapped down the squares. "It's all there."

He briefly glanced down and swept the little pile toward his side of the table with all the rest. "Looks about right."

"Aren't you gonna count it?" Geddy asked.

"He doesn't have enough fingers," Oz quipped. Pardie's slimy grin fell.

Geddy coughed to cover his guffaw. "That's it, then?"

He nodded to one of the other players, the Udsar, who grumbled something under his breath and stood to reveal he wasn't wearing any pants. Not altogether unusual for an Udsar, but certainly off-putting. He shuffled toward a wall safe, revealing that his seat was a bidet.

Oz groaned and wrinkled her nose. "Oh, for fuck's sake."

— *Wait ... is that ...?*

"Guess you never have to leave the table, huh?" Geddy asked after him.

He muttered an incomprehensible response as he put his eye to a scanner and opened the door to reveal a metal bowl filled with coin-shaped devices. He took one out and shuffled over to them.

"Who's racing?"

"Me."

The Udsar handed Geddy the device. "Your token," he said flatly. "For the gates."

Had this always been part of it? There was no way to know. He'd never been behind the scenes like this.

"Great. Can we go now?" Oz asked, irritated.

"Need a map to the starting line?" asked Pardie, smirking, as the Udsar settled unapologetically back onto his bidet chair.

They shared a belly laugh and picked up their game where

they left off. What a racket. Was it a rule of the universe that everything eventually got shittier and more expensive?

These guys didn't take him seriously. As far as they were concerned, he was another tourist after one last pathetic grasp at glory. Geddy turned on his heels and followed the others back upstairs, fully intending to have the last laugh.

CHAPTER 11

GETTING TO THE POINT

Oz hit the nail on the head. After a long turn in space, nothing in the universe beat a hot shower and fresh towels. At Geddy's insistence, they spent the night at the Thegus Excelsior, a fancy-ish hotel right on the square. That first delicious moment when the deluge of hot water hit his head, cascading over his face and body sent a pleasing shudder down his spine. He stood there for several minutes as it dripped off his nose and chin, sending little whirlpools of grayish water down the drain.

Being stuck in the *Fiz* for weeks on end renewed his appreciation for the little things. He could hardly wait to spend some of his winnings to fix her up. With his token tucked deep in his pocket, he left at ten to get the *Dom* out and lighten her up. He told the crew to take a shuttle out to the canyon for the pre-race show.

The Ponley Point Participant Parade was a race-day staple. The game's intro only showed it between brief, frenetic cuts in which a wide spectrum of grimly determined racers processed between two grandstands so vast that they appeared infinite.

They waved and smiled, and the impossibly large crowd cheered its approval.

When he was a kid playing the game, he'd often fall asleep to dreams of winning at the Point.

"Ged-dy! Ged-dy!" they'd chant as one, and the other racers would shrink before his eyes.

In school, he would idly draw the ships he'd someday pilot there. A sinister-looking sliver of cockpit bracketed by BW-993 ionizing antimatter thrusters from an Alliance ASG-8 Ripsaw. A heavily modified ETB-44 Skybike with dual thoron injectors.

Like everything else now, the parade was a shadow of its former self. The grandstands at the finish line, near the canyon entrance, used to stretch for half a click on both sides. Now there was just one, maybe a hundred meters long, and it was half full. There was a smattering of applause as the racers glided by. An indifferent announcer introduced them as they passed.

"Piloting the Hernoc SXT is Zomed Klazok, a middle manager at an Eicrean spice company. And there's Inya Dikarelko, daughter of Topjed Dikarelko, who has won twice at the Point."

The rest of Thegus should've tempered Geddy's expectations, but the reality of it was so far removed from his childhood fantasy that it might as well have been a different race. Oh, well. This was for the *Fiz* and Eli, not for him.

"And here we have … what looks like a Ring War-era Kailorian fighter? The pilot is Geddy Starheart, a first-time racer here at the Point. Let's give him a warm Thegus welcome."

The crew was lined up at the front railing, hooting and frantically waving their arms. Denk wore the I SURVIVED PONLEY POINT shirt he'd bought with some of his winnings and jumped up and down as he stretched it taut. It brought a smile to Geddy's lips, and he waved back, though they likely couldn't see him through the glare of the window.

"Well, Eli, it's not the crowd we hoped for, but I'm lowering my expectations every day."

— *I just hope we see them again.*

"Bah! Ye of little faith."

Having passed by the mildly enthusiastic crowd, they entered the narrow canyon that led to the starting line, and all fell silent.

"They say if it's quiet enough to hear yourself breathe at the starting line, you'll have a good race."

— *I can hear it.*

"Me, too."

From the corner of his eye, he caught the wave of a hand and turned to see a familiar face come up beside him.

Zereth-Tinn.

— *Why's he here?*

"I don't know."

He was piloting a triangular craft that resembled a hybrid of a Skybike *and* a Ripsaw, though it was neither of those. He straddled a long seat covered in an iridescent green electrobubble. The engines were hidden beneath the fuselage.

Zereth-Tinn hailed him. "Nice antique, Starheart. You here to race or to clear the dust off it?" he taunted.

Was he really talking smack? Geddy figured the guy's racing days were far behind him. It seemed he had too much to lose now.

"I don't see any engines," Geddy said, peering down at the underside of his ship. "I'm guessing training wheels?"

He laughed and said, "They'll be easy to see from behind me."

"I didn't know you were racing today."

"Something told me you might give me some actual competition. And, it's my day off, so I figured what the hell."

"Where do you find these noobs?"

He shrugged. "We don't have to. They find us. It's called branding."

An authoritative-sounding voice cut in on the local channel as the canyon widened — the Point's legendary announcer, Bromby Cremecannon. At least some things didn't change.

A glowing blue line suspended in the air represented the starting line. "Racers, welcome to the Point. Proceed to your starting positions."

A numbered column of light bearing his name and photo appeared in the worst possible place. Back left. There were just twenty racers including him, so 1.9 million credits were at stake. Half of that was almost a million, which was a lot, but nowhere near the four or five he'd hoped for.

"Whup, looks like I'm in the front row. See you out on the course, Starheart," Zereth-Tinn said, peeling off to the right. "More likely you'll see me."

Geddy maneuvered the ship into its starting position at the very back of the pack and thought through his strategy. The *Dom* was nimble and super stable, but not especially fast. It would be strongest on Suicide and the Razor and weakest in the DTC and the final straightaway. She wasn't fast enough off the line to get in front, but the setup was more important than an early lead. He could make up the time later.

"You all know the rules," said Bilby. "No weapons, no AI, no scanners, and no object avoidance. Just you, your craft, and one rear camera. Your token must pass through each gate in order. The first token across the line takes half of today's pot — just shy of a million credits."

— *Good luck, Geddy. You're going to win.*

"I hope you're right. We're hosed if we don't."

"Racers at the ready."

A chill slid down his back. He'd waited a long time to hear that for real. His fingers tightened around the controls and his pulse quickened. His eyes locked on the Razor in the far distance, and everything else melted away.

"Go!"

CHAPTER 12

PONLEY POINT

t took every ounce of discipline in his body, which admittedly wasn't a lot, but when the rest of the pack took off, Geddy waited. Maybe half a second after they jetted ahead of him, he floored it and veered hard right.

Big though it was, the *Fiz* arguably had better acceleration from a dead stop than the *Dom*. She needed a little more runway than most to make top speed. But she handled like a dream here, suggesting that her primary role on Kailoria was atmospheric defense.

The only way to get her into position was to inch his way toward the front from the outside of the pack — no easy task considering everyone else was jockeying for the same position. When the time came to set up for the sneaky turn, he'd only made up half the ground he wanted and was too far outside the mouth of the canyon. But the inexperienced pilots beside him had to slow down more than him, leaving a gap. He slipped in behind Zereth-Tinn, who was in the lead, and the Eicrean businessman in his brand-new SXT.

He passed through the first gate less than a second behind.

A couple of racers who didn't set up high enough for the

sharp curve drifted through it, slamming into the jagged rocks. Ahead, the narrow, S-shaped canyon veered right into a short straightaway. To his surprise, the SXT took a primo line and actually opened up space between them. Four others were right on his six.

The sinuous canyon's margins were a graveyard for several wrecked ships. Some were wedged and crumpled under massive boulders while others lay in half-buried pieces at the base of the steep walls.

By the time they began to climb toward open sky, Geddy had opened up a couple hundred meters on the four ships behind him but the SXT had a commanding lead. He throttled up as the course tapered at the appropriately named Crotch Gate. Like everyone else, he dropped low enough to nearly scrape the ground to set up for it.

Just as the gate came into view, so did Zereth-Tinn. He appeared at nine o'clock high, clipping the wall and sending a little rockslide toward the SXT, which barely avoided them.

— *Was that on purpose?*

— Almost certainly.

The first bouncing boulder slid just beneath the *Dom's* stubby port wing, as Geddy rolled left, and he rolled right to dodge another. Just ahead, Zereth-Tinn swerved to avoid the rusting corpse of a big ship just shy of the gate. The SXT slowed to avoid colliding with him, so Geddy leaned on the thrusters and veered right, hoping like hell there was more room than it looked.

Fortunately, there was. His straighter line through Gate Two put him just ahead of the SXT and Zereth-Tinn.

— *Nicely done!*

— Believe it or not, this is the easy part.

Once through, he yanked back on the stick and punched it, climbing straight up like an Old Earth rocket. Zereth-Tinn crept back into view on his left, climbing faster on account of the lighter ship.

He'd advised Denk to be patient here, and he was going to follow his own advice. But according to the rear camera, the SXT was gaining on him, too. No matter. He only needed to be close to the lead coming out of Moonshot.

The higher he went, the darker it got. He scanned the dark blue sky looking anxiously for the glowing circle of the gate. If you came in at the wrong angle, it looked like a faint blue line against an ocean of stars.

He didn't see it at first, and apparently, neither did Zereth-Tinn abruptly changed course, inverted, and rolled upright as he zipped past overhead. Geddy did the same, expecting to see the gate just ahead. But then Zereth-Tinn looped around again and shot off to the left like a bullet. He threw a quick wave Geddy's way. A total fake-out.

"You sneaky bastard!"

He took off after him just in time to watch Zereth-Tinn slip through the Moonshot Gate barely ahead of the SXT. By the time Geddy got there, the other four had almost caught up.

Why hadn't he seen it sooner?

Still, this was where the *Dom* would shine. He nosed down and dove into Suicide Plunge with the thrusters screaming. It was all about managing his speed. Too fast, and he couldn't pull up in time. Too slow, and he'd be too far back to catch the leaders. A thousand kilometers per hour was the magic number.

About halfway to the forbidding black maw of the volcano, he rocketed past the SXT like it was standing still and closed fast on Zereth-Tinn.

They entered the volcano neck and neck at just under 1,100 kph. Geddy spilled some of that speed and started counting. Six and a half seconds. No way Zereth-Tinn would wait that long.

"A one, and a two, and a three ..."

The two ships plummeted into the building darkness and activated their lights at the same time. The faint glint of metal signaled the bottom was near. Hundreds of decrepit ships were piled there, so much that it took him a moment to find an opening. But Geddy didn't slow down.

— *What are you doing? You're going too fast!*

"Shush ... and a four, and a five ..."

Zereth-Tinn lost his nerve and fired his retros. He dropped back behind the SXT, which was still gaining on Geddy and therefore screwed.

— *Geddy!*

"... and a six, and a ... Watch this shit."

Just the graveyard of shattered ships filled the screen, he gave the stick a short flick back, immediately flipping him nose up. He hammered on the thrusters to kill his airspeed, pinning him to the seat. His vision narrowed to a pinpoint. The stick slipped from his hands, leveling them out at the bottom of the drop. They scraped the top of a crushed Ripsaw, and the last thing he saw was the SXT explode in a yellow-orange fireball.

— *Watch out!!*

His vision widened, but not before he veered into the smooth left wall of the DTC, the wing carving a long groove in the rock. A shot of adrenaline made him overcorrect, and the ship shot back to the right, nearly clipping the other side. By the time he drifted back toward the middle, Zereth-Tinn had entered the lava tube and was closing fast.

"Shit, what happened?" he asked, panting. His heart felt like it had restarted.

— *You blacked out.*

"How long?"

— *Three or four seconds.*

"Damnit!"

— You were pulling 10 G's! What did you think was gonna happen?

Geddy gave his head a hard shake to clear it and accelerated down the long, straight tube, his vision still resolving.

Ahead, a pinpoint of light indicated the exit. The throttle was open all the way. Zereth-Tinn kept even with him, smirking through his translucent green bubble. This was a two-ship race now.

They exploded out of the tube into Shoelace Canyon.

Geddy banked hard right at the same time as Zereth-Tinn and entered the deep, zigzagging canyon. Straight ahead, the eponymous shoelace route beckoned.

— What's he going to do?

"He'll take the curves. Even if he falls behind, he knows he can beat me on the straightaway. Plus, he has nothing to prove."

He was right. As Zereth-Tinn took the first curve to the right, Geddy veered left to set up for the boreholes that went straight through the curves. How many times had he fantasized about this moment?

There was zero room for error. A bird or a sudden puff of wind and he'd hit the sides. He took a deep breath and accelerated, hoping like hell she wasn't too wide.

A satisfying *whump* sounded as he swished the first hole in the cliffs, barely missing Zereth-Tinn as he set up for the left turn ahead.

— You're already getting ahead!

"Don't get too excited," he muttered. "We have miles to go before we sleep."

He slipped through the second hole and the third, only gaining slightly on Zereth-Tinn's more maneuverable ship. *Whump* went the fourth shoelace, and the fifth.

But the shoelaces angled slightly down, and the final gate was at the top of the canyon. He had to climb to get to it and whizzed through maybe two seconds ahead of Zereth-Tinn. Considering the risk he'd taken, he'd hoped for a bigger lead. It would come down to the final straightaway.

No gates remained, just the finish line. He urged the *Dom* on, skimming over the flat desert as billows of dust opened behind him.

That gave him an idea.

He dropped her down to just a meter above the ground to stir up as much of that dust and sand as possible. Zereth-Tinn had the faster ship but Geddy weaved back and forth, kicking up even more dust and blocking him from passing. All the while, his under-mounted engines were sucking in that dust. He disappeared in the cloud for a moment only to reappear quite suddenly at two o'clock high. One of his engines was trailing white smoke.

The glowing red finish line was in sight, along with nearly two million credits.

"Come on, baby. Turn it up to eleven for me …"

Even with a damaged engine, Zereth-Tinn still inched ahead. But it proved to be too much. The smoking engine finally flamed out, dropping him back into the dust cloud.

It was all Geddy needed. The *Dom* rocketed across the finish line in front of the grandstand, which was immediately swallowed by clouds of dust. He eased back on the throttle wearing an ear-to-ear grin and pounded on the console.

"Hell, yeah! Take that, you cocky motherfucker! Woo hoo!"

— *You did it, Geddy! Aku, here we come!*

Zereth-Tinn pulled even and hailed him. "Good flying, Starheart."

"Sorry about your engine. And your face."

— *I'm really not.*

— *I figured.*

He shook his head in disbelief as elation washed over him. "Ponley fucking Point."

— *Ponley fucking Point indeed.*

CHAPTER 13

CELEBRATE GOOD TIMES

Ponley Point had always celebrated its winners in grand fashion, and Geddy was happy it, at least, lived up to expectations. The surviving racers limped across the finish line, sometimes alone and sometimes in groups, while a giant projection against the canyon wall looped an "In Memoriam" reel for the three racers who didn't make it back, including the middle manager in the SXT.

A band had set up at the starting area, projecting music out over the revelers and across the flat desert expanse. Once they started playing, the crowd swelled to several hundred, then two or three thousand. Whether they were locals or tourists, Geddy couldn't have guessed.

Winning almost two million credits in the actual race he'd grown up playing in a video game should've felt more gratifying. As captain, Geddy was thrilled. The crew deserved an upgraded ship, and they would get it now.

Oz was dancing with Denk and Tardigan while Voprot grappled with the very notion of rhythm, swishing his giant tail back and forth like he was having a seizure.

Geddy leaned against the *Dom* and took a sip from his mug of ale, bemusedly watching Voprot.

— *Is that what it means to dance like no one's watching?*

— It must.

— *This is a happy occasion, Geddy. You should be out there with them.*

— I'm not much for dancing.

— *That's not the point.*

No sooner had he thought this than Oz hurried over, clearly tipsy, and grabbed his arm, yanking him toward the others.

"Come on, Mr. Buzzkill. I know you know how to kick up some dust."

His instinct was to refuse, but this wasn't just about him anymore. They were a team, and teams made little sacrifices for each other. A little dignity was a small price to pay for their help. Besides, the band was actually pretty good.

He set his beer down and sheepishly let Oz drag him out into the gyrating crowd.

Predictably, Oz was the only one who could dance worth a lick. Tardigan's moves resembled calisthenics. Denk had some rhythm, but the way he stuck his butt out only added to his already cartoonish presence. Voprot, meanwhile, dropped to all fours, lolling his head back and forth with his tongue flapping around as though in a religious ecstasy.

To that point, the only time Geddy ever danced was if he thought he might get in some floozy's pants. He honestly didn't know if he was any good or not, though he figured he wasn't half bad.

"You've got a little shake in that can," Oz teased, effortlessly tossing her thick red locks back and forth in perfect time. So light and effortless on her feet.

Before long, a silly grin was emblazoned across his face. Was it just the company, or was it that he just won *Ponley*

Fucking Point and was having his first bit of actual fun in seven years?

He hopped over beside her and bumped her with his hip. She opened her mouth in mock offense and bumped him right back so hard he stumbled. He gave a laugh and fell back into the rhythm.

Traveling the cosmos, you saw every shape, size, and color of alien species, sometimes all in the same place. You saw interspecies love affairs and bizarre sports. But in all those years, Geddy never once found himself dancing in the desert with hundreds of them. To them, he was an alien, too. If he closed his eyes, he could almost imagine a world in which killing, and being killed, for something that happened a thousand years ago never entered anyone's mind.

But that wasn't reality, and his brief moment of reverie faded when he realized that every single one of these people knew he'd won a seven-figure sum. His winnings, all cash, were in the *Dom's* emergency ration compartment, where they would remain until it was time to get the stuff they needed for the *Fiz* and bounce.

His building paranoia finally got the better of him, and he glanced over toward the *Dom*, which was parked with the others near the edge of the crowd. It was a good thing he did, because a pair of Kailorians were running their hands over the ship in a way he really didn't like. He broke away and strode toward them.

Both were younger than the late Captain Bykite, holding drinks and talking animatedly. Reflexively, he undid the latch on his holster.

"Hey fellas," Geddy said. "Something I can help you with?"

"This your ship?" asked the smaller of the two, intoxicated and incredulous.

"That's right." He puffed out his chest to appear more

imposing. Sometimes it helped, sometimes not. He sensed Oz close behind him.

"How does a human acquire a Kailorian LPC?" inquired the drunk, an undercurrent of menace in his voice.

"It came with our trawler. Dealer incentive."

The belligerent one's eye twitched at this indignity. He was about to spew invective when the other stayed him with his hand.

"My father flew in the War. A fighter very similar to this, in fact."

"My old man was a pilot in the PDF," Geddy said.

– *See? Common ground.*

The big Kailorian harrumphed. "Then he knew nothing of war."

– You were saying?

Geddy's cheeks burned. All these assholes were the same, just pushing buttons to see what trouble they could cause. But he wouldn't take the bait. Not when everyone was having a good time. He forced a smile from between his gritted teeth.

"Pound sand, bullethead. We'd like to resume our bad dancing."

"It doesn't belong to you," said the smaller in a grave tone, his face curling into an off-putting snarl.

— *He should really look into some orthodontia.*

Geddy heaved a sigh and rubbed his temples. Why did someone always have to ruin it? "And here I thought it had a clean title."

The inebriated Kailorian stumbled over and stuck his own chest out in front of Geddy, huffing and wild-eyed. Their faces came roughly level, though his blue gherkin-shaped head kept going for another foot. Oz moved around to his side, her arms defiantly crossed. A moment later, the larger Kailorian did the same.

Geddy folded his arms and looked them both over. "I've

always wondered … do you guys have a hard time finding hats?"

They ignored him. "I'm curious, *human*. How did you come by this ship?"

Geddy opened his mouth to reply, but Oz cut him off. "Our former captain was Kailorian. He fled in the final days of the War."

The belligerent one's face wrinkled in disgust as he regarded her — not typical for someone looking Oz. "So, he was a deserter *and* a coward. No wonder you worked for him."

Oz scowled and narrowed her eyes. "What's that supposed to mean?"

Even without weapons, Oz would probably turn these two into pretzels, but they both were packing. Geddy took a step back. Behind them, the band finished one song and immediately launched into another, sending the crowd into a frenzy.

"This captain of yours may have fled, but at least he was in the fight. That's more than anyone can say about a Temerurian."

Oz lurched at him, fists balled, but Geddy grabbed her shoulder, stopping her as Denk came up on his left.

"Hey Cap, everything okay over here?"

Tardigan joined them, forming a little wall between them and Voprot, who was still lost in the music. When Geddy was much younger and always up for a scrape, it was usually just him. Having some backup for once felt kinda good.

"Beldar and Drunk Smurf here were just congratulating us on the big win," he said. "Isn't that right?"

The smaller regarded Denk and Tardigan with a smirk. "A human, a Durandian, and an Ornean? Is this some kind of joke?"

"No, but we did walk into a bar yesterday."

— *Now is not the time.*

— Oh, come on, it was a perfect setup.

"And where is your former Kailorian captain now?" he asked. "Hiding from justice, I'd imagine."

"Actually, he died battling a ranse with his bare hands," Geddy asserted, though in fact, Captain Bykite merely got in its way after making the bad decision to capture a Myadan-bound zoo ship.

— *That's one way to look at it.*

He was about to say something else when both Kailorians' eyes drifted upward, fixed on something behind him. Geddy noticed the shadow fall over the group confirming Voprot had finally noticed their confrontation.

"What in blazes is *that*?" asked the larger.

"Oh, him? He's a Kigantean warrior. You think my crew is a joke? Well, he's the punchline." He turned back to meet Voprot's eyes. "Isn't that right, pal?"

"Sorry, Voprot late to conversation," he said, still panting from his exertions. "Why no dance?"

The bigger Kailorian's eyes remained warily on Voprot as he tapped his friend on the upper arm and led him away.

"You heard the big guy," Geddy said. "Sometimes, you just gotta dance."

He did his level best to boogie away from them, drawing appreciative laughter from Oz. The Kailorians chuckled as they melted into the crowd. Geddy re-fastened the latch on his blaster and exhaled.

— *I'm proud of you.*

— Don't be. If it wasn't for my friends, ol' dickhead and I would've thrown down.

— *Then I'm glad you have friends other than me.*

Up to that point, he hadn't really felt like a captain, nor the crew a real crew. But he wasn't a lone wolf anymore. He was part of a pack, and they were stronger together.

— Me, too.

CHAPTER 14

A DO-IT-YOURSELF-ER

Geddy rose early the morning after the party, bleary-eyed but anxious to take care of the *Fiz*. Ordinarily, installation and repairs were handled same day, but in a place like this, all bets were off. He made his way across the empty pedestrian mall toward the spaceport, nearly falling on his ass when his feet hit the frost-slickened bricks. Hard to believe it got that cold at night, but they were technically in a desert.

Like the town, Thegus' spaceport was state-of-the-art, though not especially large. It was cross-shaped with two full decks and large enough to handle four transports. He bounded up the wide steps two at a time and passed through the large doors when they slid open, the metal-scented air of the lower deck exhaling into his face.

Apart from a couple techs welding a patch over a small merchant vessel, there wasn't much going on. The hangar was silent save for the constant whir of huge air exchangers on the ends. At the far side, a kiosk pointed the way to different administrative areas. An arrow pointed up a flight of stairs to the warehouse, and he began to climb.

Supply clerks handled the exchange of ship-related supplies and equipment. Ordinarily, they had massive stockpiles of parts from ships that had passed through over the years. Sometimes, junk trawlers sold off their prizes there, too, but they'd screw you on the price. You were always better off at a market if you could help it, but sometimes you had to take what you could get.

But since Thegus no longer had a market, they'd be at the mercy of the clerk, whose job it was to make the spaceport as much money as possible. This one was Eicrean, a race known for being business-minded. He scanned the list and put a tick mark by only three of the twenty-plus items, then handed it back.

"Are you kidding me?" Geddy asked. "This is all you've got in stock?"

He held up his hands in mock surrender. "You think I'd prefer to *not* sell you all this stuff?"

The only things available were a tractor beam assembly, handheld weapons, and novaspheres. No shower parts, no food recombinator. The thought of more nutrimush turned his stomach, especially after the celebratory dinner they'd enjoyed last night.

"What about the hull repair?"

"That we can do."

The tractor beam was the number-one priority, so he was grateful they had a compatible one. But all the items that would've made the *Fiz* more hospitable would have to wait. At least they had novaspheres.

He heaved a sigh. "How much?"

The chandler's lips moved a little as he did some arithmetic in his boxy, bony head. "Depending on the weapons, you're looking at five fifty, give or take."

Geddy's eyes practically popped free of their sockets. "*What?*"

He gave an indifferent shrug. "The tractor beam alone … With installation, that's four, four fifteen."

"It shouldn't be more than a hundred!"

"You got another source on Thegus for tractor beam assemblies compatible with an antique Ghruk trawler? That's the price. Take it or leave it."

Having the screws put to him by some price-gouging schmuck gave him heart palpitations. Just because they were at the edge of charted space didn't mean they got to bilk Ponley Point champions out of their hard-earned winnings. Because that's exactly what this was.

"I'll give you two," he said through gritted teeth. "That's double what it would go for in the outer systems."

The guy had the nerve to lean back in his chair with his fingers laced behind his head. "Feel free to shop around. Maybe there's an old junkyard down there between the art gallery and the Nurithean spa."

After he was done laughing at his own joke, Geddy put his hands on the table and leaned down. "How much without labor?"

———

Geddy dragged a sleeve across his forehead, accidentally sending a droplet of filthy, salty sweat into his already bloodshot eyes. Every attempt to clear it just made it worse. The wiring harness he was trying to install was still in his left hand, and the cluster of connectors running to the console were still sticking out of the conduit as they had been for the past hour.

Oz and Denk were back at the warehouse sifting through piles of used weapons, and Voprot had come along to help carry them back. Morpho knew the *Fizmo* intimately, but connecting a strange third-party component to its aging systems fell outside even his expertise, so he kept working on repairs to the damaged rear shield assembly.

Above him, at the edge of the open panel, Dr. Tardigan's dangling legs bounced annoyingly against the inside wall of the subfloor as he read the instructions on the tablet.

"Is that necessary?" Geddy said. It came out more harshly than he intended.

He stopped immediately. "Sorry, I still have that music stuck in my head from the party. What did you say it was?"

"We call it rock-and-roll."

"Rock and roll. It's very catchy. Is it an old form?"

Geddy looked up and heaved an exasperated sigh. "It never dies."

He removed the thick work glove and opened his aluminum water bottle, downing it in three big gulps. In space, he avoided drinking that recycled piss-tasting swill unless he was about to pass out. But against all odds, Thegus had some of the most delicious, deep-well water he'd ever tasted.

They'd been at it all afternoon. That crooked clerk finally agreed to two seventy-five for just the Udsarian-made tractor beam assembly and the adapter kit. Geddy had been reasonably confident that he and Doc could figure it out, but they'd made little progress.

They found wiring instructions on the net, but of course, they were all in Udsar, which only Doc could read. They'd moved the assembly into place. Now they had to figure out how to connect Udsarian and Ghruk electrical components.

Once Geddy had slaked his thirst, he tugged the glove back on. "All right, now what?"

"Okay … It says connect the … happy colorful wires to the … most receptive counterpart labeled C9 and loop around the … harness bracket fastener?" He squinted and brought the tablet closer to his face. "Although … looking at it a second time, it might also say to not do that. In Udsar, the words for 'do' and 'don't do' are the same, so it's all about the context."

"The context is to finish this before I go insane."

Geddy held the wiring harness up to his headlamp and studied it for something — anything — that resembled the instructions. Neither it, nor the wires sticking out of the *Fiz's* conduit, nor the sockets on the tractor beam assembly were labeled C9.

He was about to ask Tardigan for more guidance when a voice came from the open door to the hold. "Starheart, is that you down there?"

Tardigan lifted his head toward the sound while Geddy took a couple steps up the ladder, his eyes just above the floor. It was Zereth-Tinn, dressed in fine slacks and a jacket. He peered down at him with a bemused grin.

— *What's he doing here?*

— Selling me a timeshare by the looks of it.

Geddy climbed out with a grunt and squared up to his surprise visitor, looking him up and down. "I don't suppose you know anything about tractor beam assemblies?"

He scratched at his chin and shook his head. "I had some business here, so I figured I'd pop by. Never would've pegged you as a do-it-yourselfer."

Ordinarily, he was pretty good at reading people, but he couldn't get a bead on this guy. An opportunist, clearly, but to what extent and to what ends? Sammo Yann was hard to read, too. You never wanted to play cards against a Soturian. He'd found that out the hard way.

"What do you want?"

"Just to talk." He jutted his chin back over one shoulder toward the bar across the hangar. "Can I buy you a drink? I dare say you could use a break."

A beer sounded fantastic, and he'd be within sight of the *Fiz* the whole time. He raised his eyebrows and turned back to

Tardigan, who waved him away. "Go. I need to work on my translation, anyway."

He removed the gloves and tossed them onto the floor. "Sure, why not?"

They took the ramp out of the hold and walked abreast across the capacious hangar toward a small bar called the Lower Dex. "So what's the deal with this place?"

"How do you mean?"

"Someone bet big on Thegus."

"Guess they thought it had potential," he said, not elaborating.

He had to give it to him. The guy was a sack full of charm, but so were a million shysters. They all had an angle.

A minute later, they bellied up to the empty bar and ordered drinks. Zereth-Tinn got a snifter of Zorran brandy and Geddy his usual beer with whisky back. He and Doc had been at it since mid-morning. The Thegan bartender dropped them off moments later and let them be.

Zereth-Tinn raised his glass. "To the Point."

"To the Point," Geddy said with a wink as he clinked bottles. He took a long pull of his very cold beer, which hit all the spots. "Too bad about the town."

"I gather you preferred it dingy and dangerous."

Geddy's eyebrows arched as he swigged his beer. "It was more interesting that way."

Zereth-Tinn smacked his lips and set his eyes upon the *Fiz*. "I understand you didn't find everything you needed at the warehouse."

"Quite the racket they've got going." He shook his head. "I must be in the wrong business."

"Yes, you are," he tipped his glass and took another sip.

That stopped him just before the beer reached his lips. He set the glass down with a thud. "What's that supposed to mean?"

"You're one of the best pilots I've ever seen. What the hell are you doing on a salvage trawler?"

True, Geddy could've been a merc or private security somewhere and been paid very well to pilot some badass ship. But it would've been too close to the life he'd left behind, and he had a much bigger purpose now. This guy wasn't just making conversation, though. He was feeling him out. But why?

"That's my business."

After making sure the bartender wasn't nearby, he reached into his sport coat and withdrew a square about half the size of his palm. Geddy's heart rate immediately doubled.

— *What's wrong? What is that?*

— A deep-space tracking device. Screvari-made, by the looks of it.

Geddy grimaced and raised his eyes back up to Zereth-Tinn. "Where did you get this?"

"You know what it is?" he asked, mildly surprised.

"Of course. What are *you* doing with it?"

"I was paid to put it on your ship."

"By whom?" Geddy asked.

"Don't you know?"

"The Zelnads." He didn't nod, but he didn't shake his head either.

In the space of a few days, he'd gone from being dead and forgotten to being on the Zelnads' radar. Not ideal. "So why didn't you?"

He checked around him before speaking to ensure not even the bartender was within earshot. Was it just an act, or was he really confiding in him? "Because I stood to make a lot more if I didn't."

"Do tell."

"They know you're here, but not where you're going. I can make sure it stays that way."

"What do they want with me?"

He shrugged. "Don't know, don't care."

"And what will this charitable act cost me?"

"The rest." Another sip, his eyes fixed on Geddy.

Once again, sweat beaded on his lip and his chest tightened. After buying weapons and novaspheres, he'd have around three hundred and fifty left — all the money they would need for the remaining upgrades and repairs. He wasn't about to use it to save his own ass. This smarmy lounge singer just admitted he was playing both sides.

"Eat a dick."

He chuckled to himself and took another sip of his drink. "I thought you might have something colorful to say. Which is why I'm willing to sweeten the pot."

"Go on."

"I know where your shiny little ship is."

That stopped him. He never mentioned anything about the *Penetrator*.

"How do you …"

"There are a lot of cookie jars out there, Starheart. I've got my hands in quite a few. I take it you're interested?" He tossed back the last of his drink with an expectant look on his face.

Finding the *Penetrator* was the whole point. If the information was good, it was a small price to pay. But how would he explain it to the crew? Technically, the money belonged to all of them. Was Zereth-Tinn was playing him or not? Years on Kigantu taught him there truly was no honor among thieves.

— What would you do?

— *I don't trust him.*

— That wasn't the question.

"How do I know there's not a tracker on her already?"

"You don't." He picked up the device and tucked it back into his coat. "But I've no love for the Zelnads."

"What's stopping me from walking straight over to that ship and taking off right now?"

He casually lifted his wrist and spoke into some kind of communicator embedded in his skin. "Pietro? Close all hangar doors, wouldja?"

Giant motors engaged and closed the giant doors like eyelids, activating flashing lights overhead. Zereth-Tinn's eyes never left his as he rose.

"Leave the money with the portmaster. He'll give you the information you need." He pointed at the bartender and winked, flashing a brilliant white smile. "Sorry to run off, but my first set starts soon. Dex, put everything on my tab."

"You've got it, Z."

Before he left, he placed a hand on Geddy's shoulder. "As a show of good faith, I'll send someone over to help you with that tractor beam. No extra charge." He gave it a firm pat and flashed his gleaming teeth one last time before walking away, whistling a cheery tune.

CHAPTER 15

LET'S ROCK!

After his conversation with Zereth-Tinn, Geddy returned to the *Fiz* and ordered Morpho to inspect every square centimeter of the ship for devices. Meanwhile, he told Dr. Tardigan he'd arranged for a technician to help with the tractor beam and went alone down into the *Dom to* gather the rest of his winnings. When he came out, two mechanics were already down in the subfloor While Doc watched from above.

He spotted Morpho still working on the rear shield assembly and walked over. "Morph, I need you to search the whole ship for anything that looks like a tracker. You can finish this later." Morph gathered the handful of small tools in his sticky tendrils and placed them on a rag below the open panel, then disappeared inside it. "I'll be right back," he told Doc.

The others hadn't yet returned from their errands, so he hurried up to the portmaster's office on deck three. He, too, was Eicrean and looked up at Geddy as though he was expected.

"This is for Zereth-Tinn."

He didn't even count the cash. He wordlessly swept it off his desk into a zippered pouch and put it in a safe beside him. Then he removed an envelope from the same safe and handed it to Geddy.

"For you," he said in a businesslike monotone.

Geddy ripped it open and removed a folded piece of paper. It said: AKU. DRUKARVA SHIPYARDS. FIND ISORO. He refolded it and tucked it in his pocket.

He'd already suspected it was on Aku, but would've had no idea where to look. Drukarva was a port city in the north that used to produce most of the ships for the Screvari fleet. It must be a ruin now. Aku was on the opposite side of the galaxy, probably ten or fifteen parsecs away.

He turned back to the portmaster. "Hey, some of your boys are installing a tractor beam for us. Is there someplace around here where we could test it out?"

His eyes drifted upward as he considered this. "Well, there's a small asteroid belt around one of the moons. Gaothea. That'd probably work."

"Thanks for the tip."

After leaving the portmaster, Geddy returned to the *Fiz* to find the others had spread their loot out on the floor of the hold. The subfloor panel was already back in place, indicating the mechanics had already completed connecting the tractor beam. At least that was something.

"Wow." Geddy brightened at the sight of new gear.

Denk asked, "Hey, Cap, you wanna see what we got?"

"Sure."

"Where'd you run off to?" Oz asked.

"Portmaster," he explained, prepared for the question. "He said there's a thin asteroid belt around one of the moons where we could practice with the beam."

"Okay." Denk walked slowly around their stuff. "Here, we've got some Screvari-made energy katanas."

"Energy katanas." He chuckled to himself, cocking an eyebrow at Oz. "Can't imagine who those are for."

Denk continued, "We also got some new-ish blaster pistols, two plasma rifles, and this flux cannon. It's supposed to be mounted on a ship, but Voprot liked the weight."

The thing was as long as Geddy was tall and had to weigh at least two hundred kilos. Voprot picked it up like a toy and hefted it with a toothy grin. "New weapons make Voprot happy."

Denk continued, "We also got a handful of blaster pistols, two plasma rifles, and spare parts for everything. And then here ..." he pointed to a pile of clothes and giant metal canisters, "... we've got five novaspheres, coveralls, and fresh nutrimush. It ought to hold us until we get to a proper market."

"Works for me. Voprot, help Denk get this shit stowed. Oz, prep for launch. Doc, figure out where the moon Gaothea is from here."

The crew jumped at his orders. Geddy took an armful of the coveralls and carried them off toward their quarters.

— *When are you going to tell them?*

— Later. Much later.

He was about to turn down the corridor toward his quarters when Morpho came swinging along the ceiling, stopping in front of the door. Geddy checked to ensure no one had followed him in.

"Find anything?"

Morpho twisted his body back and forth, the equivalent of shaking his head. "Good. Tell no one." He took off across the floor and returned to his labors on the shield.

On balance, their trip to Thegus had at least turned the *Fiz* from a flying warehouse into a viable salvage vessel. It had also revealed the location of the *Penetrator* and gave additional insight into how Thegus might fit into the Zelnads' plans. But the bitter taste of Zereth-Tinn's extortion remained, and no quantity of nutrimush could cleanse his palate.

———

Denk maneuvered the *Fiz* into position near an isolated car-sized asteroid in the belt around Thegus' purple-tinged moon, Gaothea. As the portmaster indicated, it was a small belt, barely visible against the swirly patterns on its surface.

Geddy and Oz had donned spacesuits and stood at the controls of the tractor beam to the right side of the closed hold door. They were designed around the old netting system, but were now mapped to functions on the new beam. Neither of them had ever reeled in an object this way, and he'd never seen her so nervous.

"It's gonna be fine, Oz," he assured her, though he couldn't possibly know that. "This is why we're practicing."

"Hope you kept the receipt."

He glanced over his shoulder. Tardigan and Voprot were in the bridge with their noses pressed to the windows aside the airlock.

"So, you ready to do this?" Geddy asked.

"Nope."

"Let's rock!" Geddy watched her face for some reaction, but none came.

"Boots on," she said. They activated magnets in their boots, locking them to the floor. "Disabling artificial gravity."

"These aren't made for walking," he quipped. Still nothing. She was too focused on the job at hand.

"Denk, I'm opening the hold door."

"Roger that."

Oz bled the air to release the pressure and activated the door, revealing the small asteroid they'd parked beside. Geddy held a binder with Tardigan's translated operation instructions. She powered up the beam, and data popped up on both sides of the screen with a glowing red reticle in the middle.

"Okay, position the reticle over the target and hit DEPLOY to activate."

Using a small joystick, Oz gave little taps until it was positioned perfectly on the asteroid. A tap of the button, and the reticle turned green. Fresh data flooded the edges of the screen, including estimates of the rock's composition and its distance from the *Fiz*. It also indicated there were no life forms detected.

"Whoa." Her big eyes lit up. "That's pretty sweet."

"This would've prevented our ranse situation."

"So would've leaving that ship alone," she pointed out. "Bykite should've listened to you."

He appreciated the reminder that she was on his side. "Okay, now it says to adjust the retrieve rate or accept the suggested rate, and the beam will engage."

The system recommended a rate of 0.23 meters per second. Oz looked to him, and he gave a shrug. "Sounds reasonable." She pushed the button, and a bright green circle of light spread across the rock, accompanied by a faint hum.

"Now what?" she asked.

"The rest should be automatic."

At first, it appeared the asteroid wasn't moving, but after a minute, he could tell it was getting closer.

A satisfied smile crept across Oz's face. "This is suspiciously easy."

"It'd better be for what it cost us."

"It'll sure be nice when we get the other stuff we need."

Guilt fell over him like a cold blanket. Before long, he'd have to inform the crew of the bargain he made with Zereth-Tinn, and that they weren't much better off. He was already thinking of ways to forestall that.

— *You have to tell her.*

— Not yet.

Little by little, the rock neared the open hold door. To his pleasant surprise, the beam guided it through the exact middle of the opening and shut off. The big, sparkling rock crept very slowly through, hovering four or five meters off the floor.

"All right, it's fully inside," Geddy said, closing the binder. "Now what?"

"We usually maneuver smaller pieces into place manually. With larger ones, we bring the ship up to meet it before we reactivate gravity. Something this size could go either way."

He considered this a moment, deciding Denk might appreciate the practice. Plus, with the hold practically empty, it didn't matter where it wound up.

"Denk, let's move the ship around this thing."

"Aye, Cap. Just tell me when it touches down."

"Roger that. Take her nice and slow."

He and Oz stepped away from the controls and clomped toward the slow-moving asteroid, which was only about a quarter of the way into the hold. He'd forgotten how much effort it took to walk with magnetic boots on. It was hard to keep up with the drifting rock.

The rock continued drifting on a line to the airlock, passing them, still well above the floor.

"Denk, the ship doesn't appear to be moving."

"The lifters aren't responding," said Denk, a tinge of panic in his voice. "Morph's on it."

As slowly as the big rock was floating, it had nonetheless passed the circle at the center of the hold and inched ever closer to the airlock door.

"Um, Oz?"

"Change of plans," she said. "Let's move."

They took big, heavy steps toward the drifting rock but

hardly gained on it. Barely ten meters now remained between it and the door. Through the windows on the far side, Voprot and Tardigan's expressions went from mild concern to outright fear.

"Denk, talk to me."

"Still no response from the lifters."

"Then go forward!"

"Shit. Thrusters are offline, too! What the heck?"

— *Deactivate your boots!*

"Oz, get ready to push me."

"What?"

"I'm gonna try to stop it."

"It's too massive. You'll be crushed!"

"Then I'll cushion the impact." He turned off his boots and locked eyes with her. "Now!"

Oz gave him a shove in the middle of his back and he launched toward the asteroid. Behind the windows, Tardigan and Voprot's eyes widened, and they took a few steps back. Geddy passed the rock with only three meters between it and the door.

But he was moving too fast. He hit harder than expected, slamming into the wall with his shoulder. By the time he righted himself, only two meters remained. Frantic, he pulled himself between the asteroid and the airlock, extending his arms in the vain hope it wouldn't crush him. At a minimum, this was going to hurt.

"Denk, gravity!" Oz cried. "Now!"

A moment before his gloved hands touched rock, Denk reactivated artificial gravity, and both Geddy and the rock immediately dropped. The rock fell straight through into the subfloor, barely one meter short of the door.

A few seconds later, Oz reached him and met his panicked eyes. "Holy shit, are you okay?"

Pain radiated from his shoulder. "I think my shoulder's jacked, but I hardly ever use it. You?"

"I'm fine. But we're dead in the water and all we've got to show for it is sixty metric tons of iron and nickel."

Geddy gave a pained grin and chuckled. "Must be Tuesday."

CHAPTER 16

A LITTLE HEART TO HEART TO HEART

Not two minutes after the asteroid dropped through the floor, Morpho restored power to the lifters and thrusters. You had to give it to him on comic timing. Once he did, they turned gravity off again and carefully maneuvered the rock back out through the hold, leaving a crater too big to jump across right in front of the airlock door.

As bad as that was, it could've been a lot worse. The rock didn't affect any critical systems, and it didn't damage the airlock seal. In that sense, at least, they got lucky.

The caved-in floor panels were replaced with others from less-used areas, and Voprot helped make quick work of that. In fact, it left a cavity where he could sleep. If Geddy was being honest with himself, facing a little peril together had bonded them in a new way. He hoped they might blow off some steam after all that, but by the time they finished dinner, Voprot, Tardigan, and Denk were ready to hit the rack.

"G'night," said Geddy as Denk waddled away yawning.

Geddy cocked an eyebrow at Oz. "Kailorian gin?"

A broad smile lit up her face. "You read my mind."

"I thought that was your job," he said with a laugh.

Supposedly, she couldn't read minds, but he wasn't quite convinced. He retrieved the bottle and two glasses from the cupboard.

— *Is this when you tell her about the money?*

— In a minute. I need to soften her beachhead.

— *Is that anything like a maidenhead?*

— Not remotely.

— *And what about me?*

— What about you?

— *She deserves to know about me, too.*

Geddy shook his head to clear it. If he couldn't shake Eli out, he could at least try to rattle him. That was the last thing he wanted to talk to Oz about tonight.

When he turned back to her, she wore a sly grin. "Even if I could read minds, yours is the last one I'd bother with."

He poured two fingers for each of them, then capped the bottle and sat back down, sliding the glass over to Oz. Their fingers brushed for the briefest moment when she took it from him. They were long and buttery soft to the touch, her nearly white skin as smooth and perfect as cream. The one thing he wanted to do after leaving The Deuce was touch a real woman, but he hadn't, and it gave him an electric thrill to touch her.

Oz pulled her hand away, raised her glass and said, "To staring death in the face once again."

"Well said." They clinked glasses and took a sip. The first taste was like paint thinner, but once it fried your tastebuds, it went down pretty good. "Listen, Oz, there's something you deserve to know."

Her smile disappeared and whatever chemistry was brewing fizzled out. "Of course. What's up?"

She leaned forward, her chin resting in her palm. Guilt nearly choked him before he could get the words out. He told her about Zereth-Tinn's intervention with the tracking device.

"Why would the Zelnads want to track you?"

"I think because I'm the common thread between their research ship and the *Penetrator*."

She frowned, confused. "Why would they want your ship?"

"I'm not entirely sure."

"Why would Zereth-Tinn want to help you?"

Geddy glanced down at his drink and mumbled, "Apparently, he's not a big fan of the Nads. Unfortunately, his little favor didn't come cheap."

Her expression changed to realization, and she sat back, a grim look on her face. "How much?"

"The rest of our winnings."

Her jaw dropped as much as her voice raised. "*What?*"

Geddy tensed as Oz's presence grew. Was this how the Kailorians felt that night at the dance? Intimidation?

"He said he knew where my ship was."

Doubt colored her expression. "How could he possibly know that?"

"He's not who we thought. He knows people. Like, *knows people*. You know when the hangar doors all shut?"

"That was him?

He snapped his fingers. "Called someone and boom! He wanted me to know he had power."

"He had you by the balls." Oz's voice was low as she shook her head.

— *Wow, she really gets you.*

"The thing is, I'm still not sure who's side he's on."

"What do you mean?" She looked back up at him, her interest piqued.

"After he extorted me, he sent over the techs who got the beam going."

"So, we're broke again." He nodded grimly. "What do we do now?" She took a drink, but kept her eyes trained on him over the rim of the glass.

Geddy ticked off the ingredients on his fingers. "We've got a working beam, novaspheres, and a semi-functioning trawler. I say we go to work."

Oz pursed her lips and gave a slow nod. "Seems like as good an idea as any."

"But listen, I don't want the rest of the crew to know all of this yet. Morale's kinda high, which seems important when you're scavenging for trash, and I'd rather not spoil it."

She leaned forward and folded her hands on the table. He met her in the middle.

"I'll keep it under my hat for now ... *if* you tell me what's up with your little space-outs."

The easy smile on his face covered his racing heart. He leaned back instinctively.

"Space-outs?"

She reached across the table and placed a warm hand over his. "I'm an empath. I can sense things. Emotions, mostly, but with you, there's ... a presence."

— *Geddy, your pulse is extraordinarily high.*

— Yeah, because this is it. Maybe I should stall.

"Presence?" his voice squeaked.

"It's like I said when we first met. You're not alone. It's almost like there's another presence in you."

— *She knows, Geddy. It's time to come clean.*

— Knowing endangers her.

— *I'd say your crew is okay with a little danger.*

He tried to swallow but his mouth was sandpaper. He sloshed down a generous swallow of his gin.

— Well, here goes.

— *She's earned your trust and respect. It's time you earned hers.*

"That's because ... I have an alien entity living in my head."

— *You might have eased into that ...*

Oz slapped her hands on the table, furious. "Goddamnit, Geddy. Can't you be serious for one minute?"

He leveled his gaze at her. "I am serious."

Her eyes narrowed as she sized him up. When she could see he was being earnest, she sat back, and he continued.

"About eight years ago, I was working in the geothermal tunnels on Earth 2 and inhaled some dust. A day later, I heard a voice in my head. He's an entity named Eli. That's the presence you sense."

"Eli."

— *I'm proud of you.*

"Yes."

She side-eyed him suspiciously. "Did he just talk to you?"

"He said he was proud of me for telling you."

"And this entity is … a *he?*"

"Well, he … er, *it* is technically genderless, but I've had a few women in my head before, which is why I need to believe he's a he."

For a long moment, she studied his face for some sign of a ruse but found none. "I'm … not sure what to say."

Geddy shrugged and finished his gin.

"I–er, *we* built the *Penetrator* to get him back to his home world," he continued. "Which, as it turns out, is the same world the Zelnads come from."

Oz's lips trembled as she fished for the words through an incredulous stare, but she didn't blink. "But … we don't know what Zelnads are. Right?"

"Eli's home is called Sagacea. It's as old as the universe. Eons ago, he and others sort of emanated from this place like seeds." He exploded his fingers and mimed them floating.

"Why?"

"Their purpose was to spread insight. Knowledge. One landed on the Deuce seventeen million years ago, and eight years ago, I inhaled him or something and his consciousness became embedded in mine. Only Eli's like this helpful friendly voice, but Zelnads learned how to take people over, mind and body."

"So Zelnads are really … Sagaceans? I'm confused."

It was hard to blame her. While he was recovering from his little space walk, Eli explained why they called themselves Zelnads, which helped connect a few more dots.

"In their language, 'zelnad' means something like 'reset.' They believe civilization has been a failed experiment and that it must end. Starting with ours and ending with their own."

"A mass genocide/suicide?" Her face went slack. "Then what?"

"All intelligent life in the universe would be wiped away like a stain. All Sagaceans, good and bad, would be dead, and knowledge and inspiration would die with them. At least, that's our working theory." Her mouth hung open as she grappled with the weight of this. "I know, it's a lot."

She leaned in and stared into his eyes from just a few centimeters away. The intensity of her look was uncomfortable, but he forced himself not to blink.

"So, who am I talking to right now?"

He gave an understanding smile. "It doesn't work that way. I'm at the stick, Eli is a passenger."

She leaned back a few inches, and he could breathe again. He couldn't imagine her face becoming paler, but somehow it did. "So he could take you over if he wanted?"

That was the elephant in the room he shared with Eli. "Maybe. But he wouldn't."

"How do you know?" she asked, seemingly unsure she wanted to know.

Geddy opened his mouth to reiterate that Eli simply wouldn't do that, but he couldn't know that for sure. Eli had slowly earned his trust and affection. Was it that crazy to imagine the Nads did the same thing?

"We built the *Penetrator* together so I could bring him home. But now, I think we have a bigger purpose together."

"What's so special about that ship?"

"It's clad in a metal called shinium. It's the only thing that can get through this sort of energy barrier around Sagacea. It seems the Zelnads want it, but we're not exactly sure why."

"How do you know you're not a Zelnad? Hell, how do you know Eli isn't?"

Geddy paused before answering, just waiting for Eli to pounce. It was a fair question, though.

— *You are not, and neither am I.*

"Because I know him better than I know myself." That should have been enough, but there was more. "He's part of me. The best part." He got up and brought the gin bottle back to their table, refilling both their glasses. After a long swallow, he continued. "Look, I don't know exactly what the Nads are up to, but I'm part of it now, and unfortunately, so are all of you. As long I'm here, you're all in danger."

Oz took a deep breath and let it out slowly. "You have to tell the others." He might be the captain, but she was giving the orders.

"I will. But I'm telling you first because if something happens to me, you'll be in charge."

"Then nothing had better happen to you. Either of you." She bit the inside of her lip, lowering her big, glassy green eyes to her glass and gave it a swirl. "What's it like, having somebody literally inside your head?"

— *Yeah, Trust Issues. What's it like?*

"It was annoying at first, but now … I can't imagine life without him. He's my best friend. We're bound together."

— *Best friend?*

— Don't get too excited. It's a short list.

Geddy could have sworn there was a wobble in Eli's thought.

He tossed back the rest of his drink and took his glass in the sink. "Stay up if you'd like, but tomorrow's a big day. I'm gonna hit it."

"Big day how?" she asked.

With a wink, he said, "We're finally gonna put the *For Sale Make Offer* to work."

CHAPTER 17

TRAWLER TRASH

The only thing Geddy didn't know about running a deep-space salvage trawler was how any aspect of it actually worked, which somehow didn't disqualify him from being captain. But Dr. Tardigan and Voprot were in the same boat, so he asked Denk and Oz to give them the lowdown. As was becoming habit, they gathered in the hold to accommodate Dorkasaurus Rex's immensity.

Denk had been with the late Captain Bykite nearly since the beginning and was most familiar with the business of running salvage, so Oz let him break it all down. For some reason, he was extremely nervous about it.

"Should I sit?" He sat on one of the stools. "Or stand?" He stood and sat again a couple times, his beady black eyes darting nervously between them.

Geddy waved his hand dismissively. "Meh. You're about the same height either way."

"Heh, heh, I guess you're right." He gave a shrill little laugh before deciding to stand. "Okay, so how does this all work ... well, the story of space salvage really begins with the Udsars, who–"

"Love it so far," interrupted Geddy. "But can you skip to the part where we make money?"

"Right," Denk said, again with the nervous laugh. "Well, most people think we just fly around space and look for wrecks, but that's just luck. And yeah, sometimes we do get lucky."

— Not nearly often enough.

— *Is that innuendo?*

— You're starting to understand me.

He couldn't resist glancing at Oz, who immediately looked away before they both started laughing. Denk continued undaunted.

"Other than that, we get salvage one of two ways — by picking up what transports or freighters throw away, or planetary salvage ops."

Clearly, the Semenovs had exclusive rights to the salvage op on Earth 2, but it made sense that other planets would bid out, at least for certain types of items. They'd used some of the planet-based equipment to extract the Zelnad research vessel from the desert on Kigantu.

"Demolition companies sometimes invite trawler crews like us to help with cleanup," added Oz. "We'll pick through to find stuff we want and keep the proceeds."

"Isn't that ... scavenging?" Geddy asked.

Oz exchanged a thoughtful look with Denk. "It's admittedly a fine line."

Denk jumped in to save her. "The point is, most people are looking for Zelnad tech these days, so a lot of what we find isn't worth much anymore, which means to get by, we need tons of it."

"What about transports and freighters?" asked Voprot.

— Wow, a complete sentence.

— *He's improving.*

"Good question, V. The big ships do all their upgrades in

space. It's easier to send the old stuff out through the airlock than to bring it to the next port with them, so that can be a big score."

"But surely we don't follow them around like ...?" A distasteful look settled on Tardigan's face.

"Bottom feeders? Sometimes, when we were really desperate," Oz admitted. "But usually we'll just hail them and ask if they have anything to jettison. They'll usually throw us a bone. Sometimes it's good stuff."

Geddy always suspected there was a very fine line between salvaging and scavenging. One seemed like a legit business, the other like begging for scraps.

"All right," said Geddy, nodding. "So where do we start?"

Oz cleared her throat. "We're barely a viable trawler right now. The ship still needs a lot of work, and until you're trained up, you three are useless dipshits. No offense." None of them objected to this characterization. "Those are just the broad strokes," she continued. "There's more to it, especially breaking stuff down. What we really need is practice. We couldn't bring in a rock without breaking the ship."

Denk's face fell. "Yeah, but sometimes it's weeks between jobs. It'll take months to train everyone up ... I mean, unless there's some secret stash of valuable space junk just floating around in orbit. Heh, heh." He laughed as though the very idea was ludicrous.

Geddy stroked his chin, squinting up at the ceiling as a profoundly foolish idea took form in his brain, swelling like a determined tick.

— *Your brain is working on something. That can't be good.*

— It's not. Forget it. It wouldn't work anyway.

— *Okay.*

— Unless ...

"Ged?" Oz asked. Her faint smile suggested she knew he'd just been talking to Eli. "Do you have an idea?"

"Yeah, but it's absurd."

"Now you have to say it."

"Old Earth."

— *Wait ... what?*

A long pause came while they exchanged confused glances.

"Old Earth is in uncharted space," said Tardigan. "We don't even know its exact location."

Geddy cocked his head quizzically. "Whaddya mean, we don't know?"

"Supposedly, humans jumped through a natural wormhole from just beyond your solar system to here. We've identified your home galaxy but only have a vague idea about your home world. Put simply, Old Earth's generally accepted position in its galaxy is a guess."

"So we find a vector to the Milky Way and hang a left. It should be right around there."

"Are you saying there's something of value there?" inquired Oz.

"Not on it, above it. It's completely surrounded by satellites and crap. I'm talking thousands. Aluminum. Titanium. Gold. Platinum. I'm pretty sure their solution to global warming was to blot out the sun with expensive shit. Clearly, it didn't work."

"No one's been there in ... what ... five hundred years?" asked Oz.

"The way I see it, there are hunters and there are scavengers. Would you rather wait for a transport to send a used toilet out with the trash or have a big score all to ourselves?"

— *It's not worth it and you know it. What aren't you telling me?*

— Not now, Eli. Daddy's negotiating.

Oz was deeply skeptical, but she was the only one who knew the full stakes. If they packed the hold with Old Earth stuff and found the right buyers, the money he'd paid Zereth-Tinn wouldn't matter. Besides, as captain, the ship's finances were his responsibility.

Doc cleared his throat. "Perhaps it's selfish, but the academic in me believes the opportunity to see Old Earth is worth the risk."

"Voprot up for anything," said the lizard with finality, folding his bulging arms across his stout chest.

Geddy's eyes slid back to Oz. "What say you, First Officer?"

"It's inconceivably risky." She turned to Denk. "Back me up here."

"Aw, jeez." He scratched absently at his head like he always did when he got nervous. "Well, it's risky for sure. We can only plot the first jump or two. After that, we're kinda on our own. We'll have to run deep scans to find our next vector but the nav gear isn't the greatest ..."

"Sorry, Ged," said Oz, her voice pained. "It's just not worth it. We've only got six novaspheres. If we run out ..."

"Between us and Earth is a whole lotta nothin'," he asserted. "No way it takes more than three jumps to get there. The way back won't be uncharted. One, maybe two jumps and we're back here, loaded with valuable metal. Doc, do you agree?"

"The captain is correct," affirmed Tardigan. "The challenge is getting there. Once we've scanned the points between, we'll be able to plot our jump back."

Oz threw back her head. "Ha! You mean the scans from this dinosaur of a ship? With no correlating data? I wouldn't be surprised if we jumped into a star."

Running out of novaspheres on the way there was the biggest risk by far, but he couldn't go to Aku empty-handed. Money might get him close to the ship, but the Nads weren't about to hand it over just because he asked nicely. He needed something to bargain with. Like whatever technology Zirhof believed took humanity across the cosmos.

"I guess I'm kinda with Oz," Denk said, stuffing his hands

in his pockets. "I say we push for the nearest port and spend some of that money we won to really–"

"The money's gone," Geddy said, the words sucking the moisture from his mouth.

Voprot pivoted his head back and forth at the others. "Voprot not understand. Where it go?"

Geddy took a deep breath and relayed the story of what happened with Zereth-Tinn. When he finished, he let the silence hang, giving the crew time to digest what he'd told them. But then Denk said a very surprising thing.

"You shoulda told us right away, Cap. We're a crew. Good or bad, thick or thin. We stick together and always have each other's backs."

"He's correct," said Doc. "We've cast our lots with you."

"Voprot want to see worse planet than Kigantu," said the lizard.

A sticky sound came from overhead, and Morpho dropped with a wet splat to the floor.

"Morph, you get a say, too." In lieu of a response, Morpho swung over to the novasphere storage unit and sat on top of it. "See? Even Morph's on board." He squared up to Oz, whose face still registered doubt. "Well?"

"This isn't a good idea, Geddy. We've been trawling for years. We always get by."

"Get by? Look around you!" He gestured grandly about the rickety ship. "We have no prospects!"

Oz looked like she might have a snappy comeback, but only folded her arms and looked away.

"Denk, isn't this is why you left Durandia? To have adventures in the stars? Guys, we have an opportunity to be the first *aliens* to orbit Old Earth. To jump further than anyone's ever dreamt into uncharted space. And to make enough money that we can finally turn this rust bucket into a proper trawler. As fancy as the *Raven*, if not more so."

Denk's protruding ears perked up. "As fancy as the *Raven*?"

— *Oh that is so cheap.*

— Means to an end.

"Think about it," Geddy said, his voice strong, sure, and captainy. "A good used trawler from this century is what — a million, million two? We fill that hold with shit from the middle of the periodic table and we're looking at three, four mil easy. We can pimp this thing out or even get a new ride."

Eli was right. It wasn't fair to tease Denk with a new ship, but captain or not, something this big had to be a unanimous decision. He wasn't wrong about what filling the hold might be worth, but he couldn't know how long it would take to do it or if they'd even survive the trip.

Denk's eyes brightened as he turned to Oz, looking for all the world like he was asking for his mother's approval or something.

Oz rubbed the bridge of her nose, shaking her head all the while. Finally, she sighed and said, "Three jumps. If we're not on Old Earth's doorstep by then, we still have two novas-pheres to jump back."

Geddy considered this a moment. It was a good, smart, conservative plan. "Works for me. We leave in the morning."

CHAPTER 18

SESEHLU SAYS WHAT?

G eddy and Oz sat in their usual spots on the rotating stools beside the breakdown bench in the hold, idly swishing back and forth and watching Doc's dance-like convolutions. There wouldn't be room for much recreation on the return trip because it would be full. The crates stacked along the starboard side would be heavy with metal, the shelves on the port side packed with valuable Old Earth artifacts. If there wasn't room for Voprot, that's a price he was willing to pay.

Doc's martial art called to mind any number of pantomimes, so Geddy and Oz amused themselves by guessing at what they were, like assigning shapes to clouds.

He struck a reverse C shape, bending way back over his heels, and made a sort of plucking motion around his head.

"Ladies and Gentlemen, the Zero-G Haircut," Oz said, doing her best announcer voice into her cupped hands.

Tardigan absolutely slayed boredom. *Slayed it*. Orneans had photographic memories, so he could close his eyes and re-read any text or peer-reviewed paper he'd ever seen. When he wasn't sitting cross-legged on his bed, Zenned out and wearing a goofy grin, he occupied himself by practicing this Ornean martial art in the hold. You couldn't look away. Entertainment was scarce aboard a working ship.

For two interminable weeks, they'd traveled in a widening spiral in search of an initial vector to the Milky Way. All day, every day, Denk vigilantly watched the scopes, bleary-eyed and understandably anxious about the whole operation. It rarely took this long to find a jump vector, but then again, no one had ever jumped this far.

The crew was clear-eyed about the risks, but they never came up. There was a scenario, however remote, where they became lost in the void, too far from home or the Milky Way to find either with the *Fiz's* mediocre deep-scan capabilities. Had it been a mission to formally map this part of space, the right vessel for the job would've been something like that Zelnad research ship. What would happen if they burned through all their novaspheres only to find that the space debris over Old Earth had largely de-orbited or been torn apart by meteoroids? What if a novasphere failed? It was rare, but it happened.

Maybe he should start being nicer to Voprot. If they ran out of nutrimush and he got desperately hungry, they'd all start to look like juicy globzoiks. At present, he was asleep and snoring in the subfloor over in the far corner. Denk, as always, was vigilantly watching the scopes for their vector.

Doc crouched low and swept his right leg behind him in a semicircle while balanced on the ball of his left foot. His arms were extended forward with his palms pressed tightly together. His head swiveled over one shoulder.

Geddy wagged his finger at him. "Ah, the Broken Compass. He won the All-Galaxy tournament with that."

"All-Galaxy what?"

"Interpretive dance competition."

"What'd he say this was called again?" Oz asked.

"I can never remember. Sizzle something?"

Boring though it was, he took comfort in this routine. He'd learned the value of discipline on Earth 2. After what they'd gone through just to get here, it felt like a vacation. A vacation with his crew. Quality time with Oz.

"Sesehlu," Doc said with closed eyes, not missing a beat, from a good five meters away.

"You heard us talking?" asked Geddy.

"The practice sharpens one's awareness," he said, sweeping his hands in a circle before framing his face. "You should try it."

"Vogue," he and Oz said at the same time, laughing. She didn't often show her teeth when she smiled, but when the joke was funny enough, she turned it on. Boy, did it light up a room.

"What happens if someone pulls a blaster on you?"

"I suppose I would educate them on the folly of violence." Tardigan grabbed his ankles and hopped like a rabbit.

"And once they fell asleep, you'd take their gun?" Denk asked.

"Sesehlu only offers a peaceful path. It is up to you whether to take it."

"We seriously don't have any games aboard? Movies? I'd read a brochure about irritable bowel syndrome right now."

"Remember," Doc traced invisible letters in the air with jerky swipes of his hands, "this was a Ghruk ship."

"So what?" asked Geddy with a shrug.

A bemused grin opened on Oz face. "You must not know much about the Ghruk."

She had his number there. Ghruk was part of the former Triad, a swampy planet with little high ground. They were short and dark green, with tentacled eyes and loose skin like dripping wax. He'd met two or three of them before, but only in passing. It was a deeply insular society, which, considering their hideous appearance, was probably for the best.

"Do they feed off boredom or something?"

"Adult Ghruk can call up lucid dreams at will. They believe there should be no idle time. Sleep, work, dream. They have no concept of boredom."

"That explains a l–"

A red light started flashing, and a shrieking alarm soon followed. Doc froze to the spot. Oz and Geddy leapt from their seats. Voprot's giant head stuck out as he sat up from his nest in the subfloor.

"Is that a prox alert?" Geddy asked, confused. Even the oldest, shittiest starship in the galaxy could steer clear of obstacles. This had to be something else.

The airlock door hissed open, and Denk came barreling breathlessly through. "Guys, we've got a problem."

Geddy and Oz leapt from their seats and ran after him. Doc and Voprot came in behind them.

"What is it?" asked Oz, marching to the back of the bridge.

Denk had returned to his seat, anxiously tapping his fingers while awaiting Geddy's command. Voprot sat on his haunches with his claws curled around the top of the copilot's seat, staring anxiously up at the scopes.

It was an approaching ship, balls to the wall at five o'clock. Something fast and big.

Again, he and Oz spoke nearly in perfect unison. Only this time, they said, "Pirates."

Running alone in a poorly defended ship far from any of the usual shipping lanes was always risky. Whereas the *Fiz* hunted for salvage, pirates sought treasure and mayhem, as they had for millennia. They were usually a mix of mercs, bitter ex-mils, and career criminals who believed the universe owed them something.

But freighters usually carried freight, and the *Fiz* had none. If they got boarded, they'd put up a good fight, but pirates knew how to infiltrate a ship. They'd eventually punch their way in, and when they found the hold empty, they'd likely kill everyone except Oz, and then they'd make which she were dead.

"Denk, get ready to floor it," Geddy commanded, hopping into his too-tall captain's chair and buckled up. They were getting this stupid pedestal ripped out at the next opportunity.

Oz and Tardigan buckled in as well. Geddy locked eyes with Voprot, who had braced himself at the entrance to the bridge.

"Look for a clear vector. The only way we lose these guys is to jump away. I don't care where. Morph, load the chamber."

Morpho dropped one of the glowing orbs into the launch tube. To his left, Oz's fingers flew across the weapons controls. The *Fiz* was woefully deficient in that department. They were only equipped with War-era disruptor banks, one of which was out of commission, and had no torpedoes or missiles. Until they had the cash to arm her properly, they were sitting ducks.

"What should I do?" asked Tardigan behind him.

"Hide. Take a couple blasters with you. If the shit hits the fan, shoot anyone who isn't us."

Doc's eyes widened, the gravity of the situation setting in. Back in the corridor, Voprot turned back, his eyes hardening.

"Voprot not hide," he growled. "Guard weak Ornean."

You had to hand it to the big lizard. He feared nothing and no one.

Geddy looked back at Doc and sighed. "Fine. Then I'd get that whip of yours ready. Doc, grab one of the rifles. Make no mistake, people, you're fighting for your life."

Doc hurried to the weapons locker and got one of the new rifles, then followed Voprot out into the hold. The inner airlock door hissed shut behind them.

Geddy spun back toward the screen. The fast-closing ship had no transponder, of course, but the boxy shape was a dead giveaway. An old Gundrun gunship four times their size, with a dense cluster of antennas at the bow that resembled the splintered end of a board. He couldn't guess at the range, but they probably tracked them all the way from Thegus. This wasn't some bunch of knuckle-dragging thugs. These guys were pros.

Denk had the engines cranked. For how old it was, the *Fiz* had some juice in her caboose, but the pirates were still gaining.

— *What if we don't find a jump vector in time?*

—I'm working on that.

—*Work faster.*

—I'm open to suggestions.

"Oz, you ready to rumble?"

"The starboard disruptors are online, but they might as well be spitballs against a ship that size."

Geddy took a deep breath. Dealing with pirates was part of the job no matter what sort of ship you were on, but they were sitting ducks and he wasn't sure what to do. Once, he might've known at least one of the guys chasing them and only needed to name-drop the Auctioneer to be considered untouchable. But that was a lifetime ago.

If they couldn't jump, the next best thing was a friendly planet. "Denk, what're we closest to?"

Denk's sausage fingers danced over the controls. A minute later, he pulled up a second screen with an estimated distance to the nearest planet. Geddy breathed a sigh of relief. It wasn't far — twenty minutes or so at their current speed.

"Hello there," Geddy said in a voice normally reserved for picking up women. He leaned forward to get a closer look. "Is that …?"

Denk looked anxiously back at Oz, who was focused on the closeup in the reticle. "It's Temeruria."

What little color was in her already pale face dissipated.

She leaned back in her chair with a haunted expression. Geddy wasn't sure why. To him, it seemed like incredible luck.

"Send a distress call and burn straight at it." For a long moment, no one did anything. Not exactly how captaining was supposed to work. "That's an order, Denk!"

"I know, Cap, but ..." he pleaded, looking past Geddy toward Oz.

Geddy turned away from the console and came face-to-face with Oz. "I can't go back," she said simply. "I was banished."

In his haste to get them out of this situation, he'd forgotten what she'd confessed to him on Caloth. The Nads delivered a targeted strike on the royal palace when she was young, killing the king. When they decided not to retaliate, she'd joined the Xellaran resistance, earning her permanent banishment, or so she said. But some old decree wasn't about to keep Geddy from making it through the day alive.

"Unless we find a jump vector in the next thirty seconds, you're gonna have to suck it up and–"

An angry, buzzy beep from the console yanked him from his musings.

"Missiles incoming!" shouted Denk.

"Do I even have to ask about countermeasures?" Geddy asked.

"Countermeasures. Ha!" Oz chuckled as she returned to her position. "That's adorable."

The rear camera showed two approaching missiles on a tightening spiral. Oz waited until they were close and blasted them with a volley from the small aft cannon. They exploded harmlessly in the distance, but it was really just a warning — prepare to be boarded.

When his eyes darted back to the screen, Geddy found the big ship looming larger still. There was no point arguing about Temeruria because they weren't going to make it. Unless they miraculously stumbled into a jump vector, this was coming down to a fight.

He bolted to the weapons locker, grateful they at least could defend themselves. The Screvari-made energy katanas were clearly for Oz, so he and Denk would take the other rifles and him the old Exeter.

Nearby, Oz was still fixated on the ship, fingers tensed on the joystick.

Geddy removed the two swords and tapped her on the shoulder. "Never mind that. We need to get ready."

Her eyes followed the blades up to his face, her expression grave. She took them with resignation. He reached back in for one of the blaster pistols, already holstered, and held it out.

"This, too."

"I don't need that."

"Backup, then."

Oz took the pistol in a huff and fastened it about her slender waist, then strapped the sword sheaths over her back. Meanwhile, Geddy strapped on his blaster.

"Denk, did you send the distress call?"

"Aye, Cap. Course is set for Temeruria."

"Then start praying."

The color drained from Denk's face. "Shouldn't we at least try to outmaneuver them?"

"We can't. Our best bet is to keep them from getting in until we pass the outer markers."

Denk set the autopilot and met Geddy and Oz at the back of the bridge. Geddy handed him a rifle. It was comically large in his hands, like the children conscripted into the Screvari army in propaganda clips from the Ring War.

"Ever shot one of these?"

He shook his head. "No."

Geddy tapped the end of the barrel. "Point this end at the bad guys and pull the trigger."

CHAPTER 19

YO-HO-HOSED

Before leaving the bridge, Geddy cast a final glance back at the display just long enough to confirm the approach angle of the pirate ship.

"They're coming up on the port side. Use the workbench and machinery for cover and don't leave it unless you have to."

Voprot was already kneeling behind the drill and mill machine, which was mounted on a thick cylindrical base. He'd donned his ranse armor and had one of the plasma rifles leveled at the opposite wall. His whip still hung from his belt.

Tardigan had taken the lift to a perfect position at the top of the shelves. They wouldn't be expecting a sniper.

Geddy turned to Denk and jutted his chin toward Doc. "Go up there with Doc."

Denk nodded and slung the big rifle across his small back, then started climbing the ladder. Meanwhile, Oz flicked on the blades of her katanas. They glowed and sizzled with bright orange energy. The smell of ozone wafted into his nostrils.

"You guys ever been boarded?" he asked loudly. No reply.

"Here's what's gonna happen." He pointed at the wall across the empty hold. "Any second, a giant hypodermic needle will punch a hole through the fuselage. Once it does, they'll send something through to soften us up. If they get in, we're as good as dead, so concentrate your fire on the opening and don't stop shooting."

Geddy and Oz crouched behind opposite ends of the workbench while the others settled into position. His heart threatened to pound out of his ribcage. It had been a very long time since he dealt with pirates — long enough, in fact, that he couldn't be sure they still used the same methods.

"I've been boarded." Oz's voice was low and when he turned to her, she was smirking. "But it's been a while."

He laughed in spite of himself. Any woman who could manage a dumb joke while staring death in the face was A-okay by him.

— *This is bad, isn't it?*

— Pretty bad, yeah.

— *We might die?*

— Depends how badly they want our big load of nothin'.

— *What about the* Dom?

— It wouldn't stand a chance. Besides, I'm not leaving the crew.

They waited, tensed and ready, for what seemed like a long time while the engines hummed, urging them closer and closer to Temeruria. Maybe the pirates had somehow scanned the hold, found it empty, and decided the juice wasn't worth the squeeze.

No sooner had he thought this than a pointy black tube the size of his leg shot through the fuselage, air hissing out through the tight space around it. A jolt of adrenaline surged into Geddy's muscles, and he trained his rifle on the opening. They should've all suited up. Too late now.

"Here we go!" he shouted.

The sound of metal on metal, like rolling ball bearings, came from the tube. Just as he was about to fire, movement from overhead caught Geddy's eye. Morpho launched himself across the hold and plugged the opening. Immediately, something spherical pressed against him from inside. His stretchy form bulged, straining against whatever was trying to get in.

"He's slipping!" Oz said.

The end of the tube was too smooth. Morpho held out for a good fifteen seconds, then shot halfway across the floor as dozens of softball-sized silver spheres burst forth.

"Light it up!" Geddy cried.

He targeted one of the spheres and scored a direct hit. It exploded with a satisfying crack, but it only spawned hundreds of smaller spheres that scattered at first, then gathered like a school of fish.

Apparently, their methods had evolved.

"Cease fire!" barked Geddy, but it was already too late. The panicked shots from the blasters had created a swarm of shiny pinballs that unfurled into silvery bugs. They raced as one toward Voprot, razorlike legs skittering across the floor.

The big Kigantean wasn't having it.

He dropped the rifle with a clang and sprang up from his crouch behind the machine with his claw clenched around the handle of his whip. He brought it up over his head and something activated inside, turning it into a glowing, hissing snake made of lightning. Dropping to one knee, he cracked the whip on the advancing horde and spun himself in a quick circle, sending a big swathe of centi-bots sparking and smoking back across the room.

But he'd barely finished striking before another wave was on him, crawling up his thick legs and slashing through his reptilian skin.

"Aaah!" he screamed. "Voprot in trouble!"

"Screw this," muttered Oz, pulling the energy katanas from their sheaths. Three surgical swipes and the bots on Voprot fell to the floor. She spun and charged forward with a fierce battle cry, slashing at the little bastards like a woman possessed.

Morpho re-entered the fray, throwing tendril after tendril out like sticky lassos to fling the bots across the floor. But they only reoriented and kept coming.

The hold door. A single hole was enough to get rid of a ranse. Only now there was an ocean of bots between him and the button, and neither Voprot nor Oz could exactly stop what they were doing and grab onto something. Besides, every last molecule of air would get sucked out before they reached the airlock.

— Any ideas?

— *How close are we to Temeruria?*

— Probably not close enough.

A finger split off the main wave and advanced on Geddy. With his Exeter pistol in one hand and the rifle in the other, he unleashed on them without any regard for ricochets.

Blaster shots from Denk and Tardigan on overwatch were helping keep them at bay, but their shots were getting so close that he could smell his hair searing as they passed by.

"Hey, watch your fire!"

"Sorry, Cap!" yelled Denk.

A sharp hiss came from across the hold, and a tiny volcano erupted along the floor beneath the giant needle as a cutting torch began melting its way through the *Fiz's* fuselage. Once it was cut, the tube would retract, taking the chunk of hull with it, and a pirate horde would pour through.

"Retreat to the bridge!" he shouted, shooting away advancing bots. "I'm gonna open the door!"

Denk and Tardigan slung their rifles and practically slid

down the ladders. Oz and Voprot continued to fight off the bots as they backed up toward the bridge, their legs criss-crossed with bleeding cuts.

Before Oz and Voprot reached the door, an earsplitting boom came from the direction of the needle. The *Fiz* gave such a shudder that Geddy lost his balance and fell to the floor. Immediately, air started sucking into the tube.

Whatever happened, the pirate gunship was gone, and the tube broke off, venting the bots and their air into space. The pressure alarm blared overhead, orange lights flashing.

The rush of wind through the tube made it shriek like a tortured soul. The vacuum tugged at their clothes as they took one determined step after another toward the airlock. Geddy got back up and overrode the lock, then held it as the others rushed through.

He glanced over his shoulder just before the inner airlock door closed. A handful of bots were stuck to the twenty-centimeter cut made by the torch, partly sealing it, but the others were still sailing out of the tube and into space.

"What happened?" asked Denk, wild-eyed and frantic. The sweat stain around his neck reached halfway down his chest.

"Look!" Doc pointed a shaking finger at the front display.

A squadron of six Temerurian ships — four escort fighters and two gunships — flew in a protective formation around them. The female squad leader hailed them.

"*For Sale Make Offer*, this is Captain Rebinha of the Temerurian Star Guard. Do you copy?"

Denk practically fell over himself scrambling to his chair. "We read you loud and clear, Captain. Boy, are we glad to see you!"

"You're out of danger, but you're inside our markers. Please slow to approach speed."

Geddy nodded his assent. Denk slowed the ship, and the whine of the overtaxed engines returned to a soft hum.

"Is everyone okay?" asked the captain.

Geddy sat beside Denk and activated the comm. "This is Captain Starheart. We've got some minor injuries, but yeah, we're okay."

"We received your distress call. Pirates have increased their activity in this sector lately. We'll escort you to the surface and see about fixing your ship."

"We're in your debt, Captain."

"Are any of your crew Temerurian citizens?"

Geddy opened his mouth, but stopped himself and turned to Oz, who was off camera. She let her weight fall against the wall, lightly tapping the back of her head on it as she looked up at the ceiling.

Denk muted the comm and asked, "What should I tell her?"

Oz pushed herself angrily away from the wall and strode into view with her arms folded tightly in front of her. The captain squinted at her. "Welcome home, Miss. Please identify yourself."

"First Officer Osmiya Nargonis."

"Nargonis ..." he checked a screen off to his side, then frowned, his eyes swiveling back and forth between her and the readout. "Just a moment."

The screen blinked out. Oz's face was stone, and Geddy started to wonder if Oz had told him the whole truth. He figured she wanted to come back but felt she couldn't. But maybe her banishment really was unbreakable. If they were turned away, he didn't have a backup plan.

When the captain came back onscreen, his expression had gone flat. "Miss Nargonis, the prince has allowed you to land."

"Lucky me," she mumbled, then returned to holding up the wall.

His eyes pivoted back to Geddy. "Captain, can your ship handle the entry?"

Judging from the look on Denk's face, landing with a giant tube sticking out of the hull would be a new experience. When it came to the *Fiz*, safety was always subjective. But repairing her in orbit would be ten times more expensive, not that they had the money.

"Only one way to know for sure," he said with a gulp.

CHAPTER 20

YOU CAN NEVER GO HOME AGAIN

The glistening blue marble of Temeruria hung in the endless void of a sector bereft of colorful celestial features. It had no moons or rings, no distant nebulae, and one yellow sun.

Geddy had only been there once to deliver a heavy crate to a specific platform at the spaceport in Medrikar, the capital. On that occasion, he never even powered down. They took the box out of his cargo hold and told him to leave. As was often the case, he had no idea what it was.

For someone in his former line of work to make a delivery to Temeruria was highly unusual. First off, it was so far from the beaten path that interplanetary trade and tourism were almost nonexistent. Second, pacifism was supposedly their most cherished value. They left the Alliance at the outset of the Ring War and declared their neutrality despite having one of the best-trained defense forces in the galaxy.

All of which had piqued Geddy's curiosity about the circumstances around Oz's banishment. If the Zelnads had indeed tried to draw Temeruria into a conflict by assassinating the king and bombing the palace, how could they remain pacifists? And why banish her for joining the Xellaran resistance when it had nothing to do with Temeruria?

The moment the *Fiz* entered their atmosphere, he and Denk realized they'd underestimated the challenge of landing with a giant tube sticking out the side. The drag wanted to pull her hard right and send them into a spin, but Denk somehow managed to guide her down the throat of the approach tunnel. Fortunately, none of their hydraulics had been affected by the hull breach, or things might have literally gone sideways.

They entered the middle hangar of the relatively small two-deck spaceport and didn't have to ask which landing pad was theirs. A retinue of guards stood in formation behind a man in an elegant black suit.

— *Pretty regimented for pacifists.*

— My thoughts exactly.

Denk deployed the skids, and they settled gently down. A perfect landing.

Geddy patted him heartily on the back. "Well done, Mr. Junt. Shut 'er down." Voprot and Doc were both a bit green in the gills after their rough, shuddering descent. "On your best behavior, fellas. Get cleaned up and meet us at the ramp."

Oz reluctantly unbuckled her jump seat and got up to return her katanas to the weapons locker. Geddy followed after her and leaned against the wall.

"Any idea what we're walking into here?"

Her ropy red hair formed a veil around her face as she stared down at the floor. "The imperious one with the stick up his ass is my father. He's the only reason we were allowed to land with me on board."

"He some kind of big deal or what?"

"Prince Bransel." Her lips curling derisively around the title. "Younger brother of the late King Rambar."

Geddy didn't think much of royalty or monarchies in general, with their fancy rules and dusty old traditions.

Birthright was no way to choose your leaders. But even two degrees of separation from a king still made Oz royalty of some kind, didn't it?

"The one who was assassinated?" She nodded, and a big piece of the Osmiya puzzle clicked into place. "Holy shit. You're saying the King of Temeruria was your *uncle*?"

She held out her hand. "Gimme your blaster."

— *That's what she said?*

Geddy fought the urge to chuckle. At least part of him had worn off on Eli.

— Not now.

He unfastened his holster and handed it to her. "Wait ... you're not a *princess*?"

Oz silenced him with a cautioning finger, her eyes shooting daggers from the tops of her eyes. "Do *not* use that word. I'm serious."

He held up his palms defensively. "Okay, okay."

"I need to Zen out for a minute."

She brushed past him en route to the bathroom. Geddy trailed behind her, bursting with questions. Suddenly, their little money problem seemed solvable. Maybe they didn't have to go to Old Earth after all.

She turned on the yellow water and bent over the sink, splashing it over her face with her eyes pinched shut.

"Hey, this is a good thing. I mean, it looks to me like they're ready to let bygones be bygones," he said, bracing himself in the doorway.

"That's how it's supposed to look," she said, water dripping from her chin. "He wants something."

"What?"

She turned off the water, and he placed a towel in her hand. "I don't know yet. Whatever it is, he won't get it from me. As soon as we get The *Fiz* patched up, we're gone. Old Earth might not even be far enough."

"What about our money situation?"

"I know what you're thinking, and it's not an option."

"Yeah, but—"

"*Not an option.*" She finished drying her face and smoothed her short jacket as she passed him and marched back out into the corridor where the others were already waiting. "Guys, there's something I need to tell you ..."

———

Oz was closest to the button that lowered the ramp, so they stood there for a few silent moments, waiting for her to hit it. But she was frozen to the spot, staring off into space.

Morpho would stay with the ship again. Geddy told him to pay close attention to what the mechanics and technicians did to the *Fiz* when it came down to repairs.

"I must admit, I'm excited to see Temeruria for the first time," said Tardigan, giddy as a school kid on his first day. "Their history is quite fascinating. Thousands of years ago, warring tribes were in constant conflict. Not until a massive gathering called the Great Confab did they finally ... agree to share the ... planet's resources. Is anybody listening to me?"

"Not really," said Denk, still rattled by the difficult entry.

"Voprot suddenly drowsy," said the big lizard crouched behind him.

— *I wanted to hear the history lesson.*

— You want to stay and listen, be my guest.

— *Dick.*

Great. That's just what I need. He must have picked that one up from Oz.

Tardigan's tone turned serious. "Temerurians are known to be gracious and extravagant hosts, but they are easily offended. We must observe their customs and express gratitude for their hospitality."

"Got it," Geddy said, looking past him at Oz, who was still in her trance. "Oz, you okay?"

She gave a start as though she'd been in a trance. "What? Yeah, sorry, I'm ... good ..."

"You want to go ahead and give that ol' ramp button a press?"

After a tension-loosening shake of her arms and legs, she took a deep breath and closed her eyes for a couple seconds, then set her jaw and muttered, "You can do this."

"See?" offered Geddy. "It's all about attitude."

Oz hit the button and the heavy ramp lowered. She met Geddy's eyes and gave a pained smile then led them down into the hangar.

Her father was much taller than she, with more severe features and highly arched eyebrows that radiated judgment. Hair as black as his clothes was pulled into a short ponytail through an ornate silver ring that matched the small, shiny buttons of a tailored tunic that ended just above the knee. There was a regal quality to him that Geddy had seen before in other powerful men. By the time Oz pulled up in front of him and the guards, he'd no doubt sized them all up.

"Hello, father," she mumbled, her eyes lowered.

To Geddy's surprise, he pulled her in for a hug. "Oh, my sweet Osmiya, how I've longed to see you!"

She halfheartedly returned the hug. "Yeah, okay. All right."

— *I'm sensing some awkwardness.*

— Yeah? You picked up on that?

"Look at you," he said, stepping back to inspect her. "The spitting image of your mother."

"I see she couldn't be bothered to come." There was a sadness in Oz's voice Geddy hadn't heard before. That special kind of sadness reserved just for family.

"Now don't be like that. She's beside herself with anticipation, but she had a feast to plan."

"Feast?" asked Denk hopefully, a hand rubbing his belly.

He lifted his eyes to regard Geddy and the crew, his smile faltering just enough to notice. "Aren't you going to introduce me to your friends?"

Oz stepped aside and gestured toward them in turn. "This is my crew. Captain Geddy Starheart, pilot Denk Junt, Science Officer Dr. Kronz Tardigan, and ... Voprot. Guys, this is my father, Prince Bransel."

Geddy took a step forward and extended his hand. "Pleased to meet you, sir. On behalf of the whole crew, I want to thank you for saving our bacon."

Bransel cocked an eyebrow. "Bacon?"

"Sorry, a crude human figure of speech. I meant to say asses."

— *Smooth.*

— *Gimme a break. I'm no good at this stuff.*

— *You don't say.*

"My daughter works for a ... human." It looked as though he might vomit on the word human. His eyes narrowed as he sized Geddy up. "How novel."

"I'm the captain of the ship, not her boss," Geddy said, standing a little taller. "We're a team."

"Yes, well, I'm certainly eager to hear of the great adventures that lured her away from her ancestral home and landed her on a salvage trawler." He gave a polite smile before moving on to Denk. "You're the one who managed to land this ... profoundly disabled vessel?"

Denk drew himself up to his full height, reaching only up to the man's chest, and puffed out his own doughy chest. He still had to crane his neck to meet the prince's dark eyes. "Yes sir, your excellency." He fiddled with his hands and looked around nervously. "You mentioned something about a feast?"

"Patience, young Durandian," he said, grinning as he

placed a hand on Denk's shoulder. It barely reached his chest. "You'll use our finest booster seat." His eyes slid from diminutive Denk up to towering Voprot. "And what … might you be?"

Clearly Bransel wasn't used to looking up to anyone.

"Voprot of Kigantu."

"A Kigantean," Bransel said quietly, studying the giant lizard. "How remarkable."

Voprot gave his toothy grin and shot his long, forked tongue out, cleaning both eyeballs with a slick, slurpy noise that made Geddy cringe. The prince stepped back, repulsed, and gave a disgusted *hmph*. He turned away and squared up to Tardigan.

"And who could've imagined an Ornean doctor working on a garbage ship? Your people must be so proud."

Tardigan stuck one foot out and swooshed his arms around in an elaborate pattern as he dropped into a deep, theatrical bow. *"Malen ka subana.* It is my distinct honor, great Prince Bransel."

"A traditional Temerurian greeting," said Bransel, seemingly impressed. "Ordinarily, we reserve such formal gestures for ceremonies, but …" he returned the gesture, *"… av ke subana la'uq."*

Tardigan's face lit up like he'd just won his first spelling bee. He opened his mouth to continue speaking, but Bransel turned away, clapping his hands together. Tardigan's mouth snapped shut.

"Well, I'd imagine you are all in need of a good cleaning and some rest." As if on cue, Denk's stomach growled loudly. Bransel turned back and smiled. "And, of course, the feast. Please follow me."

He headed toward a waiting ship in an adjacent pad, a sleek, shimmering craft about twice the size of the *Dom*, his long strides making Geddy feel like he was jogging. He sidled up beside Bransel. It wasn't just the ten centimeters Bransel had on him that made him feel small.

"It's salvage," he said.

"I'm sorry?" asked the prince, not slowing down.

"You said garbage ship. It's actually salvage."

He gave a bemused smirk as though being corrected by a human was adorable. "A distinction without a difference. And by what cruel twist of fate does one come to captain a … salvage ship?"

"Long story."

"And a thrilling one, I'm sure."

"Look, all we need is a hull patch. As soon as she's space-ready again, we'll be out of your hair."

He swatted the idea away. "Nonsense. You've had a harrowing encounter, and I haven't seen my daughter in fifteen years. I'd be most aggrieved if you didn't accept a full measure of Temerurian hospitality."

— *Remember what Dr. Tardigan said.*

— I know, I know. Doesn't mean I trust him.

— *You don't trust anyone.*

— I'm working on it.

"Of course, your eminence."

They reached the waiting ship and stepped onto the integrated lift, which came standard on most high-end ships. Temeruria was known more for its produce than its shipbuilding. Where could they have acquired such tech?

Once they'd loaded in, a force field engaged, and the elevator rose through a faint red column. They rose up into an elegant round room with three branching corridors and Bransel led them down the center into the bridge.

There was only one pilot, though she was probably superfluous. Ships this nice pretty much flew themselves.

"Aibry," Bransel said, and nodded to the waiting pilot. The woman nodded in return, then tapped a couple holographic

Outwardly, he had a rich man's affect, but something about him struck Geddy as hollow and dark. "What do you know about the rest of her family?"

"Not much. She never talks about them."

The ship slowed to a hover over the landing pad and pivoted to face the valley before touching down like a butterfly on a marshmallow. Bransel, who had strapped himself in beside the pilot, got up and came over to them flashing a bright smile. Oz was the last to stand up.

"Welcome to our humble home."

Denk, Doc, and Voprot fell in behind him. Geddy hung back with Oz. "You okay?"

"I'll be okay when we're back in space," she said flatly. "This was a mistake."

"Osmiya? Captain Starheart?" came her father's voice from the lift entrance. "Won't you join us?"

"Be right there!" Geddy assured him, then turned back to Oz. "As soon the *Fiz* is repaired, we're gone."

Her big, beautiful eyes, which had been downcast, swiveled up to him. "You promise?"

"Promise. Now let's go."

Oz grudgingly followed him down to where the others were waiting in the lift. It lowered them down to the landing pad, where they briefly passed through a spot of delightfully warm afternoon sun. A wide bridge across a statue-filled garden led to the residence. Voprot stared at everything with childish amazement and a goofy grin.

Ornate wooden doors swung open at their approach, and they stepped out into a breathtaking vivarium. Its giant glass dome reminded Geddy of Tatiana's place on Earth 3, but in place of an aquarium, an idyllic little pond fed by multiple waterfalls teemed with colorful fish. In the middle grew a real tree at least ten meters tall encrusted with vines. Natural light filled the room.

While Geddy was taking it all in, he heard Oz murmur, "Oh boy, here we go."

He followed her gaze down a hallway that led deeper into the house. A woman in a neon yellow sari came gliding toward them, both arms weighed down with tukrium bracelets that jangled as she made a dainty beeline for Oz with her arms spread.

"Oh, my dear, sweet Osmiya! Come and hug your poor, worried mother!"

Oz took a hesitant step forward and embraced her mother with the same gusto as she had with her father. It was painful to watch Oz's discomfort. Her mother's eyes were closed, a warm grin playing on her face as she squeezed her daughter tightly.

"How many tears have I cried since you abandoned your family and your home to join some ridiculous militia?"

It was hard not to laugh at Oz's suicidal expression. "Wow, Mom, that's a very accurate depiction."

Her mother scoffed, then patted her down as though checking for a weapon. "Look at you — in the full flower of womanhood, and you're wasting it. When my body was firm and sleek, I took full advantage."

"She really did," Bransel assured them.

Oz's pale cheeks burned with embarrassed rage.

A splash came from the fish pond prompting a sharp gasp from her mother. Everyone's head turned toward the sound. Voprot, who was partly hidden by the enclosure, had submerged his head completely in the water.

"Dear gods, what is that ... *creature?!*" Her hand flew to her chest, startled by Voprot's immensity and general lizardiness.

Geddy whapped him on the back and he yanked his head free with a frantically wriggling yellow fish in his mouth. As everyone stared in horror, he tossed his big head back and swallowed the entire thing. Geddy smacked his hand against his forehead.

— *Not much for decorum, is he?*

— Seriously.

"That's Voprot," Oz said defensively. "He's our ... he's with us."

"Voprot promised feast," he said, water dripping off his chin.

Bransel stepped forward, smiling through his irritation. "The feast comes later. These fish are not for eating!"

"Just for seeing?" Voprot asked, confusion flooding his eyes.

"Yes!"

"Voprot ... finish this one?"

Eager to take her parent's attention away from Voprot's horror show, Oz took her mom's hand and led her toward the crew. "Mother, I'd like you to meet the rest of my shipmates. This is our captain, Geddy Starheart, science officer Krons Tardigan, and pilot Denk Junt. Guys, this is my mother, Nandra."

They sheepishly lifted their hands in greeting as she regarded them with naked disdain. "Oh. These people are with you? sWill they joining us for the feast?"

"Is that going to be a problem?" Oz asked, her jaw clenched.

A further objection nearly made its way to her lips, but she swallowed it and began patting Oz about her nearly white face, rearranging her ropy red locks to suit her. Oz stood and took it.

"You're an absolute mess, dear. And uf," she waved her hand across her nose, "you smell like space. You will clean up before dinner, won't you? We're all looking forward to learning how you fell in with such a ... diverse group."

A long and uncomfortable silence ensued, which Nandra shattered with a sharp clap of her hands.

"Well, I have much to do before the feast, so please make yourselves at home and get cleaned up. Chafton will show you to your rooms and arrange for fresh clothes. Chafton!!"

Her shrill summons echoed through the vivarium as she fidgeted impatiently, looking embarrassed for the delay. From another hallway behind them came the sound of somebody running. Geddy whirled to see a small, frail-looking creature with thin, downy fur and a waistcoat practically skid to a stop in front of her. He was even shorter than Denk, walked with a significant limp, and had trouble catching his breath.

— *What is he?*

— Not sure. No race I've seen before.

He might have been some distant cousin of Krigor's, his former confidant back on Kigantu. Short, triangular ears stuck straight out, though not far, and his forehead was deeply creased. His bulbous nose hung partly over his mouth. Plump bags under his sad eyes suggested a lifetime of servitude.

"You ... called for me ... madam," he managed, huffing from the effort.

"Our guests need proper evening attire."

"Of course, madam. Right away."

"Dinner is at six o'clock sharp. Osmiya, we'll be in the formal dining hall."

She turned on her heels and left with Bransel in tow. As soon as they were well away, Oz hurried over and knelt to wrap Chafton up in a hug.

"I'm so very pleased to see you again, Miss Osmiya," he said, his face brightening.

She kept her hands on his shoulders, locking eyes with him. "Chafton, you're the only one I've missed. How are you? What happened to your leg?"

"I took a spill on the stairs some years ago. It never quite healed right, I'm afraid."

Didn't heal right? Looking around this place, Geddy wouldn't have been surprised if they had a live-in doctor.

Oz rose and turned to the others, keeping her hand on Chafton's diminutive shoulder. "Chafton has been with our family since before I was born. He practically raised me."

"Begging your pardon, miss, but I need to note some measurements and get to work." He took a little notebook from his waistcoat and studied them, squinting and writing down his estimates. Clearly, he had a well-trained eye. "Madam Nargonis will be cross with me if your clothing isn't ready in time."

His eyes lingered on Voprot, tapping the pen on his chin a moment before writing something down. Tucking the notebook back in, he said, "I trust you remember the way to the guest rooms."

"Of course, my dear friend. See you later."

The little servant forced a smile and turned away, disappearing down another hallway in with his awkward, painful-looking gait.

"Guess we'd better clean up, guys," Oz said, motioning for them to follow. "We're in the east wing."

She led them down yet another hallway and up a wide flight of stairs to the second floor.

After being mostly confined to the hold aboard the *Fiz*, Voprot clearly appreciated being able to draw himself up to full height in the high-ceilinged hallway.

Dr. Tardigan paused here and there to study the frescoes that lined the walls. One in particular caught his eye, and he excitedly tapped his finger on the wall. "Captain, this artwork meticulously depicts the events leading up to the Battle of Plathe. If accurate, it directly contradicts the long-held belief that–"

"Fascinating, Doc." Geddy patted him on the shoulder as he passed, barely glancing at the painting.

Oz had paused by one of the narrow vertical windows that overlooked the grounds, her hands on either side of the opening as though considering a jump.

"Don't do it," he said, smiling.

She gave a rueful shake of her head. "I wasn't gonna take her shit. Not for a second. But then she opens her stupid mouth, and it's like I'm twelve again. She's still as overbearing as ever, and I'm just as powerless."

He leaned against the window beside her and cleared his throat. "My mom had this much older brother named Oren. When I was little, he'd sometimes come by for dinner, and every time, he'd somehow get me in a headlock and rub the ever-loving *shit* out of my scalp. Hurt like hell. The first few times, it was funny, but eventually I hated it. Then I hated him. But one day, I got home from my friend's house and Mom told me he'd died."

"Was there a moral in there somewhere?"

"All I had to do was tell him I didn't like it. Stand up for myself. Instead, he died with me hating him."

She stared at the floor, slowly shaking her head. "Y'know, I nearly convinced myself I was this badass bitch, yet the moment I set foot in this ridiculous house ..."

— I'm a little out of my depth here, pal.

— *Oz may be a woman, but to her mother, she is a memory frozen in time. A child with a child's sensibilities.*

"She wants you to be the teenager she remembers. Unless you set her straight, you always will be."

Oz gave that a moment to wash over her, then straightened her back and rubbed her eyes. "That's ... shockingly insightful, Starheart."

He gave an aw-shucks shrug. "I don't know what came over me."

"Could it be Eli?"

Geddy grinned and gave her a wink. "Call it a team effort."

CHAPTER 22

GUESS WHO'S COMING TO DINNER

The vaulted ceiling of Geddy's room had to be at least five meters high. Floor-to-ceiling windows overlooked the neatly manicured expanse of lawn and gardens while the city unfurled far below like an expensive rug. Everything from the furnishings to the towels was obviously custom made and meticulously arranged, if not by Nandra herself then by someone under her direction. He couldn't help but wonder how long it had been since anyone stayed there, say nothing of how many rooms never saw a single visitor.

In the wake of the Ring War, Temeruria became the galaxy's largest supplier of tukrium. That wealth was evident in their flyover of Medrikar, but it was equally clear that the Nargonis family represented old money. Royal money.

As much as he looked forward to eating real food, clinking glasses with a bunch of snooty Temerurians wasn't exactly his idea of a good time. But if that's what it took to get some help from Oz's family, so be it.

After a long shower and a shave, he found a set of clothes laid neatly across the bed. Perfectly tailored black slacks with a fitted shirt and mustard-colored tunic that had a bit of sheen to it. He expected to look utterly ridiculous, but as he squared up to the mirror, he was pleasantly surprised by the look.

"Not bad, eh?"

— *It does suit you.*

"Although, after free-balling it the past few days, I'm not sure I'm groovin' on these pants. They're a little tight in the crotch." He adjusted himself a few different ways, unable to find a good position for his junk.

— *It's just for a few hours.*

He sighed and dressed himself down. "High fashion comes at a price."

— *Oh, brother.*

A soft rap came at the door, which was reflected in the mirror. "Come in!"

It was Tardigan, who had similar pants and a short blue robe gathered in a belt at the waist that draped over his hips like a skirt.

"Get a load of you, Professor."

His face flushed. "Oz is almost ready. I didn't dare go looking for the dining hall alone."

"I wouldn't either. We'd get lost." Geddy tried rolling, then unrolling, then buttoning and unbuttoning the cuffs of his white shirt.

— *Rolled.*

— Are you sure?

Before Eli could respond, Tardigan's hands were unbuttoning one of Geddy's cuffs and rolling it up.

— *You win this time.*

After finishing the second cuff, Tardigan stepped back to get another look. "I must say, Captain, you clean up very well."

"You, too. Like a scholar."

He sank onto the edge of the bed with his head lowered. "Disgraced scholar, perhaps."

This sad-sack BS was getting old fast. Geddy sat down next to him. "Doc, it's time we had a little talk."

"About what?"

"I don't give two-thirds of a shit what you did before joining the crew. I've done things that would make your toes curl. I expect we all have."

He showed his palms in contrition, shaking his head. "I'm sorry, Captain. I don't understand."

Geddy turned to face Tardigan, wincing at his pinched scrotum. What were Temerurian men packing down there? Mushroom caps?

"You're the unpaid science officer of an antique salvage trawler with a hole in the hull and an empty hold and you're wearing borrowed clothes. Be proud!"

Tardigan laughed in spite of himself. "Perhaps I could give myself a bit of grace."

He patted him on the knee. "That's the spirit! Now come on. Let's go eat, drink, and be merry!"

Geddy pushed up off the bed and immediately adjusted his pants. This was going to be a long night.

"Perhaps merriment is closer than you think, sir," Doc noted with a wry grin.

"Why's that?"

"Because you haven't seen what Voprot is wearing."

———

Voprot literally wore a bedspread.

On one hand, a toga was a clever solution to outfitting a tree-sized reptile on short notice. On the other, he looked like he was pledging the lamest frat in the galaxy.

"Voprot feel regal," he declared, the red and gold batik fabric swishing back and forth as he lumbered down the hall. "Want more fish."

"Not likely, pal," said Geddy, still sniggering. Voprot's face fell.

Denk's outfit looked like it had been stolen off a portly kid at a magician's funeral. He sported baggy black knickers with purple tights and a frilly purple silk shirt under a black waistcoat. As ridiculous as it was, Denk appeared delighted.

"How do I look?" he asked, turning from side to side.

Geddy and Tardigan shared a look.

—*Be nice, Geddy.*

"Surprising. Like if a bagpipe player had a baby with Zorro."

Denk's face was blank. "That's a good thing, right?"

"It's the nicest thing I could say," Geddy said, putting his young pilot at ease.

Oz was the last to join them in the hall. She emerged sheepishly from her room wearing a dark red dress that complemented her red braids perfectly. The flowy, swishy drape that seemed to define Temerurian apparel suited her far better than any of them.

Her big, expressive eyes and makeup couldn't mask her sour expression.

"Wow," Geddy said as she shuffled up to them. "You look incredible."

She allowed a sheepish grin. "Thanks."

"Well, the gang's all here. Shall we?"

"Not yet," said Oz, motioning for them to come closer. "We need a little pregame huddle." They gathered more closely around her. "God only knows who my mother decided to invite to this thing, but fair warning, she and my father have some very ... eccentric friends."

"I, for one, enjoy chatting with eccentrics," offered Tardigan.

— You don't say.

— *Maybe that's why he likes talking to you.*

— I can't tell if that's a compliment or an insult.

"I'll remember you said that. Look, just keep your head down and don't do anything stupid like eat my mother's very expensive fish." She looked pointedly at Voprot, who pouted in response. "We just need to make it through tonight."

They nodded that they understood and followed her down the hall back toward the vivarium.

Voprot paused by the pond, licking his lizard lips as though hypnotized by the koi-like fish, but Geddy shoved him in the small of his back.

"Keep moving."

Oz led them down another long hallway illuminated by skylights. The sun was low on the horizon, bathing her in golden light, making her look luminescent. She and Geddy had both left home before they were technically ready, but he'd thought the similarities ended there. Maybe she'd been running away from something, too.

— I don't know about you, but I am really looking forward to this.

— Probably for different reasons than me.

— And what are those reasons?

— I could use some entertainment.

When they reached the dining room, Oz paused at an arched doorway and gathered herself before pushing through.

The room was the size of a gym. At the center was a gigantic U-shaped table that might have been carved from a single piece of wood, with high-backed chairs that came to points like knife tips. A dizzying array of plates, utensils, glasses, serving platters, and multi-tiered dessert trays ran down its full length with room to spare for the main courses that had yet to come out.

The domed ceiling featured an intricate painting of what Geddy could only assume was the entire royal family, which included at least a dozen children. Based on how youthful

Bransel and Nandra looked, it was quite old. If Oz was pictured, he didn't recognize her.

Servants flitted about, some eyeing the arrangements and making little adjustments while others came and went through a pair of swinging doors that let in the clanks and shouts of a busy kitchen when opened and squelched it when closed.

Bransel was holding court with a handful of men in one corner, drinks in hand, while Nandra and two women stood shoulder to shoulder in another corner, whispering conspiratorially as they entered.

Nandra's outfit sprouted so many frills and folds that it looked like it was Halloween and she'd dressed as an air filter. Layer upon layer of fabric barely brushing the floor gave the impression of gliding. She regarded them with much the same distaste as before.

"Darling!" she said to Oz, her hands clenched together. "I hoped you'd remember the way."

"I only ate here every night for sixteen years," Oz said stiffly.

The others had left their private conversations and were slowly making their way across the room to get a closer look at the new arrivals. None were dressed quite so extravagantly as their hosts, but to Geddy's surprise, the getups they'd been provided weren't out of place.

The ladies pulled up well short of them and gawked in fascinated revulsion at Voprot, who tended to have that effect on people. All but one of the men hung back as well, an important-looking fellow roughly Bransel's age who regarded them with great interest. His fitted royal blue suit appeared to be a uniform.

"You must be the crew of the salvage ship," he said, his voice rough and authoritative. A puffy scar ran from his left ear down his neck where it disappeared beneath his collar.

"What gave us away?" asked Geddy.

The man stiffened. "I am Sky Marshal Komfeti."

The pronunciation of his name sounded exactly like "cum-fetti." Geddy's face reddened as he held back a laugh. Even Oz cracked a smile.

He offered his hand. "Captain Geddy Starheart."

The man shook, his hands more delicate than he would've expected. Maybe "air marshal" was a military title and maybe not.

Bransel stepped forward and said, "You can thank Sky Marshal Komfeti for the strike against your pirates."

"Thanks for blasting them, Komfeti," Geddy said straight-faced. "It wasn't a second too soon."

Stop it, mouthed Oz as Komfeti gave a tiny nod.

— *Are you sure you're a grown-up?*

— Come on, Komfeti? It's too … shall we say … juicy?

The marshal jutted his chin at Voprot. "I like to think I'm quite well-traveled, but I'm afraid I don't recognize your race."

"Voprot Kigantean."

He frowned. "Come again?"

Geddy covered his guffaw with a cough. "His English isn't the best. He's Kigantean. We're working on it."

"Kigantean?" he asked with great interest. "As in, Kigan-tu?" Voprot nodded. "I wasn't aware Kigantu had an intelli-gent race."

— Does it, though?

— *Be nice for once!*

"We not travel much."

"Now that we're all here," Bransel said, "why don't we all introduce ourselves. Casilda, would you like to start?"

Casilda was Nandra's widowed sister-in-law. Then came Komfeti's wife, Arinya. Both of them kept their distance from the crew other than a hasty hug between Casilda and Oz.

The other men introduced themselves as Zavis, Damari,

and Brodrik, all royal functionaries with long and meaningless titles who seemed indifferent to their presence.

"Shall we eat?" Oz said impatiently.

"Well," Nandra's forced smile and tone dripped with passive aggression. "Osmiya has swooped in from god knows where to declare that dinner should begin. Please find your placards and be seated." Abruptly she pivoted toward the kitchen and barked, "Eldan!"

A skinny young man who had just come through the door with a pitcher of water immediately about-faced and hurried back into the kitchen.

Geddy and the others scanned the table for their names, but only found "Human," "Durandian," "Ornean," and "?" He paused at the question mark and pointed it out to Voprot.

"Pretty sure this is you, big guy."

CHAPTER 23

A MEAL FIT FOR A KING'S YOUNGER BROTHER

Voprot looked as uncomfortable as Geddy had ever seen him and regarded the chair with abject confusion. The only places Geddy could remember seeing him sit was at the bar in Aquebba, which had benches, and the galley, which was a short stool. A high-backed chair presented a challenge vis-à-vis his gigantic tail.

— *Maybe the fish pond wasn't that bad an idea.*

— Ha! You're getting the hang of this, Eli.

— *It feels unkind.*

— That's the point.

"Nandra, Voprot's happy to sit on his haunches," Geddy said. "Besides, it brings him almost to eye level with the rest of us."

She wrinkled her nose and shrugged. "Whatever makes you comfortable. Suffice it to say, we're not used to hosting such … exotic guests."

Voprot picked up the big chair like a toy and looked anxiously at Geddy, who nodded toward the back wall. He hesitantly parked it there, returned to the table, and sat on the floor with a thud. The others also sat, with the crew on one side and everyone else on the other. As promised, Denk had a booster seat and not a trace of embarrassment about it. Nandra and Bransel sat in larger, throne-like chairs together at the head. Nandra rang a bell to summon the staff.

A parade of young Temerurians emerged from the kitchen like soldiers, each carrying a single covered plate. They arranged themselves behind the guests, and once they were all in position, set the plates down and removed the covers with a flourish. Was all this foo-foo stuff for special occasions, or did they do it all the time?

At the center of the giant plates sat a tiny nest of dark green leaves with a bright orange fruit or berry of some sort in the middle that resembled — but hopefully wasn't — an egg. Drops of red dressing that looked distressingly like blood formed an artful, if macabre, constellation around it.

Voprot and Denk both leaned down to study it, baffled, as the servants receded.

"Island ivy salad with fresh tasselberry and fluxroot oil dressing," Nandra announced, clearly expecting them to be impressed.

Since leaving Earth 2, Geddy had almost exclusively eaten nutrimush or tiny portions of pretentious food. Hadn't these people ever heard of sandwiches? Pasta? Maybe a good old fashioned tater tot casserole? Was it asking too much to want something worthy of a deep food coma?

Before they could even arm themselves with forks, Voprot's tongue shot out and slurped up the berry. Immediately, he grimaced and shuddered as though it was poison. As he gagged, all Geddy could imagine was him spewing half-digested fish across the ornately decorated table.

"Voprot no like." His growly voice echoed uncomfortably through the cavernous space. "More fish?"

Nandra's entire face puckered, her fingers gripping her

fork so tightly that Geddy thought it might bend. "This is not a restaurant."

Dr. Tardigan, who had just taken a bite, cleared his throat to fill the uncomfortable silence and dabbed at the sides of his mouth with the cloth napkin.

"It's delightful," he said. "Do I detect a hint of smoked gilifras?"

Their Temerurian hosts exchanged a look of profound surprise, even earning an approving smile from Nandra.

"You're familiar with Temerurian spices?" inquired Brodrik.

"Oh yes. I've been studying your planet for many years."

"Then you probably know more about it than Osmiya," remarked Nandra.

Oz, whose eyes were fixed on her plate, paused chewing to look up desperately at Geddy. He expected some awkward exchanges from a bunch of royals, but these people took the cake. Even the snobs on Pretensia would think this was all a bit much.

"I never imagined Orneans would indulge study in such … esoteric subjects," said Brodrik. "What aspects of our world do you find most interesting?"

Doc held up a finger as he chewed another bite. "There's so much to choose from. Your history, your culture … your delicious cuisine. But I suppose your tukrium industry is the most historically significant."

"And proud we are of that legacy," said Bransel, smiling. "It has been our good fortune to fill the supply gap left by the collapse of the Triad."

"Admittedly, I'm not as familiar with some of your more recent history, such as the awful attack on your palace."

All the Temerurians stopped eating and drinking at once, including Oz, who stared at Tardigan like he'd broached some taboo topic, though she hadn't told them it was off limits.

"What do you know of it?" asked Komfeti.

Sensing the shift in the room's temperature, Doc scrambled to downplay the topic. "Oh, very little. Simply that the attack was unprovoked, and that great King Rambar lost his life. One can only guess at the Zelnads' aims."

Their salads gone with the exception of Voprot's, the servants reappeared with even larger plates and revealed their contents in the same fashion. It was a bird with four wings — presumably the same flocking birds they marveled at as they flew to the compound. A grainy stuffing spilled forth from its body cavity. It actually looked and smelled quite delicious, but they hadn't struck Geddy as game birds.

"Yellow-crested caricoot marinated in dark ale with wild cesave stuffing," announced Nandra with an elegant wave of her hand, oblivious to the fraught conversation in progress.

"Is that what my daughter told you? That it was the Zelnads?" spat Bransel.

"Well, I ... um ..." Doc glanced over at Oz, and Komfeti exchanged a dark look with Bransel and Nandra.

"The truth, Dr. Tardigan, is that we never learned who bombed the palace or why," affirmed Komfeti.

Geddy wasn't always good at reading people, but he knew a lie when he heard it. If Oz knew, they knew.

"But who would've done it if not the Nads?" asked Geddy.

Nandra cleared her throat and smiled pleasantly. "Surely this isn't a conversation for the dinner table. Please, luxuriate in the delicate flavors of your ..." The *tink-tink* of utensils drew Geddy's attention to Denk, who was shoving forkfuls of the bird into his face. Voprot's plate was already empty. The women across the table all looked like they might barf. "... caricoot."

"I don't know what this is, Mrs. Nargonis, but it sure eats good," Denk said with his mouth full, bits of bird stuck to the sides of his fuzzy little face. He hadn't heard a single word of the charged exchange.

Komfeti locked eyes with Geddy. "The Zelnads would never attack us. If anything, they'd come to our rescue."

"What?" Geddy asked. "Why?"

"Because they're our customers," Bransel replied. "And very good ones. Other than perhaps overcharging for novas-pheres, we have nothing to fear from them."

— *Temeruria is in bed with the Zelnads?*

The entire crew stared at him as though he'd unwittingly spilled some awful secret, but was utterly confident in his assertion. After a moment, his face softened with under-standing.

"Judging from your expressions, it seems you've bought into the narrative that the Zelnads are some kind of 'evil empire,'" he said, supplying air quotes.

Geddy barked a laugh. "Narrative! That's rich."

Oz's father bristled. "You disagree. Please, edify us."

— *Walked into that one, genius.*

— Shit.

"They've been buying up tukrium for years, but no one's ever seen more than a ship or two. A few weapons here and there. Where's it all going?"

Bransel gave an indifferent shrug. "Temeruria refines and sells the strongest metal in the galaxy. What becomes of it after that is no more our concern than a baker to his bread."

"Speaking of bread, could someone pass the butter?" asked Denk, not slowing down in the least.

"It doesn't concern you that a mysterious group with unlimited funds is buying up all your tukrium? That they control the novasphere supply?"

"We know all we need to about the Zelnads," Bransel explained. "They don't cause trouble and they pay on time."

"Uncle Rambar didn't trust them," said Oz gravely. "Maybe neither should you."

"Says the girl who went off to fight in an entirely unrelated conflict," Nandra hissed, silencing her.

"You don't know anything about it, mother." Oz stared murderously at her over the tops of her eyes.

"I know your side lost miserably. And now you're a glorified ... trash collector." She shook her head in disgust. "In a flying junkyard with three morons and whatever *that* is." She pointed directly at Voprot.

— *Well, this is going off the rails.*

When it came to details about her past, Oz was a cipher. Like Denk said, she'd never spoken of her life on Temeruria, her family, or her years on Xellara. Did she fear this same judgment from others? These people were nightmares. If she couldn't muster her own defense, someone would have to do it for her.

"First of all, there's only one moron on my ship, and you're looking at him. Second, your daughter is the best fighter I've ever seen, and I've seen a lot. And she's also selfless, and kind, and perceptive. You should be proud of her."

Geddy stole a glance at Oz. A corner of her mouth twitched upward.

"Yeah!" Denk said, hitting his fist on the table. "And she knows right from wrong."

"Which is more than I can say for you people," added Geddy. "She's the glue that holds our ship together. Besides the actual glue, I mean."

"The un-flyable ship from which we are presently extracting a pirate harpoon?" Bransel sneered.

— *So much for asking them for money.*

— Yeah, not looking good on that front.

"Look, we appreciate your help. Truly. But all this ..." Geddy gestured around him at the high ceilings, the piles of food, and the muffled clank of pots from the kitchen. "You want to do business with the Nads, be my guest. But I don't want any part of it. Starheart out."

Geddy stood so abruptly his chair fell back and the pointy tip at the top snapped right off. Without bothering to right it, he strode toward the door.

— *Starheart out?*

— It felt right in the moment.

— *You know you can't really go anywhere, right?*

— It's the principle of the thing, Eli. It's the principle.

Denk and Voprot followed suit.

"Voprot out, too."

— *It actually worked there!*

Tardigan dabbed at his mouth as he rose. "Perhaps I don't have a monopoly on shame. Good evening to you all." He still took the time to re-fold his napkin and push his chair back in.

Bransel, Nandra, and their guests were dumbstruck by such a rejection of their hospitality. Their heads swiveled to Oz, who was still in her chair. As Geddy reached the door, he stopped and looked back at her, giving a nod to remind her of their earlier conversation. He wasn't much for giving advice, but Oz had been right to leave this place. Just beneath its bucolic veneer was a deep moral rot, and none of them should have any part of it.

"Some things never change," Oz said, getting up herself and quickly wiping a tear from the corner of her eye.

Nandra rose, indignant, ringing the bell violently. "Osmiya, you are a princess of Temeruria and we are your family! Return to the table at once!"

Oz spun back toward her just short of the door. "I'm no princess, and you're not my family." She nodded over her shoulder toward Geddy and the crew. "They are."

"Your ship will be ready by first light," Bransel called after her. "I suggest you be on it before the welds have cooled."

Oz spun and threw a fork she'd concealed in her hand, so quickly and accurately that it was already stuck in her father's bird before anyone saw what she did. Bransel stared incredulously down at the fork, then back at her.

"We're done, father." She marched through the door and down the hall.

"Does this mean we're not staying for dessert?" Denk asked, falling in after her.

Geddy patted him on the back and sucked in air through his teeth. "Afraid so, buddy."

CHAPTER 24

NAD IT UP

The morning after their contentious and troubling meal with the Nargonis clan, they were escorted back to the spaceport by Bransel's personal pilot. The workmanship on the hull patch allowed the hold to pressurize, and that was good enough for Geddy. The sooner they were out of there, the better.

Once they cleared Temeruria's atmosphere, Denk pulled up the approximate coordinates for Old Earth and started searching for the longest vector he could find. With just five blue balls, there were no jumps to waste — two there, no more than two back, and one to spare.

To know the location of the *Penetrator* but not go straight to it was torture, but his chief responsibility now was to the crew. With a little luck, they'd return from Old Earth with a cargo hold full of valuable salvage and one helluva story to tell.

He lay on the bed in his quarters, drumming his fingers on his chest as he stared up at the corner of the ceiling where dust had collected, suggesting air slowly escaped through it. Whether that was by Ghruk design or a sign of the ship's deteriorating condition, he couldn't be sure.

— *You're sure this is the right play?*

— No, but it's our best shot at a big score.

— *When do we go to Aku?*

— After this. You heard Zereth-Tinn — the Nads are looking for me. As far as I'm concerned, they're on our schedule now. Besides, we can't just show up on Aku empty-handed.

— *What are you talking ab–*

A gentle rap came at the door.

"Come in, Doc."

Tardigan poked his head in. "How'd you know it was me?"

"You're the only one polite enough to knock."

He entered and plunked down on the chair in front of the fold-down desk and gave a sheepish grin. "Old habit, I guess."

"I dunno about you, but I'm glad to be back in space. Oz's family was a nightmare."

"Actually, Captain, that's what I came to discuss."

Geddy sat up in his bed and propped up his pillow to lean against it. "Oh yeah? What's up?"

He heaved a sigh. "Their business dealings with the Zelnads have me very concerned."

Having been part of many shady business deals himself, Geddy was less shocked by Temeruria's opportunism than the others likely were. Funny how fast principles went out the door once piles of money entered the equation. Their posture might be different if they knew what the Nads were up to. So far, nobody really did.

"With good reason."

"How familiar are you with the Triad?"

"As much as the next guy."

The Triad was a centuries-old trade partnership between Kailoria, Ghruk, and Aku. They were positioned in a nearly equilateral triangle around the Exiod Ring, an asteroid belt rich in tukrium. Back then, Temeruria only mined what they needed for their own modest fleet.

Ghruk handled the mining side of the operation, Kailoria refinement and processing, and Aku shipbuilding and weapons. For decades, Aku's biggest and best customer was the Alliance, a trade and defense partnership between twenty-one worlds that then included the Triad planets and Earth 2.

At some point, however, the demand for tukrium inexplicably skyrocketed. These new buyers, the Zelnads, were from both Alliance and non-Alliance worlds with no clear thread to connect them besides a seemingly bottomless well of money.

As the price of tukrium rose, however, so did tensions. Alliance planets suspected one another of building a secret army while the Triad struggled to meet demand, accusing each other of graft and corruption.

No one could pinpoint exactly when hostilities began. All anyone knew for sure was that it got ugly fast. The Alliance tried to mediate the Triad's dispute, which only succeeded in convincing them leave the Alliance.

As the Triad descended into a full-scale conflict amongst themselves, the Alliance decided on a military intervention. The Triad suddenly found themselves fighting both each other and a well-equipped Alliance ostensibly looking to keep the peace. The death toll was staggering. World after world broke ties in protest, and the Alliance began to crumble. Its leader went into exile, and member planets divided the Alliance's assets amongst themselves.

The Triad planets were never the same.

"Then you know that tukrium became extremely scarce after that."

Geddy nodded. "When I was growing up, tukrium ships were practically tourist attractions. The only tukrium thing we had was a chef's knife, and Mom kept that under lock and key."

"The collapse of the Triad would've thrown a wrench into the Zelnads' plans."

"Hence their interest in Temeruria."

"As king of a pacifistic world, King Rambar never would've trusted the Zelnads with his tukrium. Especially not knowing why they wanted it."

The late King Rambar, Oz's uncle, had been killed when she was still a kid. Her account of why was much easier to believe than Bransel's and his cronies. "And he was in their way."

"That is one possibility, yes."

Geddy locked eyes with Tardigan, his face grave. Could Oz's father have had a role in taking out his own brother, the king, clearing the way for a lucrative tukrium deal with the Nads? Having met the guy, it didn't seem like crazy talk. If it turned out to be true, Oz would blow a fuse.

"You think Bransel had something to do with it?"

"And possibly Sky Marshal Komfeti, especially if the palace was bombed from the sky."

As troubling as it was to imagine, it made perfect sense. Temeruria's decision not to join the Alliance likely cost them in terms of trade. A king who refused a lifeline from the Nads just on principle could easily have become a target.

"Have you shared this with Oz?" Geddy asked.

"Not yet."

"All right. Let's keep it that way for now. I need her focused on the–"

Denk's frantic voice cut him off, distorted and scratchy from the dented little speaker in the upper corner of the room. "Guys, you'd better get up here. We've got company, and it ain't pirates."

———

Geddy sprang from bed and followed Tardigan out the door. Morpho and Voprot burst through the airlock doors at the same time. They joined Oz at the back of the bridge. Geddy was about to ask the obvious question, but the front display said it all.

A heavy freighter the size of a city, flanked by two destroyers shaped like half-pyramids and a dozen triangular fighters, was headed straight for them. He didn't recognize the design of the freighter, one of the biggest he'd ever seen, but he sure as hell recognized the warships. He called the destroyers schnozzes.

"Zelnads," Geddy muttered.

"They must've come out of a jump, but I never saw a gate," Denk said apologetically, his face ashen. "They weren't there, and then they were. What do we do?"

— *They'll know it's us!*

— I'm not so sure about that.

— *Why?*

— As far as they know, I'm still on Thegus. What about you? Can they detect you?

— *We're too far away. Plus, right now, it's you they want.*

"Nothing," Geddy answered Denk.

"They're here to pick up a tukrium shipment," spat Oz, her expression as dark as he'd ever seen it. "Tukrium my own father is happy to sell them."

Geddy glanced furtively at Doc. Her anger made all the more sense in light of his theory, as did her decision to leave and never come back.

The screen's border flashed yellow, and Denk pivoted his chair, terror filling his innocent black eyes. "They're hailing us."

When Geddy hesitated, Oz seemed to sense why and stepped forward. "Let me do the talking. Apparently, they're buddy-buddy with Temeruria now."

He hated the idea of her covering for him, but it made the most sense. "Good idea. But be cool. We don't need any attention."

Voprot was resting on all fours in the shadows, gawking at the whole scene. Geddy stepped behind him, keeping out of sight. Oz smoothed her jacket and drew herself up before giving Denk a tight nod to activate the comm.

The face that appeared on screen was a square-jawed Zorran-turned-Zelnad with short-cropped white hair and an expressionless face. Pointy cheekbones protruded from his deep orange skin like he habitually fell asleep on a beach, with concave cheeks and a mouth a little too small for his teeth.

"*For Sale Make Offer*," he said, his voice even and authoritative. "Alter your course at once. You are impeding an established trade route."

"Trade route?" Oz said in a defiant tone. "It's fucking space. You don't own it."

— *Uh-oh.*

— On second thought, she may not be in a good headspace right now. But I'd be lying if I said I wasn't curious about how this'll go.

"Alter your course," he repeated gruffly.

Oz didn't flinch. "Or what?"

The lieutenant was taken aback, like he'd never imagined being questioned. As much as he didn't want trouble, Geddy couldn't help but grin. Everyone's fear of the Nads was based on their far advanced technology and unknown motives, which really were excellent reasons, but that didn't mean everyone had to lie down for them.

The Zelnad cocked his head and said the obvious. "Or … we will run into you."

"I've got a better idea. How about *you* change *your* course?"

Denk, who was already wound tight, looked as though he might compress into a diamond.

— Where's popcorn when you need it? This is great.

— *She certainly is bold.*

The lieutenant's face hardened. "Put your captain on screen."

"He's on the shitter. Now look, we're not on a collision course, and if we were, we have this thing called a control stick that makes the ship go in different directions."

Promisingly, he hesitated. "Scanning your military capabilities." He glanced at a display to the side, frowned, and gave it a confused tap. "You have … no military capabilities."

She shrugged. "See? No problem."

"What is a Temerurian doing with a Ghruk ship?" he asked.

"What're we, on a date? Tell you what — we'll move a few meters to port so we can both get on with our day. How would that be?" she said, arms crossed.

— *I hope we are never on the receiving end of this.*

— It's kinda hot, though, right?

The young man didn't know what to do and apparently had nobody to ask. He sighed, exasperated, and glanced down at another display.

"Your suggested course adjustment is acceptable."

Oz stuck out her arms and mockingly paced back and forth, mocking him in a flat, old-timey robot voice. "*Your suggested course adjustment is acceptable. Battery low. Must recharge.*" Then she laughed and gave a dismissive wave. "You're too much. See you never!"

The screen blinked out, and with shaking hands, Denk eased them into the narrow alley between the destroyers and the fighters. The strange-looking fighters seemed too small for pilots. For all he knew, they were flown by androids or synthetic organisms like Morpho.

The freighter had to be ten times the size of the Project Rearview transport that evacuated Old Earth. How much refined tukrium could it hold? How many ships could they build with it?

They already controlled the entire novasphere supply. Once they took over the tukrium trade, they'd be untouchable.

Denk held their course, and after a few minutes, the freighter and its fearsome escorts glided past. As soon as they were in the clear, Denk's whole body relaxed and color returned to his cheeks. Geddy emerged from the shadows and stood beside Oz, whose gaze was still fixed straight ahead. She angrily wiped a stray tear from her eye.

He never knew what to say in these situations. Leaning in, he nudged her gently with his elbow. "You did good."

She huffed, her face filled with tension, but said nothing.

"Captain, I found us two solid jump vectors. We should be to the first one within the hour."

Without taking his eyes off Oz, Geddy said, "Good. Set a course. Voprot, prepare the hold for a jump."

Voprot nodded and slinked away toward the airlock. After a moment, Oz turned away and went after him. "I'll help."

— *Women are complicated.*

— Buddy, you have no idea.

CHAPTER 25

OEEEEEE!

Denk executed a full burn toward the jump vector, eager to gain as much distance as possible between them and the Zelnad convoy. Oz figured their destination was the main tukrium refinery on the far side of the planet, which meant they likely couldn't track the *Fiz* even if they wanted to.

Obviously, Zereth-Tinn knew to look for him, but whether the Nads really asked him to put a tracker on his ship was still an open question. Geddy's gut told him they didn't really know where he was going or in what ship.

Oz had returned to her seat at the weapon controls. Voprot sat with his back against the wall at the back of the bridge, his tail stretched out across the floor. Tardigan was boning up on Old Earth history in his quarters. Morpho was perched on Denk's chair, ready to deal with the next inevitable mechanical issue.

Denk maneuvered the ship into perfect alignment with the vector that supposedly pointed like an arrow to Old Earth. They probably wouldn't get all the way there, but by the time they entered uncharted space, they'd at least be pointed toward the Milky Way.

Everything beyond that would require a deep scan to find the next jump vector. Each jump burned a novasphere whether it was twenty thousand kilometers or twenty parsecs, and they couldn't know exactly where the fargate would spit them out. It should be space, but it could be an atmosphere like Kigantu.

Would five novaspheres be enough?

"We're staring right down the throat of that vector, Cap," said Denk, his voice a bit shaky.

"Very good, Mr. Junt. Morph, load up a blue ball." Morpho slung a strand of himself down to the hopper and opened it, then dropped one in the launch tube.

Geddy rose and returned to the captain's chair. As usual, Oz was already a step ahead of him. He turned on the intercom and said, "Prepare to jump."

Thirty seconds later, Denk turned and gave a thumbs-up. "Ready, Cap."

Geddy locked himself tightly in. The Temerurians' workmanship on the patch was about to be put to the ultimate test. A hull breach would leave only the warp shell between them and the forces of a jump, and that would be catastrophic. If the repair wasn't secure, a single jump could tear the ship apart.

"Ever jump this far before?" Oz asked quietly.

"I rarely left the system. You?" She shook her head.

"I'll feel better when I'm on the other side of the universe."

"Mr. Junt, let's take a Sunday drive."

"Aye aye," Denk replied, and launched the first novasphere into space. The tiny, glowing blue ember shot out into the void before it burst outward and instantly froze, opening a shimmering oblong gap in spacetime that never stopped looking like a celestial vagina. "Activating warp shell."

A low hum tickled his feet as the translucent green bubble enveloped the *Fiz*.

"Old Earth, here we come."

Denk eased the ship forward into the slit, held open by forces beyond comprehension. Every time he felt a pang of guilt about his ulterior motive, he reminded himself it really was in everyone's best interest.

— *Earlier, you said something about not going to Aku empty-handed. What did you mean?*

— Ssh. Don't ruin the coolest part.

— *But–*

— LATER.

He refocused on the inner border of the gate, wreathed in an impossibly beautiful purple and blue corona that flowed and rippled like a reflection in a pond. On the other side was more space, stupendously far away, but otherwise exactly the same. Geddy's fingers dug into the armrests and he took a deep breath.

The initial shudder felt like they'd run into something large and unyielding, not unlike the Zelnad superfreighter. Then, the feeling of being sucked into a vacuum cleaner the size of the universe. In half a blink, it was over. His ears popped painfully as they exited the jump. His joints ached and his eyes felt too large for the sockets. Maybe his body hadn't fully healed yet.

At the moment, they were nowhere. No Temeruria, no Nads, and barely two stars to rub together. But it was still charted space, and the nav system knew where they were.

"Denk?"

"All systems green, Cap!" Denk reported.

"Launch number two when ready … er, I mean …"

"He knows what you mean," said Oz with a roll of her eyes.

Denk aligned the ship to the next clear vector, which fell nearly on the same line. A few hundredths of a degree here could mean light years on the other end, so precision was critical. He launched another novasphere, and the same purple slit opened up.

Geddy stared straight ahead, mesmerized. They had a beautiful view of a distant nebula, greens and purples and golds that looked like space itself had contracted and then frozen mid-explosion.

A sudden throbbing pain formed at his temples. He sniffed, but it was too runny to be snot. He touched a fingertip to his nostrils, and it came away red. Before anyone noticed, he wiped it on the inside of his jacket.

— Well, that's not great.

— *You should stop. Give yourself time to recover.*

— I'm fine.

"Mr. Junt?" Geddy asked, feeling like the last burst of gravitational waves had shredded his cartilage.

"All systems are green. But this is where the nav data ends," Denk said, his voice tinged with nerves.

"Then let's fire up that scanner. What're we waiting for?"

Tardigan came running into the bridge, his face knotted in worry. "Don't jump again!"

Geddy whirled in his chair. "Why not?"

"Which estimate are we using for Old Earth's position?"

Something about his tone sent a shot of adrenaline through his heart. "Whatever's in the IAS database. Why?"

He paled and grew somber. "Oh, boy …"

"Something tells me I don't want to hear whatever you're about to say," Geddy said.

Tardigan gulped. "It's just that … you see, Old Earth's exact position has been a matter of some debate in the academic community."

The veins feeding his headache began pulsing. He swallowed down the pain. "We already knew that. Get to the point."

"Old Earth data is based on its celestial equator. We use supergalactic coordinates."

Voprot sat up. "If jump to wrong place ..."

"We fucked," said Oz.

— *He's right, Geddy.*

— I know, but so am I.

— *About?*

— Just trust me.

"You're telling us this *now?*" Geddy asked.

"It was an oversight, Captain. It won't happen again."

Oz threw up her hands. "That's it. We're going back."

Geddy pumped his hand in a calming motion. "Just hold on a sec. How far off could we be?"

Doc scratched at his chin. "It's difficult to say, especially over such vast distances. I'd say half a parsec or more."

That was very, very far, but not unreasonable — about ten times the width of the solar system, well within the bounds of human-charted space.

"We're at the edge of charted space here, right?" Geddy asked. "Can't we convert the coordinates and plot a new vector?"

"I can only make a best guess."

"But if we reach the Milky Way, we can find Old Earth based on its own data, right?"

Doc nodded, albeit reluctantly. "In theory, yes, if we can identify some features in the data set. But Captain, I must emphasize the risk of–"

"Being well and truly fucked?" Oz interrupted. "Yeah, I second that. Captain, a word?"

Denk's eyebrows gave an *uh-oh* flare. He and the others all looked away as Geddy crossed the bridge to Oz, who was seething.

— *I thought we wanted to avoid getting on her bad side?*

— Let me handle this, please.

He pumped his hands up and down in a calming motion. "Look, this was never a sure thing, but we're so close. One more jump and we'll–"

"Cut the bullshit, Geddy," she snapped. "We're already in over our heads and you know it. This isn't about the money."

— *She's got your number. Now we'll find out what you're keeping from me.*

"That's *all* it's about. We made this decision as a crew."

"No, it's about your ego. And maybe some twisted idea of what a trawler captain's supposed to do, but mostly your ego."

His sphincter unclenched. If he had to confess his ulterior motive to her, he'd have to tell the whole crew and reveal that yet another of his half-truths had put them in harm's way. If he could deliver on his Old Earth promises and fill the hold with loot, he'd tell them everything and all would be forgiven. Eli, Sagacea, the Nads … all of it.

"You forgot guilt," he said.

She nodded toward the others, who, of course, had been eavesdropping. Morpho was stretched on the ceiling above them, listening intently.

"One more. But if Old Earth isn't right in front of us, that's it. We go back. No salvage is worth dying for."

— *Oh, come on. Are you really gonna let her and the others follow you on this errand of yours, whatever it is?*

— *We need to do this, and so do they.*

He heaved a sigh and nodded, then turned back to Denk. "Mr. Junt, proceed with your scan."

Denk gulped and initiated the scan. The screen filled with a globe of little dots representing all celestial bodies within the scanner's range. The nav computer then searched for potential vectors to Old Earth, rotating the globe around rapidly until a green line shot through the cloud. A virtual camera zoomed along the line until it ended at the rotating blue planet and the estimated coordinates.

"There she is," Geddy said, smiling. "Right where we left her."

Tardigan came forward and studied the screen, anxiously wringing his hands. He pointed excitedly. "Yes, see there? Those measurements are clearly equatorial. Denk, can you convert those to supergalactic?"

"Nope."

Doc pointed to the navigator's station where he usually sat. "Any nav system should be able to handle that. Don't you know how to use it?" he asked of no one in particular.

"Everything's in Ghruk," said Denk.

"It's a Ghruk ship. How do you operate anything?"

"Don't ask," Geddy said. "Can you figure it out?"

"Perhaps."

Tardigan cracked his knuckles and took a seat at the dusty old terminal. After switching on the holo-displays, his fingers danced across the strange, foreign interface as he keyed in the old coordinates and converted them. A moment later, the vector on the front display began to change as the computer hunted. Another green line appeared showing a new vector to Old Earth.

"That's my best guess as to Old Earth's location."

"How far off would we have been?" Geddy asked.

"One point seven parsecs, give or take," replied Doc.

"How good is your best guess? This is our last shot."

"It's a better estimate, Captain, but it's still an estimate."

Geddy didn't like estimates. He liked knowing the score. Placing this kind of trust in anyone was an unprecedented leap of faith, but they'd placed far more in him, and with considerably less reason.

"Understood. Let's buckle up and do it. How long to get the ship into position?"

"Not long. The new vector's close."

Geddy glanced back at Oz, not for approval but to show

he'd heard her. She was wrong about the ego thing, but not about being decisive and sure. He just hoped like hell he wasn't leading them astray.

The crew strapped in as Denk did a short burn in the direction of the vector's origin, then slowed and maneuvered them into position.

"She's lined up and ready to jump," Denk said.

"Then let's get going. I'm hungry."

Denk launched the novasphere, and they slipped through again. This time, he felt the impact, but his eyes kept trying to flutter closed, which didn't jibe with his excitement. Time for Old Earth to show its pretty face. More than anything, he wanted to be right.

G-waves racked his body like a paint mixer. Supposedly you blacked out for a second or two, but he never felt anything but that sudden, violent compression, like passing through a narrow pipe. They'd instantaneously traveled a mind-blowing distance. He unbuckled himself and rose, stumbling a bit.

"Everyone okay? Denk?"

"Systems are nominal, Captain."

He squinted at the screen, but it was black and speckled with stars, just like most of space. No planets at all, especially not a blue and green one. "What am I looking at? Where are we?"

Denk swiped past a number of screens, shaking his head. "That's a great question."

CHAPTER 26
MIGHT AS WELL JUMP

Oz joined Geddy at the back of the bridge, staring at the nearly blank screen in front of them. He'd been so certain they would come out right in front of Old Earth that he thought the display had malfunctioned.

"See anything familiar?" Denk asked hopefully.

That was so dumb on so many levels, it made Geddy's head swoon. Between that and jump fatigue, he wanted nothing more than a nap. But rest would be impossible until he knew they weren't hopelessly lost in the void.

"Sorry, Denk, but none of these particular pinpoints of light ring any bells."

Oz's eyes were burning a hole in his back. At best, he'd proved her and Eli right. At worst, he'd doomed them all. But he wasn't ready to give up hope yet.

"We should run a spectroscopic scan," Doc suggested. "Cross-reference it with our Old Earth data. Even two stars will help determine our position."

Geddy nodded to Denk, and he initiated the scan. A few minutes later, the nav computer found not two, but four likely matches, and his heart leapt.

"Ha!" exclaimed Doc excitedly, returning to his seat. "Now it's a matter of simple triangulation. Just give me one minute ..." Again, his fingers flew over the baffling interface.

A bead of sweat formed on Geddy's forehead. He surreptitiously dabbed at it with his sleeve, hoping Oz wouldn't notice.

"Voprot sleepy," said the big lizard, who had stretched out against the wall.

"Almost there, big guy," Geddy agreed.

Tardigan leaned back in his seat, chewing thoughtfully on the inside of his lip. "Well, Captain, there's good news and bad news."

Geddy gulped. He didn't want bad news of any sort, especially as it related to their mission. "Gimme the good."

"We're in the right galaxy."

If that was the good, he already knew the bad. "But we're still nowhere near Old Earth."

Doc lowered his head and looked away.

"In other words, we're lost," said Oz.

"Maybe, but we're making great time," Geddy offered.

She gave him a look that could've melted tukrium.

Doc turned his chair so everyone could see his holo-display, which showed a rendering of the Milky Way. He pointed to a blue spot on the right side of the giant spiral. "This is us."

"And Old Earth?"

He moved his finger ever so slightly toward the center of the spiral. "Right around here."

Geddy nodded, encouraged. "That looks really close."

"If you consider a light year close."

Geddy gulped. One light year was fairly small in astronomical terms, but even at a full burn, it would take years to get there. A knot formed in Geddy's stomach as reality set in for everyone.

They had to make a fourth jump. A jump from which they might not return.

— Am I having a heart attack?

— *No. Just a conscience.*

He heaved a sigh and rubbed his throbbing temples, his eyes so puffy and red it was getting hard to focus. Had he ever been this tired? Had all the jumps messed with Doc's calculations? Even Morpho seemed depleted.

"Looks like we have a decision to make," Geddy said.

Oz said, "Not to state the obvious, but–"

He cut her off, not wanting to hear the, *I told you so* in her tone. "It'll only leave us with one novasphere. I'm well aware."

"So, there is no choice," she said. "We have to go back ."

Oz looked from Voprot to Tardigan to Denk and finally back at Geddy.

"For what it's worth, I believe the risk is relatively low," Doc said "We've scanned the interstellar space between here and our galaxy. Once we reach Old Earth, we can reconcile the data and should be able to make it back in one jump."

Oz scowled, shaking her head. "Zero room for error doesn't sound like low risk to me."

Geddy's head floated, and he grabbed onto the back of a chair, steadying himself as the wooziness passed.

— *Your body needs to recover, Geddy.*

— Not yet.

— *Then at least give Oz time to cool down.*

"Let's take ten. Think about it, and we'll have a vote when we ... um ..."

He about-faced and strode toward the bathroom, fighting to stay upright as the whole room tilt under him. Before he knew it, he'd stumbled and half fallen against the wall on the left opposite Voprot, steadying himself on the cold metal.

"Captain?" Voprot asked. "Are you okay?"

A bead of sweat dripped from his nose. His tongue stuck to

the roof of his mouth. Waves of dizziness crashed over him again and again, causing his knees to buckle. As he slumped to the floor, he sensed Voprot dive to catch him, then everything went black.

———

— *Geddy.*

Eli's too-familiar androgynous voice pushed through the darkness and into a narrow sliver of consciousness. He didn't know where he was, how he got there, or even whether the flashes of memory unspooling in his addled mind were real or dreams.

— Am I dead?

— *You wouldn't stop, so your body stopped you.*

— Are we there yet?

— *No. Dr. Tardigan's been monitoring your condition.*

He cracked one eye open to find himself again in the *Fiz's* tiny infirmary. An IV ran into his arm, the bag nearly empty.

— Then why wake me up?

— *Because we need to talk.*

Geddy had hoped to wait until they were on Old Earth's doorstep to confess his motives to Eli. Then there would be no turning back. But it seemed they were already at that point.

— Why do you have to be so nosy?

— *Because there is more at stake now. Why are you doing this? And don't say space junk.*

Geddy told Eli about the quantum cube he'd helped Zirhof partly decrypt and his theory about the mythical jump technology that supposedly brought humans to Earth 2. If true, it could only have originated on Old Earth. The cube referenced the work of a JPL scientist named Dr. Birgit Nilsson, who was part of the secretive Project Rearview. Could she have figured out a way to manipulate spacetime that even the Zelnads hadn't figured out? If so, it represented something the Nads would surely trade the *Penetrator* for.

— The only way we get our ship back from the Nads is to force their hand.

— *But if this tech exists and you hand it over to them, they'll be unstoppable. The* Penetrator *won't even matter.*

— I said I'd offer it. Not that I'd give it to them.

— *What do you mean?*

— If this advanced jump tech really exists, it would make novaspheres obsolete.

— *Which would take away their biggest source of cash.*

— Exactly. We find it, jump back, and offer to exchange it for our ship.

— *Do I really need to explain how flawed that plan is?*

— I just came up with it. It's a beta plan. It'll improve with age.

— *Like you?*

— Exactly.

— *I was being sarcastic.*

CHAPTER 27

SALVAGETTE CITY

"Gang, here's the situation," Geddy said, still woozy from jump fatigue.

Oz and Doc were seated to either side, with Denk and Voprot at the back of the bridge. Morpho was perched on Denk's shoulder.

"We've used three blue balls, and there are two left. To get to Old Earth, we need to use a fourth. Doc seems confident that we'll come out right in front of the OE, and that with what we've mapped between here and home, we'll make it back in one long jump. But if he's wrong on either count, we're hosed."

— *You have to tell them about your ulterior motive.*

— Not yet. Finding it's a long shot. I sold them on a sure thing.

"Look, I know this isn't a democracy, but I'm making it one. Either we're all on board with another jump, or we go back empty-handed."

They exchanged indecisive looks. Nobody wanted to be first.

"We're farther from our galaxy than anyone has ever

ventured," Tardigan said, his eyes meeting the rest of the crew's. "This is the forefront of discovery." He drew himself up to his full height and squared his jaw. "And I am confident in my calculations."

Geddy nodded and turned to Voprot. "What say you, Voprot?"

"Voprot go where you go."

He couldn't help but smile. The big fella was growing on him a little.

"Denk?"

He shuffled nervously back and forth, opening and closing his small hands. "Boy oh boy, this is rough. I dunno ..." He glanced at Oz, whose expression remained impassive. "I wanna pilot a better ship, a proper trawler, and this maybe helps us do that. I guess I'm sayin' I'm in, Cap."

Oz's face fell. Morpho formed into the shape of a head and nodded. Obviously, he was on board.

"First Officer Nargonis," Geddy began, wringing his hands. "It comes down to you. If you're not in, we don't go."

She sat with her legs splayed, elbows on her knees, holding her head as she shook it. "You know my position. Of all the ideas that ever were, this may be the dumbest." She heaved a sigh. "But ... screw it." Her eyes settled on Doc, then moved to Geddy. "Where one of us goes, we all go."

The tightness that had formed in Geddy's chest relaxed, and it was easier to breathe. "Okay, then. Mr. Junt, prepare to jump."

"Aye, Cap," Morpho hopped down and loaded one into the chamber while Denk returned to the controls. Geddy and the others strapped back in.

— I sure hope this works.

— *It will. I know it will.*

Once they were in their positions, Geddy gave Denk the thumbs-up. He launched the novasphere and eased the ship through the slit. Again, he felt like his whole body got hit with a bag of hammers, but the sight on the front screen drew him shakily up to his feet along with everyone else.

There, hanging in space like a child's mobile, was Old Earth.

Geddy blew all the air from his lungs, closing his eyes and giving silent thanks to whatever combination of luck and grace brought them to the doorstep of his ancestral home. When he opened them, Oz was looking at him. All he got was a tiny nod.

"Is that it?" Denk asked innocently.

"I believe it is."

He laughed, and soon they were in a big, somewhat smelly group hug.

The oceans were blue, of course, but the land masses were the same pale, sickly brown as Kigantu. They appeared much smaller than in photos, the coasts having long since been subsumed. Very few clouds obscured their view, and nothing was white — not even at the poles.

A bleary-eyed Voprot hauled himself off the floor and sat on his haunches beside them, marveling at the sight. From a distance, it could've been Temeruria or Vyeph or any of the so-called "goldilocks" planets, though it was a good deal smaller than any of those.

The moon, unfortunately, was on the opposite side. Had they passed near it, he would've liked to see whether anything was left of Selene base, the multi-domed installation that inspired the Bubbles back on Earth 3. Unless it had been pummeled by some big asteroids, it probably still stood, but investigating it served no purpose. It wouldn't be worth as much as the stuff in orbit, anyway.

"Denk, scan for metal debris. There should be some big signatures."

Denk's stubby hands flitted across the console and brought

up a fresh display revealing colored dots that formed a shell around Old Earth like a swarm of bees. Was this how it felt for deep-sea explorers to find what they were looking for after months of fruitless searching?

"My heavens," muttered Doc. "There must be thousands of pieces. It can't all be debris."

"They're mostly satellites, but a lot of junk, too," Geddy explained. "Rocket bodies and such. The aluminum's not worth much, but the titanium, gold, and platinum?" He cocked an eyebrow at Oz. "That's cash money, baby."

Her flat expression suggested she was still pissed at him, but even she couldn't deny the excitement of it. "Won't mean much if we don't make it back."

"What's the plan, Cap?" Denk asked, the excitement of a big payday glinting in his beady eyes.

"Start with the titanium. Haul it in, break it down, and jettison the cheap shit. Electronics and solar arrays should contain most of the precious metals. We keep at it until we're full."

"That could take weeks. What about your ship?"

In fact, this was all about getting back the *Penetrator*, but she couldn't know that yet. Not until he knew whether the story the cube told was really true.

"You've saved my ass twice. My ship can wait."

If Zereth-Tinn hadn't extorted him, they would've been on Aku already, and the crew would have some cushion. But if this mission went well, they'd be set up for years, he'd get the *Penetrator* back, *and* possibly save the universe.

Doc gave a rueful shake of his head. "It's more beautiful than I imagined. Though, scans indicate a surface temperature of nearly seventy centigrade."

"Yeah, but it's a dry heat," Geddy quipped, his energy renewed. "Denk, can you scan for just the valuable metals?"

Denk laughed, but quickly stopped when no one joined him. "Oh … you were serious. No."

"The new tractor beam can," said Doc. "I read it in the manual."

Thinking of how inaccurate Doc's translation was didn't exactly inspire confidence. "All right. So let's start with the biggest pieces and scan them before hauling them in." When no one objected, he continued. "Oz, you and I'll run the beam. Doc, help Voprot prep the hold and figure a good way to keep inventory."

"Voprot happy to earn way," he said, attempting a smile that contorted his face.

"Oz, let's get suited up. Denk, pick us out some winners."

———

It was eerily quiet as Geddy and Oz stood inside the open door of the hold, Old Earth filling their entire view. Denk was carefully backing them up toward the largest piece in the area, a dilapidated space station composed of enormous interconnected tubes. Its solar arrays had long since been shredded by asteroids and other junk, and something had punched a hole in the side big enough to see through.

Far below them was the continent called Africa, which was sometimes referred to as the "dark continent" in his elementary studies. He never knew why. An aversion to lights, maybe?

Looking at the pale brown land masses below, it was hard to imagine they were ever covered in green like Temeruria.

"That's good right there, Denk," said Oz. She turned to Geddy. "Let's get to work." She clomped across to the tractor beam console as fast as her magnetic boots would allow.

Geddy followed her over and watched as she powered up the new beam.

"This is gonna change our fortunes, you'll see," he assured her.

"I hope you're right," she said, her voice flat.

She carefully aligned the crosshairs over the center of the space station and activated the beam. The red laser played across the grimy, punctured surface as it drifted closer to the open door, calling up a list of the metals detected. Mostly aluminum, as expected, but plenty of titanium and platinum as well.

Oz consulted a flashing number on the console. "It's too wide. I'll swing it around the long way."

"Won't it be too long then?"

"Don't worry, I've got a workaround."

The station eased in through the door very slowly this time — a lesson learned the hard way from their disastrous test run with the asteroid. Voprot's and Tardigan's faces were pressed against the airlock window, watching with anticipation. As it neared the far side of the hold, it became clear that it was, indeed, about ten meters too long. Nonetheless, she lowered it to the floor.

Oz engaged him with a smirk and hit the button to close the hold door.

"Oz, the sensors are showing the door's not clear," warned Denk over the comm.

"It's not. I'm overriding it."

"Are you crazy?"

"Remember that job we did over Tamlox?" she asked Denk.

"Oh *yeah*," Denk recalled. "I forgot all about that."

As the big, heavy doors began to close, lights overhead added urgency to Denk's warning. She ignored them, keeping her finger on the button. An unpleasant metal-on-metal sound echoed off the hold's walls as the doors crushed the station's fuselage like an empty beer can. One door was shaped like the edge of a blade and the other was its concave counterpart. He'd never noticed it before.

"It's designed for this?" Geddy asked.

A few seconds later, the modular station broke away and the panel on the wall indicated a seal. The hold began to refill with air. Geddy let out a long breath.

Oz turned to him. "A little trick Captain Bykite taught us."

Once the oxygen levels were safe and artificial gravity restored, Geddy and Oz removed their helmets, stepped away from the tractor beam console, and strolled down the length of the dilapidated vessel. The airlock doors opened, and the others came through.

"Hoo-eee," Denk said with a whistle. "This thing's seen better days."

"Kind of like the place it came from," Geddy noted ruefully as he ran his hand over the flags of the long-gone nations that had conducted zero-G research aboard the vessel.

"With their technology, this must have taken months to assemble. Years, even," said Tardigan, his eyes intensely curious. "Won't it take us a long time to break down?"

"I have an idea about that, too," said Oz with a twinkle in her eye.

CHAPTER 28

HAVING A BLAST

"Wait ... you're serious?" asked Geddy.

Oz had just finished explaining that, after they rifled through their haul for intact pieces and any Old Earth memorabilia, Voprot could simply blast it with the flux cannon on the lowest setting, effectively exploding it into more manageable pieces.

"I saw it demonstrated at TrawlerCon a few years back," Oz said. "It worked like a champ."

— *TrawlerCon?*

Voprot, who had been nearly useless since Kigantu, perked up at the opportunity to finally contribute. But Geddy envisioned him lifting stuff, maybe helping sort the metal. Shooting recovered satellites with the cannon never entered his mind.

"Dumb question, but won't that blow a hole straight through the hull?"

Flux cannons were nothing to be trifled with. Old-school, sure, but still powerful as hell. Even if it didn't cause a hull breach, it seemed it would take longer to pick up the pieces than it would've to disassemble it.

"Would you just trust me for once? My god, you're worse than my mother."

— *I'd have to give her that one.*

"Okay, but I'm watching from behind the airlock in case Voprot gets sucked into space."

"Voprot accept risks." The lizard attempted a wink.

— That could be considered an act of war by some races.

— *Best to keep him out of any important negotiations.*

Even Oz decided the best place to watch this experiment was from the bridge. She joined the others as they retreated through the airlock. Meanwhile, Voprot retrieved the cannon from where he'd stashed it.

Before the doors closed, Oz stuck her head back into the hold. "Remember, Voprot, the lowest setting."

"Voprot understand."

She exhaled heavily as the airlock door hissed closed behind her. They arranged themselves along the rectangular window.

— *Is this really going to work?*

— We'll find out soon enough.

Voprot's sinewy muscles bulged under the terrific weight of the cannon, though he didn't appear to struggle with it. He held it sideways while he adjusted the setting with his claws and leveled it at the space station.

Geddy gave him a thumbs-up. "It's been real, big fella," he muttered.

Voprot pulled the trigger.

A purple-green wave of energy surged through the long barrel of the cannon and into the center of the station. Two full sections exploded into a pile of metal, wire, and circuits. To Geddy's everlasting surprise, most of the debris dropped straight down onto the floor. The pieces ranged from a few centimeters to a maybe a meter across.

A self-satisfied grin crept across Oz's white face. "Told you."

Geddy could only shake his head in disbelief. They'd still have to sort through all the pieces with handheld scanners, but the first half of a tedious job was over in only a few seconds. The fact that nobody got killed was a bonus. Based on their time together as a crew so far, that amounted to a pretty damn good day.

Voprot looked back at the airlock and gave a toothy grin before blasting the rest of the station to smithereens. By the time he finished pulling the trigger, pieces were scattered over the entire floor of the hold.

"Okay, people," said Geddy, feeling as though their luck was finally starting to turn. "Let's get to work."

Doc opened the doors, and they pushed through, anxious to assess their haul. Oz made a beeline for the breakdown bench, pulled the filthy old scanners out of their cubby holes, and handed them out while Denk rolled out large bins and lined them up along one edge, whistling a tune and happy to be back in his element. He pointed to them in turn.

"Titanium, platinum, gold. Anything else like vanadium or iridium goes in here."

Morpho dropped from the ceiling and landed with a wet plop in the middle of the pile. He immediately began flinging hunks of metal out into the designated bins with astonishing accuracy. After what he'd seen Morpho do, it shouldn't have surprised Geddy that he could distinguish metals.

One by one, they fanned out and started scanning, forming little piles. After a time, they fell into a rhythm where Morpho gathered up the piles and dumped them, leaving the others to sort.

It was surprisingly satisfying to work together as a team and get into a good flow. After about seven hours, no usable parts remained, and the bins were nearly full.

By that time, though, Geddy's knees and back were screaming for rest. After four jumps, even Voprot and Morpho looked run down. Denk secured the bins, then they trudged back through the airlock. Denk turned off artificial gravity, and they watched the remaining pieces lift off the floor in unison.

"Now for the really fun part," said Oz, nodding at Denk.

Denk opened the door to the hold, and the escaping air sucked the rest of the station pieces out, scattering it into space. What Geddy figured would take days had been accomplished in a few hours.

After it closed, he turned and smiled at his team, feeling for the first time like a real captain. A yawn overtook him and after it passed, he said, "Good work, everyone. Let's get some shuteye and do it all over again tomorrow."

CHAPTER 29

GOING DOWN?

For two weeks, they salvaged and learned about Old Earth. Chinese and Russian vessels had the most titanium, but American pieces had more precious metals. They became one big sorting machine that got more efficient as they went. Smaller satellites were broken down in three or four hours, allowing them to finish at least two and sometimes three in a day. The bins filled, Denk sealed them up, and Voprot hoisted them up on the shelves.

This didn't solve their problem about potentially not getting home, but assuming they did, the payday would be worth it.

Once they ran out of crates, they only brought in enough pieces to fill the floor. Geddy figured three more days ought to do it, which was about all they could take, anyway. The days had blended into one continuous work session, and they were all getting on each other's nerves. Tardigan liked to list titles and abstracts he'd memorized from his favorite research papers. Denk hummed incessantly. Oz lamented her horrible family. And Voprot ... was simply Voprot.

Oz and Denk estimated they had two or even three million

worth of salvage, but that didn't even count the memorabilia, which had nearly filled an entire shelf. There were gloves, EVA packs, coveralls, patches, photographs, and a surprisingly intact *Hustler* magazine from October 1996 that Geddy immediately claimed for himself.

During his time working for Tretiak and the Double A, he learned that people with money were always interested in utterly unique items, and Old Earth relics fit the bill. When he was a kid, the Old Earth Museum of Space Exploration where his mother worked got broken into several times, which was just one of the reasons why pretty much everything on display was a replica.

As far as he knew, though, the quantum cube that wound up with Zirhof was the only piece to go missing from the vault. The research it referenced, if it still existed, was on Old Earth itself. He'd treaded very carefully with Oz during the salvage operation and had been waiting for the right time to broach the subject of going to the surface.

One evening after dinner, he poured himself a finger of Kailorian gin from their dwindling supply and sat in Captain Bykite's old chair, which they'd finally gotten around to lowering. Perhaps the day would come when he felt comfortable in it.

"I still can't get over how much it looks like Temeruria," said Oz from behind him.

Temeruria was half again as large and was largely covered in green except at the poles, but otherwise it bore a striking resemblance.

"Hey," Geddy said, spinning the big chair around to face her. Her normally giant, alert green eyes were uncharacteristically droopy and her ropy red hair hung limply about her shoulders. All she had on was a pair of shorts and an oversized T-shirt that left little to the imagination. It was hard to focus on her face. "What're you doing up?"

She settled into Tardigan's usual spot in the navigator's seat and put her feet up on the nav console. The only light was reflected from Old Earth, showing off the muscles in her long, deadly legs.

"Too tired to sleep, I guess. What's your excuse?"

"You might say I like to watch."

She gave a smirk. "That's not hard to believe."

"Nah, I just realized we'd been here two weeks, and I still hadn't just sat and looked at it."

"And? What does it make you think about?"

He'd seen Old Earth so many times growing up, yet something about watching its slow rotation was new to him. More real, somehow. Maybe his brain had treated it more like a myth.

"I mostly try to picture myself there. Before things got so bad, I mean."

She tilted her head. "What's it like?"

A smile crossed his lips. How many summers had he spent there in his mind? His fondest memories were of a time and place he never experienced. "It's simple. At least, it seems that way to me because I'm just a kid. It's the 1960s, and the Apollo space program has captured everyone's imagination. My old man's just been tapped to be an astronaut, and my mom ... she teaches history. Everywhere I look, there's hope, and it feels like ... It feels like humanity is finally gonna get out of its own way." A tear came to his eye, but he resisted the urge to wipe it away.

Oz pursed her lips and gave an appreciative nod. "Sounds great."

"And then disco ruined everything."

"What's that? Some kind of planet-killing asteroid?"

He considered this briefly as he took a sip of gin. "You're not far off. Anyway, I'm starting to get it, y'know? This salvage business ... it reminds me of an Old Earth saying. 'One man's trash is another man's treasure.'"

"I like that," she said, nodding appreciatively. "Back home we used to say everything has value to someone."

"Ours is better."

She chuckled, but her smile quickly faded. "Listen, Ged ... I owe you an apology."

"For what?"

"If I'm being honest, I thought when we got here — *if* we did — it would be a big waste of time. Turns out it was worth the risk. Probably."

A pang of guilt shot through him. Yes, they were here to make back what he'd lost and finally get ahead of the game, but that was only part of it.

"Please don't apologize." She leaned forward, listening intently. "I had another reason for wanting to come here. A selfish one."

"What's that?"

— You're really going to tell her?

"I wanted to see Old Earth with my own eyes. But not just from space."

She frowned and slid her feet off the console, leaning forward as she studied him. "You want to go to the surface."

"The epicenter of space research on Earth was the Jet Propulsion Laboratory. My mom talked about it all the time. I'd give anything to see it just once."

"Then you should," Oz said matter-of-factly. "It's not like we're coming back this way anytime soon."

"You don't think it's too dangerous?"

"I'll come with you."

He didn't want company. Not for what he was really there to do.

"That's not necessary. Besides, it's a deathscape."

She waved his flimsy protest off with a roll of her eyes.

"Nothing the suits can't handle. Isn't my primary duty as First Officer to keep your dumb ass safe?"

Geddy's knee-jerk reaction was to protest further, but the offer was Oz's version of an olive branch. Going it alone now would only raise her suspicions. All he needed was some time alone in the basement vault. As long as they split up, he'd have it.

"Well," he said, forcing a smile, "you're a hard girl to say no to."

"Few men have." She raised her eyebrows, slapped her palms on the top of her thighs, and rose. She yawned and reached for the ceiling, lifting her T-shirt up far enough for Geddy to see bare skin.

— Nobody would say no to that.

— *Be strong, Geddy. Be strong.*

"After the morning haul, we'll take the *Dom* down while the guys prep to leave. By the time we get back, we'll be ready to bounce."

"Sounds like a plan." And a good one at that.

"I'm hitting the rack. You staying?"

"Just a while longer," Geddy said, wanting to watch Earth's lazy spin a little longer. "I'll be right behind you."

"Good night."

"Night."

— *I hate everything about this plan, but you're right. We will need the leverage.*

— I'm not crazy about it either, pal, but our hard work's about to pay off. With a little luck, we can go to Aku with something other than our dicks in our hand.

— *I don't have a dick.*

— Be glad. They only make you itchy and impulsive.

CHAPTER 30
ESCAPE TO LA

The next morning, the crew went through their usual routine. Golden showers for everyone but Voprot, followed by rations of nutrimush and a brief Sesehlu session with Doc. Then Geddy and Oz donned their suits while the others waited behind the airlock for them to haul in the morning's loot — a Korean communications satellite. Once the door had closed and the hold re-pressurized, they took off their helmets and headed straight to the short ladder that led down to the *Dom*.

Denk peered down through the opening looking very concerned. "You guys sure about this?"

"It'll be fine, Denk. We'll be three, four hours tops," said Geddy. "Maybe I'll even find us some very old liquor to help celebrate our windfall."

That eased any and all concern. "Good call!"

Denk closed the hatch, and Geddy descended the ladder after Oz. She hung her helmet on its hook and buckled in while he ran through the preflight checks and spun up the engines. After being in the *Fiz* day in, day out, it was nice to have a change of scenery.

He opened the doors in the ship's belly and poised his finger over the glowing holoscreen. "Releasing clamps in three ... two ... one ... mark."

The clamps opened, and he eased the *Dom* out of its housing. Once they'd cleared, he angled it down and pushed the thruster controls forward. They shot off like a bullet, and he set a course for a large city once known as Los Angeles.

"I assume you know where you're going?" Oz asked.

"Pasadena, California."

Having analyzed the composition and density of the atmosphere, the *Dom's* display painted a wireframe tunnel representing the optimal approach. He switched to manual control.

"No autopilot?" she asked.

He shook his head with a cocky smirk. "I like this part too much to let a computer do it. Besides, I've had some bad experiences."

"Atmosphere's not as bad as I thought," she said, consulting the readout. "Carbon dioxide's high."

"Yeah, that was their chief export. You're sure the suits can handle the radiation?"

"They can handle space, so ... yeah."

"Right."

The atmosphere hit like a wall, and the *Dom* threatened to shake his eyeballs out of their sockets. Geddy glanced over at Oz and noticed she'd closed her eyes, her fingers dug into the armrests.

"You look a little g-green in the g-g-gills," he said in a rattly voice.

"I'll be f-fine," she replied tersely, still not looking. "Unlike you, I'm n-not a f-f-fan of this p-part."

Back when he and Denk went down to Earth 3, a far more challenging entry, Oz was perfectly happy to stay aboard the *Fiz*. Maybe that was why.

After a few jarring seconds, the air smoothed out, and they shot through wispy clouds toward where the West Coast of North America met the Pacific Ocean. At about ten thousand meters, the footprint of a sprawling metropolis took shape, and he could just make out a handful of islands along the coast. From there, it was easy to discern the grid layout, buildings long since hollowed out by heat and fierce winds crisscrossed by streets and highways. It wasn't all that different from Laguna, only half the city was underwater.

Oz finally opened her eyes, checked the temperature readout on the display, and gave a low whistle. "Sure enough, it's almost seventy."

"If not for the suits, you could work on your tan," he joked. Oz's creamy complexion was just this side of pure white.

"What did it used to be? You know ... before."

He shrugged. "More like thirty, thirty-five at the outside."

"You're lucky your mom taught you stuff. All my mom ever taught me were manners and respect."

"Doesn't seem like they stuck," he quipped, earning him his first real laugh since they had their falling out.

Compared to the elegant, curved towers and lush greenery of Temeruria, the city was kind of a dump. Then again, it had been abandoned and weathered for more than three-hundred years.

"So where's this place we're going?"

"Jet Propulsion Laboratory. It should be in the northwest corner somewhere."

He nosed down a bit more, leveling out at seven hundred meters as they headed inland. All he had to go by was his memory of a map that accompanied the permanent JPL exhibit back at the museum on Earth 2. There had been a green patch at the edge of the city butting up to mountains and forest. That was Pasadena.

"What are we looking for?" Oz asked, surveying the decrepit remains of the city with great interest.

"A cluster of white buildings with nothing much around it. Right by the mountains."

She pointed off to the left. "Like those?"

The buildings were coated in a patina of dust, but he recognized their plain, sturdy architecture immediately. Indeed, a building near the city side still bore a giant circle with the faintly visible outline of the NASA logo.

"Exactly like those." He grinned like a schoolboy.

He made a lazy circle around the complex, which, save for a crumpled section of roof, was remarkably intact.

Again, a tear formed at the corner of his left eye. He wiped it away immediately but Oz caught him.

"Holy shit, is Geddy Starheart *crying*?"

"Must be the dust."

The cracked remnants of a parking lot just below them offered an adequate spot to land. He put the *Dom* into a hover and lowered it gently to the ground, then shut down the engines and blew out a lungful of air.

"Let's suit up."

———

After triple-checking the seals on their suits and helmets, Geddy lowered the ship's ladder. A gust of wind sent a puff of radioactive dust into the *Dom*, so he hurried down and motioned for Oz to do the same.

Once the steps retracted, they took careful steps across the cracked pavement, half expecting a fissure to open beneath their feet. A number of cars were still parked in the lot, their paint worn away by wind and grit.

"What, exactly, are we here to see?" Oz asked.

His actual destination was the Project Rearview Resource

Lab, a top-secret section of the Building C basement, but Oz didn't need to know that.

"It's kind of embarrassing."

"Looking to round out your vintage porn collection?"

"I wish." He sighed, the breath temporarily fogging his climate-controlled helmet. "No, my mom gave me this dumb little rocket when I was a kid. It was just a toy, really, but it meant a lot to me. Unfortunately, it's still on the *Penetrator*."

That, at least, had a mote of truth to it. There really was a toy rocket still inside his and Eli's ship, but he'd taken it from the museum gift shop as an afterthought the night he got wasted, right before Sammo Yann stole it.

Oz gave a knowing look. "Wow. This really *is* a sentimental journey, huh?"

"It's really just an excuse to look around a bit. Nothing I've got my heart set on."

"No, no, I'm down for a little side mission," she said, consulting the display on her arm. "Where should we start?"

Geddy shrugged. "I have no idea. Divide and conquer?" Her expression changed abruptly from confidence to concern. Before she could protest, he added, "Relax. Have gun will travel." He gave his trusty Exeter D6 a pat.

"I dunno, Ged ..."

"We'll meet back here in twenty minutes. If you get back before me, give the horn a toot."

"What the what?"

"Old Earth joke." He pointed toward Building C, then D on opposite sides of the parking lot. "I'll start her, you start over there. Holler if you find anything."

Oz was clearly uncomfortable, but their success and his charm had her in a buoyant mood. "Fine, but you're gonna owe me."

"Can't wait."

They parted company and he let out some air he'd been holding back.

— *You didn't have to send her on a wild goose chase.*

— No, but it's better this way. If we don't find what we're looking for in twenty minutes, it's not here, or it never was.

On reaching Building C, he found the lobby door shattered. Looters, probably, or squatters. What kind of shit went down here after all the people chosen in the lottery left on the transport? It must've gotten ugly. He stepped inside, flicking on the lights of his helmet.

Space-related artwork and placards decorated the lobby walls starting with Robert Goddard, posing with his rocket in 1926 right beside the broken door.

— *Who's that?*

— The original Rocket Man.

He continued around the perimeter, but the only doors were for bathrooms and a utility closet, so he crossed to the central elevator bank. Right away, he spotted an unmarked door in the corner near the elevators. Unsurprisingly, it was locked. One blast from the Exeter at low power took care of that. As he'd hoped, it held a narrow staircase. Four flights down, he found another door with some kind of biometric security. Again, his pistol made quick work of it and he stepped through.

The falling door sent up clouds of fine dust, turning his helmet lights into two clearly defined cones. The timer on his arm display indicated that five minutes had already slipped away.

— *Is this it?*

— Dunno. We're looking for something that says Dr. Birgit Nilsson.

Long ago, this room would've been filled with bulky, hot-running computers. Now, a triangular arrangement of workstations stood at the center around a clear cylinder that housed a quantum computer, an odd-looking contraption that resembled the guts of a jet engine set on one end. The liquid coolant in the cylinder had long since evaporated, but he didn't need the computer — only the data it had compressed and encoded onto cube storage.

The back left corner formed an office in a U-shape. Other than an ancient workstation similar to those in the center, there was only a coffee mug.

Geddy started rifling through the drawers, which were mostly empty except for a few office supplies. But at the very back of one in a little black plastic tray were assorted coins, a small notepad, and two nametags enshrined in cracked, yellowing plastic.

NILSSON, B.

— Well, hel-lo, Birgit. Think she was hot? She sounds kinda hot.

— *Let's stay focused.*

There weren't files to go through, and any archived data would've been stored in one of two places — the cloud or in quantum cubes. Either way, she wouldn't keep them just sitting around.

Upon covering the rest of the room, he discovered a blast door with no visible controls and no handle. He gave it a thump with his fist and judged it to be very thick.

"How the hell's this supposed to open?"

— *Well, now, let's think about this for a moment.*

— Fuck that.

Geddy stepped back, drew the Exeter, and blasted it at full power. The shockwave knocked him on his ass, and billowing dust enveloped him. When it cleared, he found that the door, which likely had been designed to withstand a nuclear blast, was still intact. But enough of the concrete had been blown away to reveal the vault beyond.

— *Always with the shooting.*

— I'm honoring my ancestors.

Another blast, this time from further back, and a hole opened in the concrete big enough for him to climb through. The vault was no more than three meters on a side, with a shelving unit along the back wall. Among the handful of items on it was a molded plastic tray bearing three quantum cubes.

— Yahtzee.

He carefully picked up the tray and dumped the cubes into his open hand. They were of a dark gray metal with a matte finish and tiny identifiers etched into the side. PRA001, PRA002, and PRA003.

— PR. Project Rearview. The A probably means archive.

— *Is that what you were looking for?*

"Let's hope so. It might just be a bunch of porn, but if so, it's probably all of it. So, win-win."

A garbled voice crackled through his comm.

" … the fuck … We've … now!"

Geddy absently rapped on his helmet as though that would do anything.

— *You're twenty meters underground and surrounded by concrete.*

He took off at a trot toward the open door and climbed the stairs as quickly as possible in the suit, panting pathetically as he reached the top landing.

Once he exited into the lobby, Oz's voice rang like a bell. She was breathless, too, though not so much as he. "You'd better be dead in there, you asshole!"

— Uh-oh.

He'd just hurried past the elevators when Oz came barreling through the door, wild-eyed and frantic.

"What's wrong with your comms?!"

"What's the matter?"

"We just got a distress call from the *Fiz!*"

"What?! What happened?"
"They've been boarded!"

CHAPTER 31

BABY, IT'S STORMY OUTSIDE

For a long moment, Geddy stared back at Oz like she'd just said something in ancient Bonzokian. The wind had started to gather outside, creating little vortices of dust that crept across the ruined parking lot like wandering spectres.

"What do you mean 'boarded?'"

She blinked away her incredulity. "I'm not speaking in metaphors here! That thing when someone enters your ship without permission??"

"Okay, okay. By who?"

— *Whom.*

— Dude, seriously?

"I don't know. I was looking for your stupid trinket when my comm started clicking. At first, I thought it was a malfunction, but then I realized it was UDC. B-O-A-R-D-E-D."

UDC, or universal distress code, was similar to Morse code but almost exclusively for starships. It was the closest thing to a common language that they had, at least in the days before translator implants.

"You sure they didn't mean to say, 'bored?'"

"Geddy, this is serious!"

"Who knows UDC? Not Voprot, obviously."

She shrugged. "Doc for sure. Probably Denk."

"Did you respond?"

"Yes, but I have no idea if they got it."

Geddy's mind raced to think of who could have boarded the *Fiz* and how. No way it was pirates. No one could've followed them, either. Could there be some human colony that survived?

— *What about the Red Raven?*

Oz noticed his momentary distraction and raised her eyebrows expectantly. "What's Eli got?"

Geddy's brow furrowed. Was he that easy to eavesdrop on?

"He wondered if it might be the *Raven*."

She shook her head. "No way. Tompanov couldn't possibly follow us through four jumps."

He opened his mouth to speak but stopped himself short. A billowing tan cloud was racing across the barren cityscape at an alarming speed. His eyes widened, prompting Oz to spin around. The building wind heralded the approach of a storm that had blown in off the ocean, sweeping up a few million metric tons of dust with it. It would envelop the *Dom* in a minute or two and the lobby seconds after that.

"Shit. Let's get out of here." Oz took a step toward the ship, but Geddy stopped her.

"No time. Come on." He pulled her in the direction of the open basement door.

"But–"

"We can't take off before it hits. Follow me."

He raised his arm and activated the *Dom's* anchor system from the console in his suit. Four thin cables shot from the underside and punched through the cracked pavement, then tightened down. He hoped they'd hold. If the storm flipped her over, they'd be royally screwed.

They jogged across the lobby, retracing his boot prints back to the unmarked door. He stuck his hand through the hole he'd blasted and yanked it back open, then motioned her down the stairs.

"What's down here?" she asked.

"Just go!"

She did, and he cast one glance back at the storm before following her down. Against the approaching wall of dust and debris, the *Dom* looked like the very sort of toy he was supposedly looking for. They activated their helmet lights.

Oz reached the bottom and turned back to him when she saw the other demolished door. She was about to say something when a low howl of wind from up top quickened her pace. She followed him into the computer room and closed the door as much as possible, then he helped her slide a nearby cabinet in front of it for good measure.

She made a slow circle around the room, her lights lingering on the triangular arrangement of workstations and the quantum computer. A moment later, she noticed the gaping hole where the vault door used to be and squared up to him.

"What is this place?" she asked, her tone suspicious.

"Top-secret research," he said. "Near as I can tell, it had something to do with Project Rearview. That was the group of nerds who figure out how to reach your galaxy."

He nodded, suddenly feeling like his suit's climate controls weren't keeping up. It galled him to lie to her, but it was truly for her own good. "I was about to head upstairs but this door caught my eye."

"Enough that you blasted it open?"

— *You have to tell her.*

— But I don't even know what I found. It could be nothing. It probably *is* nothing.

He gave a sheepish grin. "I figured anything behind so many doors would be interesting."

Oz swung her lights over to the computer in the middle of the room and took a few steps toward it. "Like that?"

He joined her beside it, nodding in appreciation. "It's a quantum computer. Not as advanced as positronic ones, but advanced enough to find us a new home."

"You think it's worth something?"

Zirhof would give his left nut for something like this, assuming Zorran men had nuts. He only cared about the data on the cubes, but the computer itself was indeed quite valuable, and it legitimized his exploration. Plus, it might actually be the only way to read the cubes in the first place.

"Absolutely. Will it fit in the Dom, though?"

A mischievous grin played on her face. "I'm sure we can. What's in here?" She nodded toward the ruined vault.

"Nothing much," he said. "Whatever it was, it probably ended up on one of the *Rearview* ships."

She took a quick scan of the otherwise empty vault and stepped back out shaking her head. "I dunno. If I was leaving for a new life on the other side of the universe, I'd leave my secrets behind."

"Why's that?"

"Because secrets only destroy things." Nodding at his arm display, she asked, "How's your O2?"

Geddy consulted his readout. He had just under forty minutes of air. If the storm kept raging, they'd somehow need to make it to the *Dom* before they suffocated.

"Thirty-eight minutes. You?"

"Thirty-one. Probably because I ran here. You're welcome, by the way." She unzipped a pocket of her suit and fished something out that she concealed in her palm. "To prove you were here."

He took it from her and held it up to the light. It was a very old little replica of a space shuttle. Turning it to the side revealed it was the *Challenger*. The initial thrill of seeing it gave way to sadness. A whole section of the museum back on Earth 2 was dedicated to the accidents and missteps that made *Rearview* possible. Then came the guilt of sending her on a bull-shit errand when he knew she'd go out of her way to find it.

"Wow, I can't believe you found this."

"Third office I looked in. It was under glass. Is it important?"

"Historically, yeah."

"Is it a spaceship or a plane?" she asked.

"Kind of both. They called it a space shuttle. It carried cargo into orbit. Maybe even some of the satellites we've been salvaging. It was reusable. It was a pretty big deal at the time."

"How long ago?"

"Phew," he said, running the numbers in his head. Math wasn't his strong suit. "Like 450 years. There were six shuttles."

"What's special about this one?"

"It didn't come back."

"Oh."

He turned it over in his hands once again and then held it up and moved it between them as if it were flying. She gave an appreciative nod and smiled. "Thank you, Oz."

"What do you think's happening up on the *Fiz*?"

A big chunk of his brain had been turning that question over as they talked, but so far, he'd come up empty. "Boarded" couldn't be literal.

"I'll bet it's a prank. They probably started celebrating without us. There was still a half bottle of gin. Plenty to get those lightweights wasted."

She shook her head doubtfully. "I hope you're right."

The low rumble outside had fallen largely silent.

He thumbed over his shoulder. "I think the storm might've passed. Let's get this computer disconnected."

It took about ten minutes to remove the cylindrical housing and the power and data cables from the elongated appliance, but he was glad for the idea. Zirhof would get a semi when he showed up on Zorr with it. Mercifully, it wasn't especially heavy, and they could both manage it. They carefully carried it up the stairs and into the space between the central elevator banks, peering out through the broken doors to ensure the storm had indeed calmed down.

Knee-high sand dunes had already been deposited across the floor, erasing all evidence of their footprints. Wind still whistled through, and visibility was no more than a hundred fifty meters. Geddy could just make out the *Dom*. Taking off would be dicey, but once they got above the wind, it would be fine. He just hoped there wasn't any damage to their ship.

"Let's get the fuck out of here," Oz said.

He nodded in agreement and they carried the computer back through the empty front doors.

"Life's a beach, eh?" he said jokingly. Oz didn't laugh as she trudged toward the ship through the loose sand.

The good news was, the tethers held the *Dom* fast to the ground. But the ship faced JPL, meaning the thrusters had taken the full brunt of the sandstorm. He lowered the steps, and they guided the computer inside, strapping it securely in place across the extra seats.

Girding himself for bad news, they went back outside and looked up at the engines. As he feared, the thruster bank was caked with sand. Oz joined him, frowning.

"Well, that's not good," she said.

"Nope."

"Won't it blast away when we fire her up?"

"Maybe. Or it might turn to glass and fry the inductor coils. We've gotta get up there and clean it."

"Ged, I don't think that message was a prank. We need to see what's going on."

"Y'know, once upon a time here, they used to say cleaning was women's work."

She cocked an eyebrow. "The same people who turned their own planet into an irradiated blast furnace?"

"That's them." He widened his stance under the thrusters and interlaced his hands, then gave her a sly wink. "Here, I'll give you a boost."

CHAPTER 32

DO THEY BECOME BUTTERFLIES?

Geddy and Oz finished cleaning sand and dirt out of the thrusters with four minutes of O2 to spare. There were spares in the *Dom*, but after the distress call, they wanted to get up there as quickly as possible. The moment he fired up the *Dom* and retracted the anchors, he gratefully peeled off his sweaty helmet. While Oz was completing their preflight checks, he patted the pocket of his suit to ensure the quantum cubes were still there.

A minute later, they were in the air. The same fierce westerly gale that had deposited a small country's worth of dust on old Los Angeles had freshened and was blowing it deep inland. His gaze lingered a moment on the desiccated corpse of the city.

— *It must have been nice once.*

— Lots of things were.

He nosed her up and punched it, breathing a sigh of relief when the thrusters didn't seize. All systems remained comfortably in the green as they left the atmosphere of Old Earth for the last time.

Geddy thought he'd gone to the surface with no expectations, but his profound disappointment suggested that wasn't exactly true. Some part of him expected to feel a connection to this place, a sense of nostalgia for something he knew but never experienced, or at least something that aligned with his fantasy. Listening to his mother talk about it for all those years had shaped it into a nearly magical place, and he'd hoped some might be left. But whatever charm it once possessed had long since been swallowed by the unyielding forces of degradation.

Oz reached for the comm to try to hail the *Fiz*, but Geddy stayed her hand.

"What the hell?" she asked, scowling. "We need to find out what's going on."

The same question had been tumbling around in his mind, but trying to contact them now was a bad idea. Whoever sent the UDC message had done so surreptitiously. Announcing their approach didn't make any tactical sense.

"We have to assume something's really wrong."

"All the more reason to get in there and find out!"

"I'm with you, but ... do the escape pod doors open from the outside?"

Weeks earlier, when he was still learning his way around the ship, Geddy found the four empty escape pod tubes. Denk had accidentally launched them when testing out the buttons on the Ghruk control panel, which he'd done at Geddy's own request. Opening the dropship bay doors would trigger ship-wide alarms. Going in through the pod tubes wasn't without risk, but it was the stealthiest option.

"I think so. Why?"

"Then we could land the *Dom* on the roof and get in through the tubes. Where do they come out?"

"The maintenance shaft above the port side of the hold."

"Good. No one could hear us up there. How sure are you that we can open them?"

"Seventy percent, maybe. But we would have access to the cameras."

"We have cameras? Do they work?"

"Bykite liked me to keep an eye on our … temporary employees," she explained, referring to their former practice of helping out drifters in exchange for some light labor.

"Score one for the guy, at least. I'm gonna make a wide circle around her first," Geddy said.

"They could be watching," Oz noted.

"If they are, then they already know we're here. The bridge looks dark."

Keeping five hundred meters between, Geddy made a slow pass around the sides and back. Either there was no ship, or there was, and it was cloaked. But the hold door was closed, and everything appeared exactly as they'd left it.

"Maybe that's a good sign," he offered.

"I'll swap out the O2 canisters," Oz said, disappearing into the rear of the ship.

He watched anxiously after her over his shoulder, worried that she'd discover the quantum cubes while futzing with his suit and confront him, but she finished without a word and returned to her seat.

Starting well above the top of the *Fiz*, he eased the *Dom* down gently onto the roof, trying to be as delicate and smooth as Bransel's ship. Once he powered down and engaged the magnets on the skids, Oz handed him his damp helmet and they checked each other's seals. The Exeter was still strapped to his thigh, and Oz retrieved one of the new pulse rifles from the locker. Not exactly her preferred weapon, but her blades were still on the *Fiz*.

"Ready?" he asked.

She checked her weapon, slung it over her shoulder, then nodded. "If this is a prank, they got us good."

"If all that's waiting for us in there is a drink and a laughs,

I'll take the joke. Until we know, we should stay off comms until we're inside."

Oz went radio silent and gave a curt nod.

Geddy lowered the steps, stopping just short of the hull. He felt the escaping air through the shiny gray fabric of his suit and stepped out as softly as he could, wincing when the boots clunked on. There was no way to tiptoe in the damn things, so every step announced their arrival. But between the air exchangers and the relentless hum of the engines, he doubted they'd be audible.

Oz knelt down and opened a small panel beside one of the circular pod hatches. After keying in an override code, the stout latch retracted, and a little puff of air escaped from around the edge. She swung the door the rest of the way open and eased herself inside. Once her boots reached the bottom of the empty tube, Geddy followed and pulled the door closed behind him, waiting for the hiss of the seal.

By the time he joined her, the chamber had re-pressurized. As soon as the light turned green, Oz cracked the inner hatch and slipped through.

The shaft was barely wider than an air vent, too short even to crouch. Even for Ghruk, it would've been cozy. Geddy's pulse spiked immediately, hoping he wouldn't have to spend more than a few minutes in the enclosed space.

— *You've got this, Geddy.*

Geddy took a deep breath and felt his heart slow down.

— Thanks.

No sooner had he closed the inner door than something dark smacked his face shield with a wet *splat*, a quivering mass of synthetic protoplasm with a knack for saving his life.

"Morph?" he asked in a low whisper, breaking the helmet's seal and pulling it and Morpho off. "Boy, are we glad to see you."

Morpho slithered atop the helmet, quivering, as Oz's thick

locks tumbled back out of her helmet. Her face twisted in concern. "What's going on?"

Ordinarily, Morpho's uniquely expressive form of body language was easy enough to understand, but his frantic gestures and pantomime weren't going to cut it this time. Oz stuck out her hand, and Morpho latched onto the back of it like a desperate barnacle, digging his little black filaments into her skin.

— *Did you know she did that with him?*

— No, but I guess it makes sense.

— *We should chat again sometime. I enjoyed his company.*

— I'll see about a play date.

Oz closed her eyes, nodding as Morpho spoke directly in her head. "Morph sent the UDC message. There are three of them ... Doc and Denk were taken hostage ... Voprot's locked inside the fuselage of that space plane we found."

"Three ... three what? Who are they?"

"He doesn't know. Some sort of ... caterpillar, maybe? He's not making much sense."

— Morpho may have gotten into the gin.

— *Are caterpillars warlike?*

— Only if you're a leaf.

"Does he know what they want?"

Oz listened for a moment. "He says they want passage to our galaxy ... He hid the novaspheres ... But they're threatening to kill everyone if we don't take them with us."

The idea of giant, intelligent caterpillars taking over the *Fiz* struck him as preposterous, but then again, he'd encountered plenty of weird shit over the years. If they'd found their way to Old Earth, maybe some other species had, too. Something they hadn't seen before.

Morpho unplugged from Oz, and she rubbed her hand where it had reddened.

"I didn't know you could, you know ..."

"Commune with Morpho?" Oz asked. A realization washed over her and her eyes widened. "Wait — you did, too?" He nodded. "*And* Eli?" He nodded again. "What was *that* like?"

"Like the world's least sexy threesome. But back to the caterpillars."

"First, let's get out of these suits."

He gave her a wink. "Thought you'd never ask."

They stepped out of their suits, leaving them in a pile, and picked up their weapons. He followed her along the narrow corridor in the direction of the bridge at a deep crouch that made his legs burn, Morpho rolling along after them. Just before the ladder that came out at the end of the hall near the crew quarters, Oz stopped by a panel with a bank of six small screens and set her rifle down. A few button presses later, they flickered to life.

The camera in the bridge made it appear empty, confirming his suspicions. A second camera on the airlock also showed no signs of life. But the four cameras in the corners of the hold were a different story.

Doc and Denk were chained to the foot rest at the base of the breakdown bench. Menacing over them were two corpulent aliens that did, in fact, resemble a pair of fat, hairless caterpillars. Their skin was shimmery and translucent, almost like plastic. Beneath it, Geddy could make out the shapes of slender, pulsing organs. Eight stubby legs terminated in claws that called to mind a bony starfish. They were curled around old-school laser rifles that looked suspiciously human-made. Zirhof had one exactly like them in his private museum.

The creatures' faces, if you could call them that, were puckered like assholes with an industrial-looking mouth part like the business end of a nose-hair trimmer. Tiny black eyes were set to the sides above it. Alien, certainly. But not entirely unfamiliar to his eyes. What the hell did it remind him of?

"What the literal *fuck*?" Oz whispered, her upper lip curled in disgust.

Geddy's eyes slid over to the adjacent screen, which revealed the third creature. It stood guard beside the door of a large plane-like ship he instantly recognized as a Virgin Galactic suborbital transport. Through the front window, he could just make out Voprot's giant head.

— *Is that their ship?*

— I don't think so.

Oz, sensing his conversation with Eli, turned to him, her eyes desperate. "What'd he say?"

"He has no idea what they are. But I might."

"Well? What planet are they from, then?"

"I think they came from the moon."

CHAPTER 33

SMARTER THAN THE AVERAGE BEAR

G eddy explained to Oz that, in the early 2000s, a small Israeli lunar lander crashed on the surface of the moon, not far from where Selene base would later be built. Its primary cargo was a container that held, among other things, thousands of tiny, hardy animals called tardigrades. They could survive extreme conditions, including the vacuum of space. Just add water.

The incident was afforded a few paragraphs on the timeline of his mom's museum along with a anticlimactic image of the crash site. But that only explained their origin, not their colossal size, intelligence, or aims. How they got there and what they wanted was anyone's guess.

Oz studied his face for a few seconds to gauge whether he was serious. "How do we take them out?"

"I dunno. Foot race? Maybe a high-stakes game of uguinok?"

"Something tells me they don't play uguinok."

Still baffled at how they got here, he took another long look at the screens. Leaning against the wall beside the hold door, opposite the tractor beam controls, were three dark shapes arranged on the floor resembling backpacks.

— *Could they have … flown here with those things?*

Maintenance on Selene base was largely done by workers with packs that were basically smaller, souped-up versions of the old NASA EVA systems. In theory, they could be modified to have enough thrust to escape the moon's gravity.

Oz rose in a huff. "Screw this. I'm gonna turn 'em to goo."

Geddy had the same impulse, but until they knew what they were dealing with, it didn't seem smart to go in with guns blazing, especially with their friends taken hostage.

"That's your plan? Run in shooting?"

"Isn't that your go-to plan?" She asked pointedly. He couldn't argue. "Plus, just look at them. I can take out all three before they even know I'm there." She ducked down and continued toward the top of the ladder.

"Wait!" he hissed, but she wasn't having it.

It wasn't like him to advocate for an actual plan, but this wasn't the time for bravado. He hurried down after her.

When he reached the bottom, he stole down the corridor and hugged the wall as he tiptoed into the bridge, where Oz was already strapping on her katanas.

"Oz, stand down," he commanded.

Her eyes narrowed as she met his gaze. "Oh, *now* you're gonna act like a captain? Gimme a break."

— *Geddy?*

"We need a plan."

"Just trust me." She tightened the strap around her back sheaths and took a defiant step back toward the airlock. He blocked her way. "What're you doing? Let's go."

— *Geddy.*

"They put Voprot in time-out. You really think they're gonna just pop like water balloons? Use your head, Oz."

"Like you used your head burning through four novas-pheres? Also, are you gonna answer Eli or not?"

She pushed past him and peeked around the corner before slipping around it. He sighed and rubbed his eyes. A headache was forming at his temples while a creeping dread inched down his spine.

— This is not good.

— *GEDDY!*

— What?!

— *I can sense them. Their energy is nearly identical to mine.*

— Sense what?

— *I think they're Zelnads!*

Ever since the meeting with Zirhof where he learned a massive scientific advancement and not luck may have brought humans to the other side of the universe, the question foremost on Geddy's mind was *how*. How could a species that ruined its own planet — twice — somehow solve the mystery of sustained interstellar travel, only to bury the secret?

Maybe the same way a former henchman who didn't know dick about shipbuilding made one capable of traversing the cosmos. The same way a bunch of marooned tardigrades grew large and smart and flew here in jetpacks. Shit didn't always make sense.

"Oz, wait!" he whispered urgently, dashing to the corner.

But he was too late.

Oz activated her sizzling blades. As soon as she opened the outer door to the hold, the creatures reared up and turned in unison toward the sound, guns at the ready.

Geddy drew his Exeter and dashed frantically after her, pulling up short of the door.

"Oz, stop!"

But the shooting had begun. Oz charged at the two guarding Doc and Denk with a feral scream. She dashed ahead and slid on her knees, her hair scraping the floor, as their laser blasts sailed just over her. She swiped her katanas at them, but instead of slicing them in half, the long claws at the ends of their stubby legs clamped on to her blades and, with astonishing speed, yanked them right out of her hands.

In a flash, one of the creatures guarding Denk and Doc struck out with one stubby arm, burying its claw deep in her left shoulder. She yelped in pain and tried to roll free, but they pinned her to the spot. Blood soaked through her shirt and pooledon the floor beneath her shoulder.

Geddy's face grew hot. He hugged the side of the open airlock as close as he dared, both hands on the pistol.

Shit, shit, shit.

"We know you are there," came a wet, computer-aided voice through the open doors. It sounded like a robot begging for a swirlie to stop. "Come out now or we will suck her dry."

— *Geddy, don't even think about it!*

— Give me a little credit here, E. There's a time and place for juvenile wit.

As Geddy pressed himself to the wall, Morpho came swinging along the ceiling and hung down in front of him, swiveling angrily back and forth as though shaking some nonexistent head.

"How about I tag in and you can suck *me* dry instead!"

"For fuck's sake, Geddy!" Oz growled.

— *There's not much to say.*

— I just gotta be me.

"We have been waiting a long time. Many generations were required for us to evolve these forms."

"Well, you look great," Geddy said. "No shame in carrying around a few extra pounds."

"You will teach us how to operate this spacecraft, and then we will take it," said the giant creature.

"Ha! Boy, did you pick the wrong ship — on multiple fronts. Even so, I'm not exactly crazy about the idea."

"We are built to last," said the giant tardigrade, digging its claws further into Oz's shoulder. She screamed in agony. "Can you say the same, human? Nice job ruining your planet, by the way."

Geddy looked anxiously at Morpho as a series of sharp thuds came from the spacecraft in which Voprot was imprisoned. When the tardigrades turned toward it, Geddy whispered to Morph, "When I say now, open the hold doors."

— *What? They'll survive, but you and the crew won't.*

— Yes we will. Without those packs, they're dead in the water. I figure we've got ten seconds before all the air escapes. We suck them out, close the door, and re-pressurize.

— *What about Voprot?*

— He's got plenty of air. We'll get him out after.

— *I dunno, Ged.*

— You got a better idea?

— *Let me talk to them.*

— Like, telepathically?

— *No, through you.*

— What, are you gonna swap stories from back home?

— *No, but maybe I can buy you time.*

— Time for what?

— *To have a better idea.*

"*Now*, human, or we'll eviscerate her. Toss out your weapon."

Geddy nodded to Morpho. "Go. Be ready."

Morpho latched onto the edge of the airlock and slung himself back toward the bridge. Geddy placed the Exeter on the floor, kicked it out, and emerged with his hands up.

The tardigrades tensed at his approach, leveling their rifles at him. "I'm unarmed."

"And yet you are not alone."

— It's as I feared. It can sense me, too.

"You know I'm not."

The three creatures exchanged a look, if you could call it that, and turned back to him. The nearest one to him, presumably the leader, tottered toward him on its comically stubby legs, its plasticky translucent skin shimmering in the bright lights of the hold as it swayed this way and that. Beneath its taut skin, organs visibly pulsed and churned. It stopped a couple of meters short and peered down the darkened corridor that led to the bridge.

— Keep it focused on you.

"I'd shake hands, but I'm guessing that's not your thing. Or juggling, come to think of it. I'm Geddy, by the way. Is it Mr. Igrade or Mr. Tard?"

Oz was right in front of the breakdown bench to which Tardigan and Denk were tied. The moment that door opened, he'd grab hold of her. Worst case, she'd grab one of them.

"You know what we are."

Any kid that had elementary biology knew that the microscopic creatures hitched a ride from Old Earth to Earth 2 riding on the *outside* of the *Rearview* transport and still survived the trip.

"I know you crashed on the moon about four hundred years ago. Congrats on your evolution, though your face could use another century or two."

The pulsating monstrosity cocked its head, studying him up and down. "I sense you are one of us, but somehow … not."

He shrugged. "Well, I have been told I'm a walking contradiction."

"I wish to speak to our kindred."

Geddy gave a nervous chuckle and glanced at the others on the floor. Neither Denk nor Tardigan had the faintest notion what was happening.

— He is not a Sagacean anymore. He is a plague.

— You really want to lead with that?

— Geddy!

He cleared his throat. "He, uh, says you're a plague. But I'm sure he means it in a nice way."

The tardigrade gave his head a rueful shake. "Join us. There is no need to subjugate yourself to this meat puppet. Take control of him and bring us to the others."

Suddenly, it all made sense. Wayward Zelnads wound up on the moon and took control of the tardigrades. Now they wanted to join their legions of pals back home.

— Tell him he can go f–

"Sorry, skinny, this flight is full. But I can offer you a voucher toward a future journey."

The tardigrade made a slow circle around him, the long, needle-sharp claws of his lower two legs clicking on the metal floor. "Tell me, human, what has your … passenger told you about Sagacea?"

"That it's nice in the fall? Frankly, I was only half listening."

Again, it dug its starfish claws into Oz's shoulder, eliciting a pained shriek that pierced Geddy's heart. "Tell me what you know."

— This is pointless. Flush them into space!

— Not yet.

"I know you want to destroy it and wipe the slate clean. I'm just not sure why."

The tardigrades exchanged what he could only assume was a look of surprise, though it seemed likely they communicated telepathically.

"It does not matter why. It must be done."

— Tell him we're done, then blast them out. That would be cool.

"Speaking of which … Now, Morph!!"

He ducked and ran as the alarm sounded and dove toward Oz's other side, grabbing hold of her good arm.

"Hold on tight." He hooked his leg around the leg of the bench beside Doc. The surprised tardigrade whirled toward him, swinging the rifle in their direction with one of his other arms. But the door had already begun to open, and hurricane-force winds whipped Oz's hair as the *whoop-whoop* of the pressure alarm blared overhead.

The one guarding Voprot got sucked out first. Geddy flipped himself over and stretched out just as his Exeter skittered along the floor. It was too far away!

"Gimme your leg!" Doc yelled.

Geddy unhooked his leg so Tardigan could grab it with his arm, letting him extend just far enough to snag the weapon. He flipped back over and uncorked on the one with its claws in Oz. The barrage cut it in ragged halves, and the lower part flew backwards through the widening gap. Seeing what was about to happen, he scrambled to wrench the upper half away from Oz, but the escaping air beat him to it. She let out a horrid scream as it ripped forcefully free of her.

"Morph, close it!" he screamed, though he had no idea if Morpho could hear him over the noise. He hadn't factored that in.

The tardigrade in charge was lying prostrate, clinging to the narrow gaps in the floor grating as its plump body stretched toward the vacuum, lengthening like an earthworm by a good meter. Its rifle was long gone. Unless the door closed in a few seconds, none of his heroics would matter. His lungs screamed as each breath took in less oxygen than the last. Ice began to form on his arm hair. His tongue began to tingle.

The door was still more than half open. To Geddy's horror, the ship holding Voprot started oscillating as air passed over its wings. Having seen this, the tardigrade turned its expressionless head toward Geddy and let go.

It slammed into the underside of the Virgin Galactic space plane and burst like a bug on a windshield, jostling it just enough for the exiting wind to give it lift. It twisted as though in a banked turn as Geddy and the others helplessly watched.

Had it happened a second later, the doors would've stopped it. But the combination of forces guided it almost perfectly through, and the plane tumbled out of the hold. Two seconds later, the doors clamped shut with horrible finality.

CHAPTER 34

YOU SUCK, FATSO

For the first time since bailing out of the *Penetrator* with his pants around his ankles, Geddy thought he might really die. His vision was so blurred he couldn't tell whether the door had actually closed or not, nor if the sound of rushing air was the last of the oxygen venting into space or fresh air spilling in through the overhead vents. This time, Morpho couldn't save him.

"V ... Vopr ..." Geddy tried to say, but he couldn't draw breath.

Tardigan's hands were around his own throat, his face purple and his eyes red and bulging. He was trying to blow the air from his lungs as fast as possible to keep ahead of the oxygen leaving his blood. Oz was on all fours, loudly gasping as her red hair formed a little cage around her face. Denk was curled in a ball sucking in labored breaths.

Geddy's vision had narrowed to a pinpoint, but just before darkness overtook it, the blaring pressure alarm mercifully turned off, and air hissed back in through the vents, blowing directly down on him. He lifted his face to the forced air and drew in a deep breath. The refilling of his lungs prompted a

coughing fit, but he was alive. They were all alive. Except…
His chest tightened as the sight of Voprot's fear-filled eyes
stared at him through the ship window before it blew out of
the *Fiz*.

A thin, sticky sound came from the airlock, and he turned
to see Morpho bounding across the floor like a living, liquid
rubber band. He made a beeline for Oz and latched onto her
arm. She gasped, rolling over onto her left hip, her feet curled
under her.

"Morph, slow down." Still rubbing her throat, her face
knotted in panic. "Oh *shit*."

"What the (*cough*) is it now?" Geddy croaked.

"The plane is gonna fall all the way down to Old Earth!"

The *Fiz* had been angled away from the planet this whole
time, hauling everything in straight to the hold. When the
space plane got sucked out, it didn't carry a lot of speed, but if
it reached the atmosphere, Voprot would burn up with it.

"I'm going after him!" Geddy stumbled toward the airlock,
his fingers still clutching the Exeter.

"Geddy, wait …" Oz began, getting to her hands and knees
before a fit of coughing stopped her.

— *Can you use the tractor beam?*

— It's too far away and too big.

— *How will you stop it in the* Dom?

— I'll figure it out when I get there.

He hurried up the ladder, scrambled down the maintenance shaft, and climbed back into his suit. Once his helmet
locked in place, it filled with air.

He re-opened the pod tube, climbed up inside, and waited
for the pressure to equalize so he didn't shoot out like a bullet.
That ate an agonizingly long minute. After opening the outer
hatch, he clomped back across the roof to the *Dom*. Once
inside, he powered her up without even waiting for the cabin
to pressurize.

The scopes flicked to life and immediately found the plane. It was already sixty-four clicks away and accelerating as it fell to Old Earth. Geddy locked on and plotted a course to intercept.

— *You're not gonna do what I think you are, are you?*

"It worked once," Geddy said, as if Eli were sitting in the seat Oz had occupied earlier. "It'll work again."

— *The impact will crush the fuselage!*

— Not if I match its velocity exactly … as it's changing and tumbling end over end.

— *Your words, not mine.*

Geddy frowned and punched it. They rocketed off toward Old Earth, dodging the thick cloud of space junk. He hoped the hull of the ship wasn't damaged or his rescue mission would become a retrieval of a giant Vopropsicle.

He punched it, quickly closing the distance to the tumbling ship. The console chirped, confirming that cabin had finally re-pressurized. He twisted his helmet free and took a few deep breaths to slow his racing heart. Now to figure a way to do this without dying.

A few seconds later, it finally came into view — a shiny, flat triangle on an off-axis spin.

"Computer, how far is that ship from the atmosphere?"

— *It will only respond to Kailorian.*

There had to be a way to do it manually, but given the ship's confusing array of buttons, it would take too long. He activated the comm, hoping someone had made it to the bridge. "Denk? Doc? Anyone there?"

"Here, Cap," Denk croaked. "Have you got him?"

"No, how do I ask the computer to show his distance from the atmosphere?"

He paused. "Boy, that's a new one for me. I can't think of a time when I–"

"Get Doc!"

Denk's muffled voice repeated the request to Doc, who immediately jumped on. "Captain, my Kailorian is a bit rusty, but I believe it is *juhr ET in talik num trat.*"

"Computer, did you get that?"

— *It won't understand that, either, dumbass!*

— I can't multitask. You know this.

"Juhr ET in talik num rat."

"Trat!" said Doc."

"Grrr … juhr ET in talik num trat."

The computer's reply came through in English, but only because the implant could translate. "Tracked object will reach atmosphere in one minute and twelve seconds."

As he pulled even with the ship, it continued rotating, giving him a brief glimpse of Voprot's terrified face in the window each time.

— *Can you really match its velocity flying backwards?*

"We're about to find out."

A pair of scanner probes protruded from the front of the *Dom* like a two-pronged fork. If he could somehow wedge the tail section between them and stabilize it, maybe he could arrest its descent and stop the spin. It would take some fancy flying even though just a few minutes earlier, his brain was starved of oxygen.

"One minute to atmosphere," warned the computer.

"Captain, are you still there?" came Doc's frantic voice.

"Thanks for the assist, but I'm kinda busy right now."

"Captain, there's no way you can stop that ship. It has too much momentum."

"I'm gonna wedge it between the antennas and hit the gas. It'll work"

"They're not strong enough. You have to let him go."

— *He's right, Geddy. Voprot doomed.*

"No, Voprot not doomed!"

He urged the *Dom* ever faster toward the plummeting craft

and passed it. It glinted like a knife in the sun as it raced Earthward. Once he was comfortably past it, he flipped around so he faced away from the planet.

— *This is not our mission!*

— It is now.

The scopes displayed Voprot's speed and acceleration. It would hit the *Dom* in five seconds. He kept the ship in the reticle as he feathered the thrusters, doing his best to match its speed.

An alarm sounded, joining the blinking light. Thirty seconds. If he couldn't stop it before then, he'd have to bug out. Unless he'd miscalculated and the *Dom* got crushed like a can as the two ships collided.

Voprot's face passed again mid-tumble, and Geddy realized how much this maneuver was like the bottom of Suicide Plunge. It worked then, and it would work now. It had to.

His heart banged in his chest at triple the rate of the countdown clock and sweat dripped from his forehead. Twenty seconds.

As the nose passed, he guessed where the tail would come around. When the fin reappeared, he tapped the stick forward and sandwiched it between the *Dom's* probes, pretty as you please. The ship's out-of-control rotation abruptly stopped and Geddy was aligned with its long axis.

Fifteen seconds.

Now for the fun part. He eased the thrusters forward to make sure the ships were touching, then dropped the hammer.

Geddy's old man could withstand incredible g-forces, and he'd inherited at least some of that, but getting caught between thrust and momentum on this level made it feel like his organs would squirt out the sides of his chest. For a long few seconds, he couldn't breathe again, and his consciousness again began to slip. If he so much as blinked, Voprot was dead.

— *You need adrenaline! Get angry!*

The readout showed them slowing but not nearly fast enough.

"Come on, you piece a' shit! Is that all you've got?!" he screamed at the *Dom*, pounding the controls like a madman.

"Ten seconds to atmosphere."

The thrusters were maxed out. It really *was* all she had, and it wasn't quite enough. If he didn't un-stick himself from the ship before they hit the atmosphere, all three of them would die. The size of his emotions surprised him. "Sorry, buddy. Voprot d–"

"Wait for me!" came Oz's voice through the comm.

The screen tracked another object inbound at high speed. When it came into view, he spotted a bright blue-orange flame streaking toward him. At first glance, he thought it was a missile, but once magnified, he realized what it was.

Oz had strapped on one of the tardigrades' jet packs, and they were much more powerful than he thought.

"You've gotta be shittin' me ..." he muttered.

She swooped down to his left, matching his speed and giving a pained smile through the face shield of her suit. "You're gonna want one of these!"

"Get under him! Everything you've got!" he yelled. What a badass. Her shoulder had to be hamburger from where the tardigrade had punctured it.

Oz positioned her uninjured shoulder against the back of the plane and fired her thrusters. A thin ringed cone of flame stretched out behind her.

The edge of the atmosphere was less than half a kilometer or so below them. It was gonna be close.

"Five seconds to atmosphere."

Another alarm sounded, this one an insistent staccato. The inductors were overheating. If they crapped out, they would all burn up.

"Come on, baby, all plunge, no suicide ..."

Their velocity dropped to 600 kph, then 300, then 100. To his right was the continent of Australia.

When his eyes returned to the screen, it reached zero, and they were moving back toward the *Fiz*.

"Wooo hooooooo!" he cried, slapping his thigh. "Oz, we did it!"

"I can't believe that worked," said Doc over the comm. "All you have to do now is get into range. Denk's got the beam ready to reel the plane back in."

Geddy throttled back to a gradual stop and Voprot's derelict vessel slipped away, continuing toward the *Fiz* as though it had just taken off at low speed.

Oz did likewise and let herself drift in front of him, giving a sheepish grin. "Voprot saved."

"Maybe he'll prove himself useful someday."

Oz laughed. "I'm sorry. I know better than to just rush in without a plan. My emotions got the better of me."

He frowned, feigning offense. "Yeah, come on. That's *my* thing."

"Can we go home now? Old Earth kinda sucks."

"Actually, there's one more thing I need to do." She cocked her head. "Our friends can survive space, but they won't survive me."

A sly grin crossed her face, and she gave a mock salute. "Meet you back at the *Fiz*, Captain. Happy hunting."

CHAPTER 35
COMING CLEAN

After Geddy blasted the drifting, frozen tardigrades to smithereens, he returned to the *Fiz* and made his way to the hold. Doc was looking over Voprot, who was seated on the edge of the raised maintenance deck. The moment he saw Geddy enter through the open airlock, he sprang to his feet, ran to him, and wrapped him in a bone-crunching hug.

"Geddy, you save Voprot!"

"You want to thank me, prove yourself useful."

"Voprot promise."

He held Geddy like a doll until he managed to squirm free of his monstrous embrace. Oz came walking over wearing a self-satisfied grin, and it was much more pleasing to hug her.

"You okay?" he asked. "That took some brass balls."

"I figured I was already making bad decisions today, so why not one more?"

Other than being terrified, Voprot emerged physically unscathed from his ordeal, although the fuselage of the old low-orbit space plane turned out to have two finger-sized meteoroid holes that had nearly depleted his air.

Now that they knew the relative positions of the two galaxies, Denk had already found a vector back home. But the entry point lay well beyond the solar system and would take a couple days to reach. That was fine because everyone needed a little shuteye.

After taking turns sleeping for a few hours, they gathered around the hexagonal table in the galley. Denk recounted the series of events that led to their being held hostage by the Zelnad tardigrades.

They'd presumably spotted the *Fiz* from the moon, jetted their way to the aft door of the hold, and waited. No sooner had Oz brought the plane inside with the tractor beam than they swooped in with their packs and rifles. Caught completely off-guard, Voprot was forced to surrender and imprisoned inside the plane. For good measure, they forced Denk to weld the door shut.

"Morpho watched the whole thing from the ceiling." Denk looked up, and they all joined him. Morpho jiggled as if confirming the story. "He to the UDC transmitter and sent you the SOS."

"What did they say to you?" Geddy asked, searching through the cabinets for a fresh bottle of gin.

"Well, only the one talked." A haunted look settled on Denk's face. "He ... er, it said a lot of the same stuff that you heard about civilization and what not, but it didn't make a lick of sense. I had no idea what he was talking to you about."

Geddy turned away, now desperate for that gin. He opened another cabinet and breathed a sigh of relief.

— Bingo.

He poured himself two fingers and downed it in one long swallow, feeling their eyes at his back the entire time.

— *Is it time?*

He refilled the glass, then returned to the table.

— Looks that way.

He sank back onto the hard metal stool opposite Oz. She gave a small nod, and he scratched absently at his scruffy beard, taking a long slow breath.

"Guys, there's, um… something I need to tell you."

As he had done with Oz, Geddy recounted the story of how Eli came to live rent-free in his brain. Doc was enthralled, but Denk and Voprot needed a lot of help. His detailed admission hung in silence for several seconds as they grappled with everything.

Denk was the first to speak. "Cap, I'm just gonna put this out there … you were alone on Earth 2 for seven years. Is it possible you might have just, y'know, made Eli up?"

— *That's a fair question.*

— And a hard one to disprove.

— *I am real and you know it.*

"Believe me, Denk, I'm crazier than you know, but he's as real as any of you. Just … incorporeal. But also my best friend."

Eli didn't say anything, but Geddy felt a warmth spread throughout him.

"And he lives in your brain." Denk still looked skeptical.

"Voprot want brain friend, too."

— *If we get to Sagacea, I can make that happen.*

— Let's keep that a surprise.

Denk continued, "Okay, but … where is this Sagacea? I've never heard of it."

"No one has. It's at the origin point of the universe."

"Is that a long way?" His head swiveled from Oz to Doc.

Doc replied, "The universe has been expanding for about fourteen billion years, so yes, it is likely quite far away."

"That's not the point," Geddy said. "Eli is what you might call an outlier of his species."

"How so?" Doc asked, infinitely curious.

"Sagaceans are energy-based beings that float through the universe. Sometimes, they sort of merge with living things and nudge them toward discovery. Insights. Knowledge — the kind of things that give rise to civilization. That's how it was for eons, but now, growing numbers of Sagaceans have decided to take people over." There was no easing into this one, so he blurted it out. "They call themselves Zelnads."

There was a collective gasp as they all pulled back, including Oz. Not even she knew that little detail. She shook her head to clear it. "Wait — are you telling us that those things were–?"

"Zelnads, yes. We know they want to destroy us, but we don't know what they're planning. All I know is that it has something to do with my ship and finding Sagacea."

"How do you know Eli's not one of them?" Denk asked.

"Because I'm still me. If he wanted to take control of my consciousness, he would've done it by now."

"I've sensed Eli's presence almost since we first met," Oz assured the crew. "His intentions are pure."

So far, this was going much better than Geddy dared imagine. At least everyone was trying to understand, which was more than he could say for most people.

"They can sense each other, can they not?" Doc asked. "That is why the leader referred to Eli as 'kindred.'"

"Yes. So we have Zelnad-dar, but it works both ways," Geddy said.

"Why they not like us?" Voprot asked.

"Well, big guy, hey think civilization is an experiment gone wrong."

"A hard point to argue," noted Doc with a flare of his eyebrows.

A dark realization swept across Oz's face. "They're building an army."

"Maybe," Geddy admitted. "It would explain their advanced tech."

"Evil brain friends no kill Kigantu!" Voprot slammed his fist into the table leaving a softball-sized dent.

Geddy looked at Denk and sighed. "Add a new table to our list."

"But if their technology is so far ahead of ours, what would they want with your ship?" Doc inquired.

"There's a barrier around their world. Some kind of energy field. The *Penetrator* is covered in the only metal that can pass through it, hence the name. It's some kind of tukrium alloy Eli calls shinium. You remember that derelict Zelnad research vessel we found? Eli thinks it may have found Sagacea but couldn't make it past the barrier. If so, maybe the crew got vaporized, and they sent it back. But that's just a theory."

"I have never heard of shinium," Doc said. "Is it abundant on Earth 2?"

"Apparently, but it's deep."

"Do they know that is where the ship came from?"

"I have no idea. All I know is that we need to reach Sagacea before they do, and my ship's the only thing that can reach it."

"If we can find Sagacea in the first place," Oz noted.

"That's about the size of it, yeah. The research vessel might've shown us the way, but it's in the wind. The *Penetrator*, however, is on Aku."

This new information surprised Doc. "How do you know that?"

"Zereth-Tinn. I don't know how he's connected to all this, but I believe he's on our side."

"So he's one of those nice extortionists," said Oz.

All eyes remained on the table as the crew grappled with this new information. It was a lot to take in. But Geddy was glad to have it off his chest. Oz convinced him they were truly in this together, and now they all knew the stakes.

"Listen, I can't ask any of you to come with me to Aku. You've got enough loot to set yourselves up for years. But this isn't about some ship anymore. It's about–"

Oz rolled her eyes at him. "Geddy, we're all in! Now can we jump back or do you need to finish your speech?"

CHAPTER 36

AKU! BLESS YOU!

To Geddy's great relief, the long jump back to their home galaxy got the *Fizmo* most of the way to Aku, but without any blue balls, it still took another four days to get there. By then, the crew was more than ready to put their feet on terra firma again. Funny how a long turn in space made you want to be on-world when the opposite was also true.

If they played their cards right, the crew could sell their loot *and* track down Geddy's ship. Dealing with Aku's subterranean black market had its share of risks, even more than the Hau Bazaar on Caloth, but it could also command higher prices if you had the kind of stuff they needed, which the *Fiz* almost certainly did.

Since the Virgin Galactic plane was largely intact save for the door, Geddy decided they should set it aside with the other pieces of Old Earth arcana and sell them later to a collector like Zirhof. Taking it back to the Double A on Kigantu wasn't exactly an option, but he still had contacts in that world when the time came.

The only contact that mattered now was a rough character

named Balzac, who wasn't nearly so hilarious as his name would suggest.

Geddy used to run a lot of weapons and armor back in the day, and not always for Tretiak. Delivering a load to tribal warlords on shitty planets like Gethenia and Bonzok, whose favorite pastime was civil war, didn't pay that well, but it wasn't all that dangerous either. Much of that gear came from Aku.

The Screvari, Aku's native people, were nothing if not enterprising. After the collapse of the Triad, Aku's former shipyards and machine shops began to manufacture everything from weapons to engines. Really, anything that required their legendary metalworking skills. Balzac, as big and mean a Screvari as Geddy had ever seen, was in charge of at least one such operation.

In half a dozen trips to Aku, he only met Balzac in person once, on his last visit. That was only because the disruptors in Tretiak's first ship, *Auctionaut I*, had targeting issues. He hung out with Balzac for a few hours while his crew got it sorted. Like most of his kind, Balzac hated Kailorians and Ghruk and felt indifferent at best about everyone else. They chatted and clinked glasses while the repairs were completed and got absolutely pickled. He couldn't remember anything they talked about, but they sure had a great time.

At least, until it came time to pay for the very expensive repairs.

Geddy must not have been watching his accounts closely, because he only had a little more than half of the total Balzac demanded. Balzac accused him of being a Kailorian spy, and for a tense several minutes, Geddy was sure he'd be executed. Eventually, Balzac had little choice but to agree to a much lower price, but the damage was done. Balzac let him go but told him to never show his face there again.

The whole crew gathered in the bridge to watch their

approach toward Aku. It was a small and featureless blue-black planet near the galaxy's edge. The lava that covered its entire surface billions of years ago had solidified into a giant, cobalt-rich ball bearing, hence its bluish cast. Like The Deuce, it relied on geothermal activity for power. Its thin atmosphere was hot and high in sulfur compounds, so everything was inside or underground. Long tunnels under the planet's surface linked everything together, which was why there were no outside lights save the spaceport in Drukarva, the only one left as far as Geddy knew.

"Anyone else been here before?" They all shook their heads.

Denk stared at the screen. "The spaceport should be straight ahead, but I don't see anything."

"It's there," Geddy said. "Trust me. You can't see the landing lights until they're in your face."

"What's our plan?" Oz asked.

"To find a guy named Balzac." He paused for giggles, but none came, not even from Oz. "Hopefully he'll have a use for our junk."

"What about your ship?" inquired Denk.

"Money's our first priority. I need to make sure you guys are taken care of in case something happens to me."

"Voprot protect Geddy," the lizard declared.

"In case *what* happens to you?" Oz asked. The look on her face told him she couldn't take many more of his secrets.

"Balzac and I had a minor misunderstanding last time I was here. It's probably long forgotten."

A gruff Screvari voice came over the comm. "*For Sale Make Offer*, we have you on approach vector two-two-six mark three. State your business."

"We've come to barter with a guy named Balzac," Geddy said, drawing himself up in his chair.

"I need you to be more specific."

"They all look the same to me," he said with a shit-eating grin. Disappointingly, Oz only closed her eyes and shook her head. "Aw, come on, that's gold!"

"Without someone to vouch for you, we can't clear you to land. Especially not in a filthy Ghruk ship."

Geddy grimaced. He couldn't exactly blurt out that the Balzac he knew ran counterfeit weapons out of an abandoned factory. In the past, he flew right to one of the silos and skipped the spaceport altogether.

He struggled to recall details of their conversation a decade earlier. There was a photo on the wall in his office, a much younger Balzac hurling a glowing red ring at a multi-armed robot that reminded him of an octopus. He was a big deal back in the day but got badly injured and walked with a hitch as a result. What was the damn game called?

He hit mute on his comm and turned to Tardigan. "What's the big pro sport on Aku? I'm almost certain it starts with a K."

"I'm afraid sports are not my area of expertise, Captain." He gave an impish little grin. "I guess you might say I am more of a ... nerd, if that makes sense."

"It definitely does."

Doc wrinkled his nose. "... however, I believe it's called grimring."

— *That doesn't start with a K.*

— You know what does? Keep yer yap shut.

After unmuting his comm, he said, "All I know is that he was one helluva grimring player."

A pause, then, "You know grimring?"

He laughed, wide-eyed with panic, desperately searching the crew for anyone who could feed him some information. "Do I know grimring? Why I ... uh ..." No such luck. "I certainly know it well enough to have a spirited conversation with my dear friend, Balzac, the grimring legend."

— *When all this is over, you should get into improv.*

— I am good at pretending to care what you think.

"Hold your position."

He exhaled and let his shoulders hunch forward. A tense thirty seconds followed, but the official came back onscreen and said, "You're cleared to land on platform 5C. Prepare to be boarded for inspection." Then he blinked out.

Oz popped out of her chair outraged. "Inspection??"

"Relax, they're just paranoid," Geddy said, pumping his hands up and down. "It's a Ghruk ship. They just want to be sure no Ghruk are aboard."

"Why they hate Ghruk?" asked Voprot innocently.

"Not because they're beautiful, I can tell ya that."

The approach tunnel appeared, and Denk followed it in. As the *Fiz* glided into its assigned platform, Geddy scanned the hangar to see what kind of traffic it had. It was the usual assortment of Screvari ships, old Xellaran cruisers, and small freighters. Not a single other Ghruk or Kailorian ship among them.

The moment the skids touched down, a four-man security retinue approached and motioned for Denk to lower the ramp. Geddy gave him a thumbs-up.

"Just be cool. We have every right to be here."

A few seconds later, the first Screvari head appeared. They had angular, pale gray faces, with patterns of deep wrinkles that resembled a drawn curtain. Their eyes were slightly smaller than humans and uniformly black. They were intimidating at first, but once you got to know them a bit, they turned out to be just as sad and bitter and put-upon as everyone else.

Translator chips were usually so good at context that it really seemed everyone was speaking and inflecting in modern English. But for some reason, they struggled with Screvari. They all sounded imperious and threatening to his ears.

The squad, none of whom moved with the slightest haste,

paused at the top of the ramp and looked around, frowning at the inferior Ghruk workmanship. Geddy would have done the same. Screvari-made ships kicked ass.

"I'm sergeant Uhrin of the DSA. Who is the captain?"

"Geddy Starheart at your service." He stepped forward and drew himself taller. "What did you say your name was?"

"Uhrin."

"Urine."

"No, 'yur-IN.'"

"Right. Urine." Geddy looked over his shoulder and grinned at his crew.

— *Ask yourself whether this is helping.*

The squad leader stiffened, unamused. "What is your cargo and purpose here?"

"Our cargo is our purpose. Metals, mostly. A few collector pieces." The sergeant glanced down through the airlock doors but didn't venture that way. "That's why I want to see Balzac."

He turned to the three men. "You're dismissed." They gave tight nods and went back down the ramp in unison, leaving the sergeant alone with them. "What do you want with Balzac?"

"He and I go way back. He'll want what we have to show him."

Only now did the sergeant wander over to the airlock. "Let me see."

Geddy opened both doors. Together they stepped into the very full hold, and his eyes roamed over it with passive interest.

The space plane, in particular, piqued his curiosity. He approached it slowly and ran his fingers over the aluminum nosecone like a kid in a museum. "So primitive. Where did it come from?"

"Between the seat cushions. What difference does it make?"

Working-class Screvari pretty much had to fend for themselves. The ruling class held all the wealth, so they'd built their own economy, importing and exporting, selling and trading under the table. It was technically illegal, but the government was very busy being corrupt.

"There's a release fee," said the sergeant.

"Of course," he said through gritted teeth.

The corners of the man's mouth lifted. "Ten thousand."

Geddy's eyes widened. "To look the other way? Forget it." No way was he paying ten grand just to talk to someone.

"You want to see Balzac, that's the price."

He'd expected to line a few pockets, but that was a big ask for a glorified hall monitor. Who did he think he was?

Still, he had Geddy by the balls, and selling their stuff was only half the mission. Nothing happened without Balzac. But he also didn't have the money. Yet.

"After I see Balzac." He twitched his head toward the shipping crates. "Call this collateral."

The sergeant nodded, a satisfied smirk on his creased face, and brushed Geddy's shoulder on his way out of the hold. "Oh, I will. Follow me."

CHAPTER 37

SHOW ME YOUR BALZAC

Before the engines had cooled, they took off again. This time, Sergeant Uhrin stood beside Geddy on the bridge, directing them to another part of the city where he hoped Balzac awaited.

"Follow that conduit there." He pointed at a particularly wide length of tunnel only discernible by the reflection from their system's bluish sun. Though it loomed large in the sky, its light was no brighter than a full moon.

"So how do you know Balzac?" asked the sergeant.

"By feel," Geddy quipped, but predictably, he didn't react. "We were business associates in a past life."

He nodded knowingly. "You look familiar. Starheart, you said?"

"Yeah, that's right. You worked for him?"

"Still do." The man cocked an eyebrow. "Most of us do." When his focus returned to the front display, he indicated a small structure at the intersection of the large conduit and several smaller ones. "There on the left. Land on the roof."

"I assume he's still involved with the black market?" Uhrin didn't seem too concerned about illegality.

The sergeant gave him a knowing look. "He *is* the black market."

Denk dropped to a lower altitude and made a slow lap to get a closer look. It certainly didn't appear to be a landing plat-form, but then again, neither had Balzac's old silo. The *Fiz* settled over the middle of a large, squat cylinder resembling a storage tank, and the top retracted to reveal a different silo that descended deep below the surface.

Slowly, Denk eased the ship down its length. Not unlike the *Fiz's* hold, the curved walls were lined with shelving and labeled bins, attended by a small army of Screvari taking inventory or fulfilling orders. A few gave casual glances over their shoulders as the *Fiz* descended, but clearly they weren't the first circus to come to town. About halfway down, two halves of a landing platform extended from either side, meeting in the middle. Denk extended the skids and settled her into place.

"Kill your engines," Uhrin instructed. Denk did so while Geddy lowered the ramp.

The smell of metal and grease assaulted Geddy's nostrils. Industry and manufacturing, milling machines, and tools.

Uhrin paused halfway down the ramp and turned to him. "Wait here." He marched across the platform toward a door that opened as he approached. It closed behind him.

"What is this place?" Voprot asked, crouching down to peek through the narrow window that wrapped around the sides of the bridge.

"Balzac's new base of operations, apparently," Geddy replied. "Shipping, receiving, and manufacturing all in one."

A couple minutes later, the door in the silo wall retracted and an older Screvari man came striding through. At a glance, it was hard to spot the difference between him and Uhrin, but Balzac had a deep scar on his chin that gave him away. And the lower half of his left arm was robotic. Maybe he'd finally get to hear the story behind that.

"Is that your friend?" Doc asked.

"Yeah, that's him." Geddy's voice was flat. He wished he knew the score between him and his old acquaintance. "'Friend' might be pushing it."

"What aren't you telling us?" Oz's voice carried a low warning.

Heavy footsteps thudded up the ramp, and Balzac appeared. As he came level to Geddy, he noted that his right eye was now mechanical as well.

— *Do you trust him?*

— I don't have much choice.

Balzac approached Geddy wordlessly and looked him over, his breathing somewhat labored. His eyes lingered on Voprot for a few extra moments, the big lizard's eyes narrowing to suspicious slits and his tongue flicking out to taste the air between them. Finally, his focus returned to Geddy.

"Heard you were out of the game, Starheart," he growled.

"Not the long game."

"What are you doing with a War-era Ghruk ship?"

"Picking up trash. I signed us up for the adopt-a-galaxy program. Pay it forward, you know? Feels good. You should try it."

"I mean I heard you were dead."

"Ah. And you want to know if it's true."

"I take it you're not working for Tretiak anymore."

"We had a falling out. Technically, two. Now I'm captain of this trawler. This here's my crew. Oz, Denk, Voprot, and Dr. Tardigan." Geddy indicated them in turn. "Morpho's around somewhere."

Balzac gave them a faint nod. "Uhrin tells me you have some product."

He grinned mischievously. "Oh yeah. Come on."

Geddy told the crew to stay put and led Balzac back into the hold. His eyes immediately fixed upon the old Virgin Galactic ship and he gave a low whistle. "Well, what have we here?"

"It's called a space plane. Sort of a bridge technology between atmospheric and space transports."

"I've never heard of such a thing. What a silly and limiting venture." He made a slow lap around it, pausing to peer through the tiny windows. "Where'd you find it?"

"You won't believe it."

"Try me."

"Old Earth."

He quickly lifted his head and gave him a *yeah, right* look. "Don't bullshit a bullshitter."

Geddy gestured toward the packed shelves and bins where all the smaller pieces awaited. "See for yourself. Titanium, platinum, gold, scandium ..."

"You're telling me you jumped all the way to Old Earth." A grin split the man's face, softening his fierce façade.

"Sure did. Took four jumps, too," Geddy said. "There are other artifacts, too. I figure the plane's worth at least seven figures to somebody."

The quantum computer was still in the *Dom's* small hold, where it would remain until he could get to Zorr.

"I'd expect so."

Balzac's lone black eye sparkled enough for Geddy to tell he was licking his chops. If anything, he'd downplayed the cargo's value with the crew. The Screvari made anything for anyone willing to pay. Everything from custom weapons to toys to jewelry. It was how the working class survived. Apparently, they were doing a little better than that now.

"None of my business, but what the hell happened to you?" asked Geddy.

"Let's just say I've made my share of enemies over the years. I'm sure you can relate."

He chuckled appreciatively. "Indeed."

"I'll send my men in to check the manifest, then I'll work up a quote. I think we can come to terms."

"Perfect." A pleased smile split Geddy's face. "But I'm hoping there's something else we can come to an agreement on."

"I'm listening."

"The Zelnads stole a ship from me. I got a tip it was in Drukarva and that someone named Isoro might know where it is."

Balzac's face registered mild surprise. "Isoro. Haven't heard that name in a while. He used to be a big deal around here, but now he's sort of a recluse."

Not knowing who or what Isoro was put Geddy at a disadvantage, but as he'd told Eli, he had little choice but to trust him.

"Can you take me to him?"

"Depends."

Geddy sighed and looked away. "All right, what the hell's *this* gonna cost me now?"

"Money doesn't interest me. What do they want with this ship of yours?"

"It's clad in pure tukrium. I think the Nads want to know where it came from."

"Which was?"

"The Deuce."

"You don't say …"

He scratched his pointy chin, working through the full implications of all this. If the Nads knew Earth 2 was a source of tukrium, they'd immediately seize control of it and only accelerate their plans. But if someone else got there first — someone with the wherewithal and means — it could be a game-changer. His fathomless black eyes sparked with some unspoken aspiration.

Balzac had been around long enough to observe and suffer from the Nads' corruptive influence on Aku. He'd surely love nothing more than to move his operations there and return to proper manufacturing, not this shady underground crap. Not only was Earth 2 abandoned, but compared to Aku's atmosphere, it was like a sparkling mountain breeze. The Screvari could move in as soon as Tatiana's salvage operation was done, if it wasn't already. But they didn't know mining or refinement, just manufacturing. For that, they would need Ghruk and Kailorian expertise.

But as tantalizing as it was to imagine the Triad worlds making nice and reforming on Earth 2, he was getting way ahead of himself.

After a moment's thought, Balzac's eyes locked on. "You know that rich woman. What was her name?"

Now he remembered what they talked about last time. He hosted a bitchfest about Tatiana Semenov that left Balzac absolutely in stitches.

"Tatiana Semenov." He mumbled her name lest he inadvertently summon her from some dark dimension.

He snapped his fingers. "That's the one! Doesn't her family practically own Earth 2?"

Balzac wanted a piece of Earth 2's tukrium, which was really shinium, and he now believed Geddy could help make that happen. But once the salvage operations were done, Tati would no longer have any say about what happened on The Deuce. It would just be another vaguely habitable exoplanet again.

He smiled conspiratorially. "You want some hot tukrium action."

"I can put ten thousand Screvari to work there in days.

Rebuild the fleet to its former glory and oust our corrupt government."

Even before Geddy left Kigantu, there were plenty of rumors about the Screvari Circle being cozied up to the Nads. Maybe the rumors were true.

"I'll arrange a meeting. *After* I see Isoro and *after* you ... you know ... take our big load."

— *First, well done. Second, are you sure about this? Don't make a promise you can't keep.*

— Like I'd ever do such a thing.

Balzac nodded. As far as he was concerned, they'd signed a contract in blood. "Fair enough. I'll take you to Isoro. It's not far."

"Okay. Lemme give the crew a heads-up."

When they returned to the platform, the crew was looking hopefully out the window. Balzac muttered something to Uhrin, who nodded, then hurried off. Geddy climbed back up the ramp with Balzac in tow.

"Well, good news, gang. Mr. Balzac has agreed to purchase our salvaged goods," Geddy said, clapping his hands together. Denk gave a fist pump, and Voprot failed to comprehend Doc's attempted high five. "It'll take a while for his people to sift through everything, but we should be sitting pretty after this."

"The ship needs a lot of work," Oz said to Balzac. "I don't imagine you could help us with some upgrades and repairs."

Balzac's eyes roamed over the dingy interior, grimacing. "I would almost insist. I wouldn't wish a Ghruk dung heap like this on my worst enemy." He thumbed over his shoulder. "There's food and showers inside if you'd like."

That put a smile on everyone's face. Geddy needed both of those himself, but they'd have to wait.

"Listen, guys, I've got to see a man about a ship. I'll catch up with you later." He went to retrieve his Exeter from the weapons locker, but Balzac stopped him.

"Sorry, no weapons in the conduits. Those are just the rules.

Voprot immediately rose to his haunches. "Then Voprot come with Geddy."

Balzac stepped in, shaking his head. "Sorry, big fella. Just him."

Oz gave Geddy a cautioning look, but Balzac's tone made it clear that this wasn't negotiable. If this was part of the game, he'd just have to play it. "Don't worry, guys, I won't be long."

Balzac acknowledged the crew silently and descended the ramp. Geddy moved to follow, but Doc reached out and grabbed his forearm.

"Captain, something about this troubles me."

"It's fine, Doc. Go enjoy yourself. You guys have earned the break."

"Just be careful," Oz warned.

Geddy took a long look at his crew and was overcome with pride. Who could've imagined his journey would lead him here? A tear began to form in his eye, but he turned and went down the ramp before it could fall.

"See you all in a few," he said over his shoulder.

— *I agree with Doc. Balzac seems too affable.*

— People can change, Eli. I mean, look at me.

— *Not a great example.*

CHAPTER 38

TIGHTER ISN'T ALWAYS BETTER

Geddy followed Balzac down to the lower conduits where Screvari moved people and goods between a series of compartmentalized mini-cities. Narrow-gauge trains shuttled people back and forth in the road-like conduit while others walked or sat along the sides like ghosts.

He'd never seen how Screvari people actually lived, but now he understood why they were short on humor. It was a depressing, congested, smelly scene. Silos similar to Balzac's held meager stores of food and water with communal living areas in between. The massive factories that had once churned out warships had been converted into makeshift facilities for black market goods.

Screvari got a bad rap. Their scary, almost demonic appearance gave people the heebie jeebies, and their rumored relationship with the Nads didn't do them any favors. The Ring War cost millions of lives, but it had cost Aku a lot more than that, and they were still paying the price. Still, this little economy was better than none at all.

The smell could charitably be described as a mix of flop

sweat and fermented meat. Unfortunately, the fresh air Geddy's lungs had been craving was a long way from here.

After a while walking in silence, Balzac turned down a much narrower and empty conduit that came to a dead end at a ladder that disappeared into the ceiling.

He nodded toward it. "Isoro's this way."

"In the ventilation ducts?" His claustrophobia was already stirring.

"The main conduit to his area is flooded. This is the only way now."

"How far?"

"Not far. A hundred, hundred ten meters at most."

He gulped, beads of sweat forming on his forehead.

— *Are you gonna be okay?*

— Yeah, no problem. I crawl through ductwork just for fun sometimes.

Geddy took a deep breath of putrid air and clambered up the ladder after Balzac. At the second junction, he stepped off and crawled into a vent so dark that he couldn't even tell for sure how big it was, which was probably for the best. Were it not for Balzac's own musky scent or the *click click* of his metal hand as he crawled, he would've felt utterly alone. Occasionally, he reached out with his free hand to brush the bottom of Balzac's boot and reassure himself he wasn't.

After what seemed like ten hours of crawling, a faint light appeared up ahead. Balzac paused. "We're almost there."

The last twenty meters saw them stalking down the duct like a pair of fat, clumsy cats. If he didn't get into an open space in the next two minutes, he was going to curl into the fetal position and pray for a quick death.

Balzac reached the square grate up ahead and gently removed it.

— *Didn't he say people use this all the time?*

— Yeah, why?

— Seems odd there would be a grate there.

— All of this seems odd.

Once Balzac crawled through, he motioned for Geddy to follow. It was a tighter fit than he would've preferred, but once his head was through, he saw they'd emerged onto a platform fifteen meters above some sort of lab that thrummed with machinery.

After crawling fully out, Geddy pushed himself back against the wall, pulled his legs to his chest, and took some deep, rhythmic breaths with his eyes closed while he waited for his heart to slow.

"Heights?" Balzac asked, just above a whisper.

"Claustrophobia," Geddy admitted.

Once his pulse slowed to a moderate allegro, he joined Balzac at the railing. At least a dozen people were below, either standing at a row of workstations in the middle or seated at banks of instruments around the perimeter.

— They're Zelnads, Geddy!

— Can they sense you?

— Probably. This is not good.

— But look!

The the edge of the room, largely obscured by bundles of elevated wiring, Geddy glimpsed a part of the *Penetrator's* left engine. Or so he thought. The shinium skin had been completely removed. A sick feeling hit the pit of his stomach.

— Aw, hell.

— Is that her?

— I think so.

— I thought he was taking you to Isoro.

— That makes two of us.

"What the hell is this?" Geddy asked, his heartbeat having picked up a few beats. "Where's Isoro?" Balzac didn't raise his head. "There is no Isoro, is there?"

When Balzac finally did look him in the eye, he'd leveled a

small blaster at Geddy's stomach. "Sorry, Geddy. The only reason I'm still in business is because they allow it."

"Ah, the old 'it's just business' argument. How original. What about Zereth-Tinn?"

"Don't blame him. I paid him to point you in my direction."

"Well, you can't say he's not enterprising. Like my ship?" he jutted his head toward the small craft at the back.

"It looked better before they stripped it."

"So what happens now?"

"They just want to talk," Balzac said.

"Then what are we waiting for?" Geddy asked.

CHAPTER 39

THE METALLURGIST

Someone on the floor sent an old lift to the platform level, and Balzac indicated with his blaster that Geddy should get on it.

"No weapons in the conduits, huh?"

"There are those who make the rules, and those who have to follow them," Balzac said. "Now go."

Balzac followed Geddy onto the lift, and it began descending to the floor of the strange lab.

— *Geddy, you will not like what I am about to suggest.*

— Don't let that stop you.

— *If this goes sideways, I may need to briefly take you over.*

— Come again?

— *They are ten steps ahead of you. You cannot defeat them. Not in combat, and certainly not in a spelling contest.*

— You said that's what make Zelnads, Zelnads.

— *I did.*

— So, wouldn't that make me one?

— *I am not like them.*

— What if they can make you like them? What if all Zelnads didn't start that way? You said Sagaceans have influenced us. Couldn't they be influenced, too? Couldn't you? You all seem to have some powerful connection.

— *That is possible. A sound logical argument for why they are doing this could be ... seductive. And nearly instantaneous, if we got close enough. If that happens, your consciousness will be absorbed into mine. Body and soul, you will effectively cease to exist.*

— Jeez! Remind me never to ask you for reassurance.

— *I cannot offer it, Geddy. There may be more powerful than me.*

— Not a chance.

— *How can you be so sure?*

— Because you're starting to make me into a better person. As far as I'm concerned, that makes you the most powerful force in the universe.

— *Thank you, Geddy.*

— Do what you need to do. But only if you need to do it.

— *Of course.*

A glance into his future only showed torture and questioning about where the ship came from and what it was made of. This was the only way to prevent a cataclysm. As the lift settled to a stop, a crowd of Nads pressed in, forming a semicircle around them.

They comprised at least half a dozen races, males and females alike. They all wore the same blank, compliant expressions, like animals to the slaughter. Each wore garb typical of their kind with no uniforms or other identifying marks.

One of them, a traditional tree-hugging Vyeph, stepped forward and sniffed at his face, then looked him up and down with intense, unblinking eyes. After a moment, he turned to Balzac. "This the pilot?"

"That's him. Name's Geddy Starheart."

"Mr. Starheart. At last we meet."

The Nad's voice was ordinary, yet somehow suggestive of millions of identical voices speaking in perfect unison. It was unsettling to say the least.

"He is a host. But not to one of us."

"What're you talking about?" Balzac asked, blinking.

"He confirmed the ship is his?"

"Yeah," Balzac growled. "Which means you and I are done." He leaned in. "This wasn't personal, Ged."

Geddy was about to unleash a stream of curses into Balzac's back side, but the Nad stopped him as he turned to leave.

"Wait." Balzac stopped, pinching his shoulders, and wearily turned back. "How well do you know this man?"

"Not very. Why?"

"Because you may yet prove yourself useful."

One of the Nads, a portly Bonzok, snatched Balzac's weapon from his hand quick as lightning. A blink later, others jumped in to immobilize him. "Hey! What the hell?!"

Reflexively, Geddy started to spin around, but he'd barely moved before their hands were on him, too, strong as vises.

The Nad in charge leaned in close again, his green-tinged humanoid face just centimeters away, the vertical slits of his pupils opened wide. His irises shone bright gold.

"How did you build your ship?"

"I guess I just kept adding stuff until it looked like a ship."

"The *material*, human! How did you acquire the metal??"

"What material?"

"You know perfectly well what material, Geddy Starheart."

"I'm sorry, I missed your name."

"If your puny mind needs such a construct, then you may think of me as … the Metallurgist."

He pivoted away, strolling toward the central row of workstations, jammed with strange-looking instruments and tools. The other Nads made way but eyed Geddy warily, ready to pounce if he made a move.

The Metallurgist returned carrying a thin shinium panel from the *Penetrator*, one of hundreds he had mined, smelted, refined, shaped, and cut to a perfect fit under Eli's guidance. Bile rose in his stomach.

"You, Screvari — are there other worlds capable of working tukrium with such skill?"

"No," answered Balzac.

"Could your friend here have done it?"

"No."

He paused right in front of Geddy, his soulless eyes like the vacuum of space itself. "Which is how I know it isn't tukrium. "I ask again — how did you acquire this metal?"

"Eat a dick, E.T."

The Nad shot his long-fingered hand out and clamped it around Geddy's throat, pinching his airway completely shut. At the same time, the others took his arms.

"We do not have time for this. But it matters not. You see, I already know."

He let go, and Geddy coughed to reopen his trachea. "Then I guess we're all done here? I can show myself out."

The metallurgist raised the panel in front of Geddy and traced it lovingly with his finger. "Tukrium is formed by forces ordinary beings cannot conceive. Forces generated during the birth of the universe.

"Over eons, stars and planets took form as we, the seeds of all knowledge and insight, radiated into the void. Beings far older than time itself. Multitudes of our kind were drawn by gravity into newly formed worlds, only to be subsumed by oceans of molten tukrium. Becoming ... one with it."

He merely reached out his other hand, and one of the others placed a small device in it that looked like a tiny black cup. He placed it on the panel and it clung even though tukrium was not magnetic.

He held it to his ear and smiled as though it was a lover. "If you were Zelnad, you could hear their voices cry out."

"I can hear them. They're saying, 'let Geddy goooo ...'" he murmured out the corner of his mouth.

"That is not what the voices are saying. They beg for home. Their spirits are what makes it special. What makes shinium different from tukrium. It also is much easier to work." He heaved a long sigh. "I, too, yearn for the day when all Zelnad can finally return home."

"Right after you stick a fork in all civilization?"

The metallurgist was genuinely incredulous at this, like it was some well-kept secret. By the look on Balzac's face, it was news to him, too.

His eyes narrowed. "Who told you that?"

"A giant tardigrade."

"A what?"

"It's like a little worm thing with eight stubby ... doesn't matter. What matters is, you can never destroy Sagacea. Not unless you plan to pile into in my ship like some fucked-up clown car."

"Your ship is of no importance to us. Only its shinium. Which you discovered on Earth 2, of all places. With luck, it will give us all the shinium we need."

"All you need for what?" Geddy asked.

"For our weapon, of course."

Had his arms been free, Geddy would've smacked his palm on his forehead. He, and even Eli had been looking at this all wrong. The Nads didn't need to drive their whole army through Sagacea's barrier or build some giant warship out of shinium. All they needed was something powerful enough to destroy it. Something that could slip through and explode. Zelnads harvested star material for novaspheres. Who knew what kind of ultra-powerful weapon they could build?

He heaved a phony sigh. "I only tell you this out of respect for your role as host, which I'm afraid must now end. This is a time for us to unite."

Before Balzac could make a move, he was seized by the other dead-eyed Zelnad puppets. "Hey, wait! We had a deal!"

"The deal was that your people wouldn't come to harm. I didn't say anything about you."

"You lying Zelnad bastard!" Balzac was a big guy, and strong, and twenty-five percent robot, but he, too, could not break free of his Nad captors. It seemed they were both screwed now.

"As for the Sagacean you apparently have befriended, it has acted selfishly." The Metallurgist gently brushed his fingers on Geddy's cheek. "I am sorry you have been the instrument of its misguided desires. If it cares about you at all, it will take full control now."

"Why? So I don't have to listen to you talk anymore?"

The smile that slithered across his face chilled Geddy to the bone. "No, human. So you won't feel it when we rip our kindred out of you."

CHAPTER 40

TRIAL SEPARATION

"Wait!" Geddy said, stopping the Metallurgist as he turned away. "What if I had something better?"

Geddy didn't want to find out what his threat meant. There was nothing he particularly cared to part with, except maybe some love handles that had formed over the past few years.

"You have nothing to offer us." He turned away yet again.

"Not even endless jumps?"

Again, he paused, slowly pivoting on his heels. "Excuse me?"

"No novaspheres, no harvesting exotic matter. Jump all you want as far as you want."

He closed the distance between them in two short steps. "Explain."

"Humans found the secret. That's how they reached this galaxy."

Geddy had no way of reading the quantum cubes from JPL, but he'd given enough thought to Zirhof's theory that it almost had to be the truth. But simply knowing that wasn't the same as handing the technology over to them. They knew nothing about the cubes, and the tech might not be on them anyway.

The Nad eyed him suspiciously. "And if this miraculous technology were to exist, what bargain would you make?"

"My Sagacean companion is no threat to you. None of us are. With this technology, you could control the galaxy. Reshape civilization as you see fit. Nobody needs to die."

He stroked his chin thoughtfully, nodding. "A most intriguing offer." After a long pause, during which his dead expression actually showed a flash of elation, he added, "Unfortunately, we already possess such technology."

Geddy's chest filled with ice water. "W ... what do you mean?"

"Oh, come now. Surely you didn't really think a human from five centuries ago just discovered how to create a bubble universe around a ship?"

Once again, Geddy thought he'd picked up a thread only to learn the sweater had already been made. Because the name on the quantum cube he'd copied from Zirhof, Dr. Nilsson, was a PhD and a JPL employee, he'd just assumed she had the fortunate insight that saved humanity from extinction.

It never occurred to him such a person could randomly be inhabited by a Sagacean just as he had. Had it landed in some no-account doofus like him, building a starship would've been the acme of achievement. But in the right brain, the synergy of intelligences may have created the holy grail of interstellar travel.

His heart dropped out of his chest. The worst-case scenario should've been that they called his bluff, but this was infinitely worse.

"You've seen our technology. Did you really think we loaded our ships with those ridiculous novaspheres like so much ammunition?" He shook his head, the same bemused grin plastered to it like a stubborn barnacle. "We can go anywhere we please. And now, thanks to your efforts, we can finally complete our mission." His eyes drifted dreamily to the ceiling. "The reset."

"Wow," said Geddy. "You must be the life of every party."

He smiled warmly. "If your companion would like to shield you from the unspeakable horror of what you're about to experience, now's the time. It would be a mercy."

— *He means to connect with me, Geddy.*

— Don't let him.

— *He may be too strong.*

— If your consciousness absorbs mine, will it make you stronger?

— *Possibly. But will disappear.*

— Yeah, well, turns out I'm not that great at disappearing.

— *I'll hold you within my consciousness for as long as I can.*

— Don't worry about me. Just try to stay you.

— *I'm sorry it has come to this.*

— It ain't over yet. I trust you.

— *I will try.*

Just like that, some cosmic switch flipped, and he felt Eli take control. Whether out of frustration, regret, or some other force conjured by Eli, anger filled him. He slaked his thirst with it. Energy like he'd never known surged through his muscles, unfolding like a map of pain as he watched. He didn't ball his fists, but they balled just the same. A dozen sets of hands held him down, but Eli could break their grip. He just had to be quick about it.

The Nad came right up to him, their eyes not ten centimeters apart. Geddy saw it, but it was more like watching himself from behind a window. He was a passenger in his own body.

Suddenly, a sharp snap came from behind. His Zelnad captors gasped in unison. Eli reopened Geddy's eyes to find that a thin horizontal, dark red line had opened across the torsos of the Nads holding down his right side. Their formerly blank, compliant expressions froze in shock. It was a full two seconds before the upper halves of their bodies toppled into each other like dominoes, opening a line of sight between Eli/Geddy and the door.

As though guided by some unseen hand, a sinuous, crackling blue snake retracted into the darkness like it had just bitten someone, gathering itself back into a vertical coil. The other Nads spun their heads toward it.

Two clawed feet the size of waterskis swung forward, followed shortly by legs the size of tree trunks and a torso draped in ranse armor.

For the second time in as many days, Geddy was actually happy to see Voprot, flanked by Doc on his right and Denk on his left.

Oz came so quietly from behind him that the two Nads pinning Eli/Geddy's right shoulder and upper arm to the floor were still fixed dumbly on Voprot never saw her blades coming. She scissored cleanly through their necks.

Those on his left fell to Denk's blasters, their chests cratered and smoking. One of the Nads holding the struggling Balzac charged toward Tardigan, who lunged forward and shot out both arms with his palms forming an X, catching the Nad/Soturian squarely in the chest. For reasons he couldn't fathom, he toppled over, stone dead.

— Where the hell's that been?

Eli didn't respond. He was somewhere else.

The Metallurgist and four of the remaining Nads darted toward the other exit. The others who had been holding Geddy and Balzac jumped to their feet to mount a fruitless defense.

The moment his captors hit the ground, Balzac took off running and didn't look back. Cowardly asshole.

And yet, Geddy couldn't move. Eli was still in charge. The Metallurgist disappeared through a door on the far side of the silo, dropping the lone piece of shinium onto the floor. All he could do was watch.

— Eli, come on! Flip the switch while you still can!

No response.

— Eli!!

A moment after Oz's energy katanas emerged like big, glowing boners from the chest-holes of two hapless Nads, a dark shape fell from her shoulder onto Eli/Geddy's face like a mask.

Morpho dug his hooks into his face. It should've stung, but Eli/Geddy didn't feel a thing. Even time didn't quite register anymore. Without Eli or any sensation to root him in the present, Geddy felt himself drifting ever inward, as though being absorbed by his own body. And weirdly, he was okay with it.

— **Eli.**

It faintly registered that Morpho, not Eli and certainly not the Metallurgist, was staging an intervention. But it also seemed too late.

— **HEAR ME, SAGACEAN!!**

The command was accompanied by a fresh surge of energy, more like pure electricity than a flood of strength. It reminded Geddy of a defibrillator.

— *Morpho?*

Eli sounded weak, like a boat that had spilled its sails. But maybe it was just far away. With Eli/Geddy's eyes covered by Morph, not even light could tether him to reality.

"Go after him!" Oz barked as another Nad, likely the last, fell to her.

"Voprot chase!" Heavy, loping footsteps bounded across the floor.

— **Bring Geddy back.**

— *I can't … I must join the others …*

— **Now, kindred! Or all things end!**

CHAPTER 41

CARRYING A PIECE

Morpho's final, desperate cry to Eli filled Geddy's brain as though blasted from a speaker, so sudden and jarring it felt like a seizure. He flopped about like a fish as gentle hands worked to guide him back from wherever his consciousness had been.

"Geddy, come on," Oz urged. "Wherever you are, come back."

He could hear them but movement was sticky and difficult, like he'd just been transferred into a new, shitty body. The last thing he remembered was a drill coming toward him. Morpho covered his face. Was still covering his entire face. That's why he couldn't see.

— **Can you hear me, Captain?**

— Where's Eli? Eli!

— *I am here, Geddy.*

— What happened?

— *Taking control of you was … easy. Too easy.*

— I called for you.

— *I couldn't hear. There were so many angry voices. Are you okay?*

— Never better.

In lieu of a reply, Morpho withdrew his sticky hooks from Geddy's face. This time he felt it, like a thousand tiny needles being withdrawn from his skin. Once his eyes finally adjusted to the light, Oz's and Doc's faces resolved over him. Denk knelt at his feet, his chipmunky face pinched in deep concern.

"The Metallurgist ..." Geddy said, sitting up quickly. His head swooned.

"He ran. Voprot went after him," Oz said, helping to steady him.

"He had a piece of the ship. Where are the others?" He rose shakily to his feet, and his vision immediately narrowed to pinpoints.

"Easy now," Doc warned, a hand on his shoulder.

A blurry memory of Doc taking out one of the Nads with a flick of his hand came rushing back. Geddy shook his head to clear it and regarded the body of the Nad/Soturian with a quizzical look. "Hold up. Did you really just walk up and kill that guy with a punch?"

"Yes," he said casually. "Why?"

"How?"

"Soturians' hearts are regulated by a nerve that passes behind the intercostal space. A well-placed blow will cause cardiac arrest."

"Fuckin' A, man. That was seseluh?"

"Yes."

"I thought it was the peaceful path," Geddy said.

"Even the peaceful path is sometimes ... bumpy."

Geddy pulled away from Oz and Doc and stumbled around the end of the row of workstations toward the far corner of the enormous room, where the partly disassembled husk of his ship still stood. By the looks of it, every last piece of its shinium skin had been removed, but was nowhere to be seen.

"Did he drop it?" Geddy's tone was more frantic than intended. "Is it still here?"

Oz and Doc followed him over, and Denk soon appeared from the near end of the workstations holding the flat, square panel. He hurried over and handed it to Geddy, who yanked it out of his hands and inspected it closely to make sure it was indeed the real thing. His nose twitched. Was it his imagination or did it still bear some of The Deuce's distinctive scent?

While he pored over it, Oz left his side to take in what remained of the ship. "This is the *Penetrator*?" He nodded. "I remember it being a lot shinier."

"They stripped all the shinium save for that one piece."

She ran her fingers over the lower part of the nose, formerly sleek and seamless but now a rough-shaped tangle of wires and actuators. "Can you put it back together?"

"I don't think so."

He placed his hands on the fuselage with his eyes closed, taking deep breaths as he leaned forward. How cruel it was to get her back like this.

— *I'm sorry, Geddy. This is all my fault.*

— Don't do that. We'll figure something out.

"I don't understand," said Doc, coming alongside Oz. "What unique properties does this ... shinium possess that it can reach Sagacea?"

Geddy sighed. "Sagaceans have been floating through space since the dawn of the universe. Some landed in molten tukrium, trapping them inside as it cooled." He held it up, lightly running his fingers over the lightly beveled edge. "It must act like a key."

Understanding washed over Doc, and his eyes twinkled. "A metal alloyed by energetic entities. Fascinating. I look forward to learning more."

Looking at the piece now, small though it was and hard wrought as it had been, knowing that countless entities just

"What about Balzac?" Doc asked.

"Oh, I imagine he'll be hanging around," Geddy quipped. Even Tardigan barked a laugh. "Something tells me we'll run into him again."

Oz cleared her throat, smirking. "If we get lucky, maybe Balzac will run into us."

CHAPTER 42
SUMBAKH, SOME DON'T

Once every six years, Zorr's three suns came into alignment in an eye-popping harmonic convergence called Sumbakh, which meant "spear" in some long-dead language. The legend held that an ancient deity went hunting and skewered the three suns all at once to demonstrate his might. Mocking his hubris, the suns merely turned his great spear to cinders. Every six years, he tries and fails, and all of Zorr goes out and parties.

After everything that happened, Geddy was ready for a proper fucking party.

Oz braved her dislike of reentry and came down with him, Denk, and Doc in the *Dominic*. Voprot, for his part, was perfectly content to stay aboard the *Fiz* with Morpho and luxuriate in his new, custom-made, Kigantean-sized bed. The Screvari had installed two privacy walls and converted a corner of the hold into a private room. That put Voprot on the wrong side of the airlock in an emergency, but he seemed comfortable with the tradeoff.

None of them had ever been to Sumbakh. Like so many other places to which he'd traveled so long ago, he never took the time. The people he would come to see almost always had a private landing pad so he hardly even went into town. How many places had he visited only to speak briefly with one person and immediately go on to the next planet or return to Kigantu?

It didn't pay to ruminate. He was finally making up for lost time.

What a day they'd had. All the public spaceports near Nova Auris, the capital of the North, were booked solid and had been for years. The only way to park the *Dom* was to purchase a Platinum VIP Package. It was obscenely expensive yet totally worth it after what they'd been through. It included a private shuttle to Miramarana Stadium, tickets to the Simpop Smythe aftershow, a private box within ten meters of something called the flashline, and all the drinks they wanted.

Any time you find yourself in a luxury shuttle drinking Zorran daiquiris at seven-thirty in the morning on your way to a concert that kicks off the biggest party in the sector, you know you're in for a long day.

Immediately upon their arrival, a group of comely young women offered them capsules of blizia, a plant they said would make it all way better, whatever that meant. Oz was a when-in-Rome type and said she'd be down, but agreed to split one with Denk just so he'd do it with her. Doc surprisingly took a whole capsule himself without hesitation. But Geddy, in a move that was immediately shortlisted for All-Time Most Responsible Decisions, decided against it. He had things to do the next day, and becoming captain of the *Fiz* had given him a renewed sense of responsibility.

Of course, even that backfired.

The so-called flashline, as it turned out, was a stripe that ran down the middle of the stadium, thusly named because it was the precise spot in that city, on that day and at the "official" time where the three suns came into perfect alignment.

Geddy figured it would be a lame novelty to tell your grand-kids about it.

Not so.

Less than a minute before the suns aligned on them, Doc Tardigan giddily informed him that the temperature on the flashline was said to hit 90 Centigrade, just for a few seconds.

"You might wish you took that blizia," he cautioned.

"Why?" Geddy asked warily.

"It makes you secrete a kind of natural sunblock. See?" Doc showed him his bare arm, which had taken on a vaguely metallic sheen, then pointed at the sky before Geddy could ask why he hadn't mentioned this until that moment. "Better put on your glasses."

"Glasses?"

Apparently, their shuttle pilot had lectured them at some length about making sure they took the special Sumbakh sunglasses along — several pairs if necessary. Geddy was already halfway through his second cocktail and thinking about the last time he was here, so he didn't catch a word of it.

"Here," said Oz, handing over a pair as she slipped on her own. "I knew you weren't listening. But you really should've taken the blizia."

"No one told me!"

He got the glasses on just in time. The full brunt of the heat lasted less than a second yet still made him think he'd burst into flames. But he held his face high and took a mental snap-shot of the three concentric suns forming a target on him and imagined a being large enough to spear it.

Once the suns had passed each other and he removed the glasses, he looked down at his hands to find them red and puffy with a thick layer of blisters. His face was even worse. The crew had a good laugh at his expense.

But that was only the start of the party. After the Simpop Smythe show, everyone from the stadium filed into the streets where hundreds of thousands of revelers had already gathered. They had an absolute blast but didn't get into their hotel until almost sunrise. Rather than pass out and miss his meeting with Zirhof, Geddy sat out on the balcony in a bathrobe and enjoyed his coffee, then got dressed and headed to the plaza before anyone else was even up.

"It's not that hot." A droplet of sweat ran down his upper lip and into his mouth. It tasted vaguely of alcohol and bad choices, but he was grateful for the moisture.

Sometimes it was nice to talk to Eli out loud. The streets were literally empty and likely would be well into the afternoon. And no wonder, because those suns were *brutal*. They cast pretty interesting shadows, though — three of them, each with a slightly different hue and sharpness.

— *I did advise you to bring water. Several times.*

He paused midway up the long flight of steps that led up to the cliffside high-rise where Zirhof's penthouse was, huffing and puffing as the alcohol sweated out of him. The levicart floating behind him with the antique quantum computer came to a stop as well. Though it followed him along at a fixed distance, requiring zero effort from him, it still seemed like he was towing it.

"Fuck, I'm outta shape. I blame you."

— *Me?!*

"Taking me over on Aku like that? I haven't felt the same since." He took another deep breath and continued lumbering up the stairs.

— *You gave me permission!*

"I think you just wanted to try this body on for size."

— *You mean this lovingly maintained temple of yours? Don't flatter yourself.*

"The secret is Kailorian gin and high G's. Y'know, I panicked when I couldn't reach you."

—*I must have been struck dumb by the majesty of it.*

"Damn skippy."

At long last, he reached the ground level and trundled across the plaza itself. A colossal fountain honoring Sumbakh spat graceful arcs of water skyward, the gentle morning breeze bearing cool droplets onto his grateful skin. Still, heatstroke was mere minutes away. He needed water, stat.

When the guard opened the heavy front doors of the lobby for him, he recoiled at the sight of Geddy.

"Flashline." Geddy said, not breaking stride, and proceeded to reception where a middle-aged Zorran woman greeted him. "Ooh. You look like you could use some water."

She pointed to a drinking fountain along the far wall, and there he slaked his thirst. He could feel their eyes on his back as he greedily slurped up huge, dog-like gulps, but he didn't care.

Having finally cooled off, he re-tucked his shirt and made an attempt to smooth it as he returned to the reception area with the levicart still trailing him.

"Mr. Zirhof is expecting you," the woman said.

CHAPTER 43

GLEANING THE CUBE

The last time he'd seen Zirhof was eleven years ago when he was still actively running the company he started. He had a sprawling country home back then which overlooked the wide and fertile river valley that cradled Nova Auris. Geddy was curious to know if he'd downsized by moving here, though that wouldn't have been Zirhof's style.

The aerivator rocketed him to the 95th floor in seconds, causing the coffee he'd enjoyed earlier to swish unsettlingly in his stomach. When the doors opened, he paused at the end of the long hallway, fully intending to find a bathroom and make himself look less like he'd just gone bobbing for French fries. The computer glided out into the hall behind him and hovered in place.

"Geddy Starheart," came a silken voice from nearby.

The lonely hallway bisected Zirhof's place, which wasn't simply *on* the 95th floor, but in fact *was* the 95th floor.

Zorrans naturally produced the same substance that blizia synthesized, giving their luxuriously dark skin a similar metallic sheen when the light caught it. Were it not for their faintly sparkled, spray-tanned appearance, they almost could've passed for human.

To his eyes, Zirhof hadn't aged a day. He could never remember the age conversion, but eleven years to him was something like four to Zirhof, who had to be north of two hundred years old by now.

Nattily dressed, Geddy liked to think of him as the rich, cool uncle he never had.

"Whaddya say, Mr. Zirhof?" he stepped forward and extended his hand.

Zirhof took it with a bemused grin, regarding Geddy's inflamed skin with the quiet acceptance a parent might show a mud-caked child. "Someone didn't take the blizia."

"Don't start with me, old man," Geddy laughed. "Pale skin is one of my many genetic betrayals."

"Did you ... walk here from downtown?" Zirhof asked, incredulous. "I could've sent a shuttle for you."

"Maybe on the way back."

Zirhof offered him a real drink, but Geddy opted for water. Another short-list candidate for the Responsible Decisions list. They chatted for a while and caught up, despite the skin on Geddy's face cracking and straining with each smile. Zirhof hadn't dealt with the Double A in several years and lamented what he viewed as its decline. Geddy briefly related the events of the past eleven years, omitting the little detail about Eli for now.

Finally, Zirhof cut to the chase.

"Well, I know you didn't come here just to bring me up to speed. What have you brought me?"

Geddy jutted his chin at the floating oblong artifact. "Just an antique quantum computer."

The old man's eyes lit up. He leapt up from the couch to inspect it, running his hands over the gleaming metal fins. "My goodness, Geddy. I didn't think anything like this made the trip from Old Earth."

"It didn't." He flashed a mischievous grin.

Zirhof's mouth dropped open. "You *went there?!*"

"I did. And there's still plenty of goodies still on the ship, including a nearly intact space plane."

"Ooh," mused the old man.

"But I have a feeling you'll be most excited about these." Geddy reached into his pocket and removed the tiny gray cubes, then dropped them into Zirhof's open palm.

Zirhof marveled at them before inspecting the tiny inscriptions with the ever-present loupe hanging around his neck. "Oh, my. These are authentic as well?"

"Straight from the Jet Propulsion Labs in formerly beautiful Pasadena, California. Specifically, the Project Rearview Resource Center."

Zirhof couldn't have been more excited if Geddy had walked in with a Stemiran harem. He gasped. "Do you think they contain the spacetime research referenced in the stolen cube?"

"That's what I want to find out. You still have something that can read these?"

"Of course," Zirhof said, a twinkle in his green-hued eyes. He turned and motioned for Geddy to follow. "Come on, the gear's in the collection room."

— *He has a room just for collecting?*

— Oh, just you wait.

Zirhof strolled down one hallway and turned down another, pushing through a set of double doors into an ornate room large enough to host a basketball game. At least a quarter of the floor was set up as a private, fastidiously curated museum exhibit displaying his favorite artifacts over his two-plus centuries. Everything from ancient Gundrun armor to Vyephian scrolls.

— *Wow.*

— Yep.

They wound through the displays to a gigantic office in the corner where an assortment of newer pieces awaited cataloguing. A smooth gray metal box about the size of Geddy's hand sat on a desk beside a holobar.

"This device can decrypt the data on the cubes. If any details of our mythical jump tech is in there somewhere, my search algorithms will find them. It'll take some time, but my stars, Geddy — this could change everything."

"Let's hope so."

"Moment of truth ..." Zirhof placed one of the cubes on a little glowing square, then powered it on. Almost immediately, directories filled the holoscreen, and he gave a little gasp.

"I assume that's a good sign?"

A broad grin spread across his smooth face. "Oh, yes. Very good."

"Mind if I spent a little time sifting through it?"

The look on his face suggested he was caught off-guard by the question. "Feeling nostalgic, are we?"

"Something like that."

"Then I'll give you some privacy." As he receded, he added, "If you need me, just ask aloud. The system will notify me."

"Will do."

"Well done, Geddy." Zirhof's eyes twinkled with childlike excitement. "Well done, indeed."

Zirhof closed the door to the cavernous office behind him, leaving Geddy alone. He'd been looking forward to this moment ever since finding them. Antiquated though they were, the cubes held mind-boggling amounts of data. A big chunk of humankind's accumulated scientific knowledge hovered right in front of him.

Reams of files unfolded on the holoscreen. He stared at

them until his focus blurred, like he was trying to look through the data into his own past. But those answers likely wouldn't be found here.

— *You cannot mean to examine all this data yourself.*

"Are you kidding? I get bored reading a stop sign."

— *Then I do not understand.*

"I dunno. I guess I want to feel close to it."

— *To knowledge? I've always considered you knowledge-adjacent.*

"No, to Old Earth. How it used to be, anyway." He flashed back to the long-abandoned JPL complex. The vault. The dust storm that almost toppled the *Dom*. It was all so sad.

He scrolled through screen after screen after screen, the file-names long and cryptic. Within each directory were more directories, level upon level. Schematics. Reams of charts and tables. Videos. Hidden somewhere in there might the answer to the question of how humans really came to this galaxy, plus thousands more he didn't yet know to ask. The possibilities tantalized and intimidated him. What did it all mean? And what hadn't his mother told him about the cube that was stolen from the museum?

The device's interface was straightforward enough. Geddy brought up a virtual keyboard and entered NILSSON, then executed the search. Immediately, the screen filled with hundreds, perhaps even thousands of hits. An electric thrill ran through him.

Not all the results were relevant. Many referenced a singer named Harry Nilsson. Others, a golf instructor named Pia Nilsson. He added BIRGIT to the search string and immediately narrowed the results by an order of magnitude.

"Hel-lo, Dr. Nilsson. Let's see what your deal was."

It immediately became clear that she was a bright star in theoretical physics. She'd been one of those child prodigies, graduating from high school at twelve and earning the first of her three doctorates at nineteen. Her papers bore titles like, "Overcoming the Problem of Negative Energy Density in Superluminal Travel" and "Predicting the Effects of Warp-Bubble Quantum Compression on Human Biology."

"Does any of this make sense to you, E?" Geddy asked.

— *At a minimum, she was well-versed in the theory of faster-than-light travel. And her research output was astonishing, so much that ...*

"So much that what?"

— *That it would lead me to believe she, was host to a Sagacean, too.*

Eli had shown him how to build a ship from scratch, and how to mine and refine shinium. He could never have done those things on his own. And Geddy wasn't exactly a towering intellect. If a wise Sagacean happened to find its way into the brain of someone like Dr. Nilsson, what kind of knowledge would that unlock? Possibly the kind that could save a race from extinction.

But again, if she'd really invented such technology, how did the Zelnads come by it? And what would it mean for the galaxy?

"We can't know that for sure, can we?"

— *No, but it is immaterial. When she passed, so would have her Sagacean passenger.*

"Let's say you're right, and that she invented the tech that brought us here. Why do the Zelnads have it but not us?"

— *That is an excellent question.*

Zirhof's obsession with the human story had always vexed him. The man had seen it all, from before the Ring War to the collapse of the Alliance and everything since, yet he'd followed this particular thread with dogged persistence. Only now did Geddy finally understand why. War was coming, and Zirhof knew it. Maybe he'd hoped the discovery of this jump technology would give them an advantage. If they already had it like the Metallurgist claimed, then the best they could hope for was to level the playing field. At least it might give them a fighting chance. And if anyone could take something from concept to creation in short order, it was an industrialist like Zirhof.

Hope surged through Geddy, and the hair on his arms stiffened in response.

"The secret is here, E. I feel it in my bones."

— *In which case your recklessness in retrieving it might ultimately save the galaxy.*

"Which would be pretty cool."

— *While technically rewarding your worst tendencies.*

"But it would still be cool, right?"

— *It would, Geddy. It really would.*

NEXT IN THE REASSEMBLY SERIES

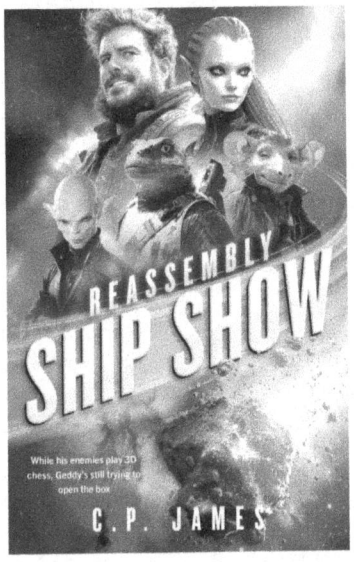

www.vinci-books.com / ship-show

Geddy thought escaping the Zelnads was tough. Now he's facing their ultimate weapon: marketing. Discover the hilarious chaos in *Ship Show*!

Turn the page for a free preview…

SHIP SHOW: CHAPTER 1
LIZARD LESSONS

If this whole saving-the-universe thing didn't work out and the Zelnads ended civilization, at least Geddy and Dr. Tardigan would never again have to teach a giant lizard how to use articles of speech.

"Vop– er, *I* see you across room?" asked Voprot hopefully.

They hadn't even introduced "the" into the mix. Too soon. Though, he did say *I* on occasion. It wasn't that he didn't grasp the concept. He just didn't like doing it.

"It's a classic for a reason." Geddy gave a shuddering yawn and leaned back in the stool behind the rarely used work-bench. "And hey, if she's your age, she might not have heard that one before." Taking Doc aside, he whispered. "This still feels weird. Isn't he like twelve in Kigantean years?"

The lessons were his idea, but Doc was concerned about Voprot's social acclimation. In this scenario, he was supposed to talk to a female at a party. A ludicrous premise on multiple levels, but Geddy didn't have a better one.

"He is an adolescent. Using his language skills in social situations is essentially … what is your human expression?"

"A Sisyphean ordeal?"

"No, I believe it is, 'Killing two birds with one stone.'"

"If you say so."

Voprot pretty much always sat on the floor of the *For Sale Make Offer's* capacious cargo hold during a crew meeting or the language lessons. His gigantic, swishy lizard tail limited him in many respects on the ship, which was made for short, snail-like Ghruk. But even on his haunches, his eyes came level with Geddy's and Doc's, which made it hard to think of him as the adolescent he technically was.

The hold felt depressingly empty. Empty crates were stacked to the ceiling along the starboard side. Sturdy shelves ran down the port wall and formed the back of the raised breakdown area called the deck. All empty, all spotless.

Their long and dicey trip to Old Earth had paid off. His old friend, Balzac, took all the metal from their scrapped satellites, which bought them a ton of needed repairs and upgrades to the *Fiz*. It still resembled an abandoned warehouse welded to the back of a service vehicle, but it was nicer on the inside now. The water ran clear-ish, he didn't have to crouch to shower anymore, and the slapdash hull repair they got as a parting gift from Prince Bransel, Oz's father back on Temeruria, had been reinforced. Morpho even got most of the items on his wish list.

It was only mid-afternoon, but Geddy could've racked out at any time. The fatigue that had kept him feeling run down and groggy for days had only deepened. It didn't make sense. Once again, he'd slept through the night only to wake up in a complete fog that never quite lifted. At least they were stocked up on coffee now. Hard to believe that counted as a win these days.

Bored with the monotony of Voprot's language lesson, Geddy's eyes drifted over to the *Penetrator*, his ship he stole back from the Zelnads. Without its shinium skin, it couldn't cross the barrier surrounding Sagacea, and he couldn't get Eli home. It was parked tight with a bunch of other junk, naked, useless, and sadly unfinished. Not unlike his reflection.

Thanks to Balzac, though, the *Fizmo's* engines' familiar low-frequency hum was even and strong. He'd gotten so accustomed to its cyclic vibration under his feet that its absence still made it seem like they weren't running at a full burn toward Gundrun.

As nice as it was to get on the ground and kick back on Zorr, it lost its charm after a couple of days. The *Fiz* was their only real home.

"Voprot have question." His giant reptilian head often tilted to the side, making him seem perpetually curious, and the shape of his mouth suggested a permanent grin. Happy, affable, curious people got under his craw after a while.

Geddy's open palm arced into his forehead. The slap echoed through the empty hold. "*I*! *I* have question! Actually, you have *a* question, but we only cover that in the advanced class."

Doc's burnt-orange, oblong face pinched in concern. "Are you okay, Captain?"

Dr. Tardigan brought a lot to the table. A flawless memory. Broad academic knowledge, including medicine. And, most vitally, infinite patience. Geddy hadn't told him about the fatigue yet, but apparently, it showed.

His instinct was to say yes. But he wasn't okay at all. Worrisome thoughts pummeled his brain like a meteor shower. Maybe that's why he was so tired. Engaging with the world was a recipe for anxiety even in the best of circumstances. He scratched at his right ear.

"Just tired and crabby. My ear itches."

Squinting, Doc leaned in to get a closer look. The ridges across his forehead pinched into sergeant's stripes. "You have a rash."

"I do?" he reflexively brought his fingers back up and gave it another quick scratch. "Bad?"

He shook his head. "Just some contact dermatitis. I'd like to keep an eye on it, though."

Great. On top of everything else, he was allergic to something on the ship. Probably Voprot.

"Yeah, okay."

"I am more concerned about your mood. You've been more surly than usual, and that is saying something."

"I'm fine. Let's just finish up here."

Doc returned his attention to Voprot. "Let's try it in conversation. Imagine you were attracted to a female. What might you say to her?"

"Voprot lick you," he said without hesitations, unironically cleaning one eyeball, then the other with his prodigious forked tongue.

"*Like*," corrected Doc through gritted teeth. "*I … like you.*"

He grinned. "Voprot like you, too."

Geddy closed his eyes and let out a long, cleansing sigh before he hopped off the stool and strode away, fistfuls of hair bunched in his fingers.

— *I'm worried about you.*

Eli, his microscopic, freeloading spore friend, had been silent for hours.

— Oh, now you chime in.

— *You do not have the patience for teaching.*

— This isn't teaching, it's punishment. On second thought, maybe it *is* teaching.

"Take ten?" Doc said to Voprot.

"Okay. Voprot butt numb."

Had Geddy been alone, he might've cried.

— Shouldn't I be *rewarded* for heroically saving him?

— *Sav–*

— If you say saving him was its own reward, I'll sneeze you back into space.

— *But–*

— I'm not kidding.

Doc put a comforting hand on his shoulder. "He's trying."

Geddy turned to him. Voprot had gotten up and was stretching each leg out to the side like he was peeing on a shrub. "Is he, though?"

They'd only left Zorr three weeks ago. Usually, time had no meaning out here, but it felt like months had passed. After finding three quantum cubes in a vault at NASA's Jet Propulsion Lab, he brought them to his rich old friend Zirhof for analysis.

It seemed they were some sort of doomsday storage media, where a good chunk of the world's accumulated data was stored. Almost an entire cube was dedicated to porn, which had never been done better or to the same degree in this galaxy. That technically made it one of humanity's most enduring contributions to all civilization in the universe.

The other, Zirhof believed, was a jump technology so advanced that it could only have been conceived by an ancient Sagacean, beings created during the birth of the universe. Beings like Eli, who was so much a part of him now that they no longer seemed like separate entities.

It would take Zirhof a long time to pore through everything on the quantum cubes. Even then, there was no guarantee he'd find anything concrete about the mythical jump tech humans almost certainly used to reach their galaxy. The tech that could only have been conceived by a very clever Sagacean.

The sale of their scrap and the old Virgin Galactic space plane had their finances in fine order for once, and the novasphere hopper was full, but their sense of urgency was lacking because they needed a break. They'd only been a working crew for about three months, during which they'd hardly had a moment's rest. With the Zelnads out there threatening all civilization, taking time to relax felt indulgent. But everyone, especially Doc, said it was crucial that they rejuvenate. And so they'd enjoyed Sumbakh while on Zorr, which made them realize they still needed to live a life worth fighting for. That meant slowing down occasionally.

"You haven't been wearing the device I gave you, have you?" It wasn't a question so much as an accusation. "If you don't want to get to the bottom of this, then I won't waste my time trying to diagnose it."

The fingernail-sized disc stuck to his forehead while he slept. It was unobtrusive enough, but the whole idea of it made him uncomfortable. He couldn't even stand jewelry.

Or maybe he didn't want to know if something really was wrong with him.

"I'll wear it again tonight."

Doc still looked doubtful, and rightly so, but his reproachful expression softened. This fatigue issue flummoxed him. "The sooner I can get diagnostics, the sooner you can get some real rest."

The device recorded brain wave patterns, vitals, and everything about his blood chemistry as he slept. "At this point, I'd eat a pan of snapping assholes to wake up rested."

Tardigan cocked his head like a perplexed dog. "How would that ever be a condition of your treatment?"

Human idioms always got him in trouble. "Never mind."

He glanced over at Voprot, who had shifted to stretching his hamstrings with his hands pressed to the hull like a hurdler. Then he arched back so far that he met their eyes upside down, then licked them again. So gross. Contorted like that, he looked possessed. You had to hand it to the big Kigantean. He never missed an opportunity to be himself.

Geddy gave a grim shake of his head and muttered, "This was an absurd idea. Why would you let me try this?"

Doc's eyes roamed over Voprot with clinical fascination. "Because beneath that simple exterior is a shockingly sensitive and thoughtful being. And what he craves more than anything, besides globzoiks, is the approval of his captain."

— *That's what I told you yesterday.*

— Hmm? I wasn't listening.

— *I am literally in your head. You can't not listen.*

They were right, of course. Voprot was pure of heart and incapable of lying. Who else could he say that about? Geddy had neither been patient nor empathetic enough with him since they met, and he didn't know why. Maybe it was because casual jokes at Voprot's expense just sailed right over him like lob shots. It was fun to swing at someone when you knew they'd duck every punch.

The airlock door slid open and Oz, his Temerurian First Officer, strode through with the look of a disapproving mother. "You're still at it? Why don't you get some rest?"

Her limited rotation of outfits typically combined sturdy, lace-up boots with dark tights and a fitted vest. It suited her very well, and nothing she wore ever looked dirty or used.

Doc checked his watch and gasped. "My goodness, have we really been at it for three hours?"

"Are you trying to say it's our bedtime?" Geddy winked at the lithe redhead.

"I'm saying we might have a long day tomorrow."

He stifled another yawn. "Why?"

"There's still a lot of chatter on the salvage bands. Whatever's going down on Gundrun sounds big."

Oz liked to peruse the net or read while monitoring the old radio frequencies used by salvage vessels. Sometimes, she said, high-paying gigs were discussed, and you could get an inside track. One such conversation hinted at a lucrative commercial opportunity on Gundrun, and for want of any better ideas, they were en route to a clear vector there.

After nearly running out of novaspheres on the way to Old Earth on his account, she certainly deserved the benefit of the doubt now. But considering how far it was to reach their vector, the information didn't feel too solid.

"I've got a feeling about this one."

Burning an increasingly expensive novasphere on Oz's hunch wasn't the issue. It was whether they should still be going after salvage work when the world might be ending. But they couldn't fight the Nads if they couldn't find them. Until then, there wasn't much else to do but try and make more money.

Geddy gave her shoulder a pat as he passed. "Then we'd better check it out. Voprot, we're done for today."

He righted himself and shrugged. "Okay." The giant lizard loped over to his sleeping area in the corner and disappeared behind the privacy walls Balzac's people installed.

"I'll see you in the morning," Geddy said.

"Eli, make sure he sleeps," Oz called after him.

— *Tell her I will do my best.*

"He says you aren't the boss of us."

SHIP SHOW: CHAPTER 2

YOU'RE MY SATELLITE

"Hey, Cap?" came Denk's voice over the tinny intercom. "Sorry to wake you, but you're gonna want to come to the bridge."

There was no urgency in his tone, but the words still dragged Geddy out of a deep state. Not sleep, exactly. Whatever it was, it could hold him in its spell all night without the courtesy of rest.

Bleary-eyed, he got dressed and looked in the mirror, canting his head far enough to see the rash by his right ear. If anything, it had freshened.

Since getting the upgrades on Aku, splashing water on his face felt and looked less like a golden shower, and for that he was grateful. He brought a couple dripping handfuls up with a slap, and a bit of the fog lifted.

The captain's quarters were slightly larger than the others but otherwise identical, with a bed in the corner and a screen on the wall beside the small closet. The side with the mirror also had a sink and a small desk he almost never used. It shared a wall with both the galley and the bridge.

After one more quick look, he exited and found his entire

crew waiting in the bridge, the looks on their faces more hopeful and alert than usual.

"Are we there yet?" Geddy asked.

Denk Junt spun around in the pilot's seat, his rodent-like features pinched tightly together. His prominent incisors hung just over his bottom lip like he'd just poked his head up from a rabbit hole.

"No, we're still en route to our vector," he said. "But we ran across this."

Doc and the others fixed their gazes on the front screen. A couple hundred meters ahead was an enormous — and very old — satellite, motionless and stark under the *Fiz's* lights as Denk made a slow circle around it. The only markings were a six-character code stenciled on the side. It wouldn't have looked out of place over Old Earth, where they'd claimed dozens of similar satellites weeks earlier.

Geddy set his hands on his hips. "Talk about your antiques. What am I looking at?"

"It appears to be disabled," Doc said. "Its transponder is not active, and its power supply is largely depleted."

"Who does it belong to?"

"Without a transponder, we cannot know for certain. I ran the registry number through IRSV and it did not match any records, however, it may predate the database."

"How old's the database?"

"Approximately one hundred eighteen years."

Deep-space salvage had both rules and an ethos regarding claims. The only truly safe claim was a craft that was clearly disabled or damaged beyond repair. However, anything not in the Intergalactic Registry of Spacefaring Vehicles was generally considered fair game. Every captain had their own policy.

Geddy's only policy was to keep his ship and his crew in business long enough to stop the Zelnads. Their financial situation was much improved, but that could change quickly.

"It still has some power, though?" Geddy asked.

"Yes. Either it is not functional or it only cycles on periodically. Deep-space satellites often do."

"Composition?"

"Primarily aluminum, though its armor appears to be high-carbon steel indicative of–"

"Gundrun," Geddy finished.

"Yes. However, Gundrun steel armor is present in virtually all spacecraft originating from this sector. It could easily be from Zihnia or Afolos, as well."

"How far are we from the nearest civilized world?"

Denk replied, "Just under half a parsec to Zihnia, then point eight more to Gundrun."

The satellite wasn't any big windfall. Depending on the components and the market, they might get a couple hundred grand or so. They were flush with novaspheres, but the repairs on Aku hadn't included any armaments. After their encounter with the pirates over Temeruria, that made him very nervous. But replacing the non-functional disruptor bank alone would easily run a million. They needed torpedoes and missiles, too, and countermeasures.

The risk was low, and they weren't close to anything. Running across dilapidated hardware didn't happen every day. Besides, once Voprot blasted it to pieces and they sorted the parts into bins, there wasn't much anyone could do.

— What do you think?

— *Legally, it seems like viable salvage. Ethically, it is a toss-up.*

"Do we know what *kind* of satellite it is?" Geddy asked Doc.

"Its design alone does not betray its core function, Captain."

The looks on everyone's faces suggested a vote would be split. As Oz often had to remind him, it was his job to lead and theirs to follow. This was a golden opportunity to be decisive.

And if the trip to Gundrun turned out to be a waste of time, at least they didn't walk away empty-handed.

"Let's bring it in."

Grab your copy...
www.vinci-books.com/ship-show

ABOUT THE AUTHOR

C.P. James writes cinematic sci-fi with humor and heart. He lives in the magical country of Ecuador. His first novel, *The Perfect Generation*, was published in February 2018. A dystopian trilogy, The Cytocorp Saga, was released in 2020. Reassembly, a humorous space opera, was launched in April 2021.